Under the effective cover of darkness, Camellion and Krestell stealthily approached the one man who now blocked the path to the house. Sherill, the man in question, was thinking he had it made until he suddenly felt the large muzzle of the Sionics suppressor pressing against his back between his shoulder blades.

Sherill let his .44 mag revolver fall to the grass. "You guys can't get away with this."

Camellion jammed Sherill so hard in the small of his back that the man cried out in pain. "Just tell me how many more guards are on the grounds. Lie once and I'll shoot twice."

"Only four," Sherill said, his voice betraying fear.

"You're a damned liar," the Death Merchant hissed. "I'm giving you a second chance. How many?"

"S-six," Sherill muttered.

Camellion didn't even bother to call the gunman a liar this time. He merely touched the trigger of the Ingram. *Bazziitttttttt.* Three 9mm round-nosed slugs zipped through Sherill's left clavicle, shot perpendicularly through his left lung, tore through the end of his liver and the upper portion of his stomach, bored through a section of the taenia coli, and came to a bloody, skidding halt in the sartorius muscle of his left leg. Sherill's chin dropped to his chest. He was dead.

The Death Merchant beckoned to Krestell. "We'll just have to go for it. Come on."

Why argue? Krestell nodded and began to creep east. The Death Merchant moved west. . . .

THE DEATH MERCHANT SERIES:
#1 THE DEATH MERCHANT
#2 OPERATION OVERKILL
#3 THE PSYCHOTRON PLOT
#4 CHINESE CONSPIRACY
#5 SATAN STRIKE
#6 ALBANIAN CONNECTION
#7 THE CASTRO FILE
#8 BILLIONAIRE MISSION
#9 LASER WAR
#10 THE MAINLINE PLOT
#11 MANHATTAN WIPEOUT
#12 THE KGB FRAME
#13 MATO GROSSO HORROR
#14 VENGEANCE: GOLDEN HAWK
#15 THE IRON SWASTIKA PLOT
#16 INVASION OF THE CLONES
#17 ZEMLYA EXPEDITION
#18 NIGHTMARE IN ALGERIA
#19 ARMAGEDDON, USA!
#20 HELL IN HINDU LAND
#21 THE POLE STAR SECRET
#22 THE KONDRASHEV CHASE
#23 THE BUDAPEST ACTION
#24 THE KRONOS PLOT
#25 THE ENIGMA PROJECT
#26 THE MEXICAN HIT
#27 THE SURINAM AFFAIR
#28 NIPPONESE NIGHTMARE
#29 FATAL FORMULA
#30 THE SHAMBHALA STRIKE
#31 OPERATION THUNDERBOLT
#32 DEADLY MANHUNT
#33 ALASKA CONSPIRACY
#34 OPERATION MIND-MURDER
#35 MASSACRE IN ROME
#36 THE COSMIC REALITY KILL
#37 THE BERMUDA TRIANGLE ACTION
#38 THE BURNING BLUE DEATH
#39 THE FOURTH REICH
#40 BLUEPRINT INVISIBILITY
#41 THE SHAMROCK SMASH
#42 HIGH COMMAND MURDER
#43 THE DEVIL'S TRASHCAN
#44 ISLAND OF THE DAMNED

#44 in the incredible adventures of the

DEATH MERCHANT

ISLAND OF THE DAMNED

by Joseph Rosenberger

PINNACLE BOOKS   NEW YORK

DEATH MERCHANT #44: ISLAND OF THE DAMNED

Copyright © 1981 by Joseph Rosenberger

An original Pinnacle Books edition, published for the first time anywhere.

First printing, April 1981

ISBN: 0-523-41325-4

Cover illustration by Dean Cate

Printed in the United States of America

PINNACLE BOOKS, INC.
1430 Broadway
New York, New York 10018

Dedicated to
Rudolf Wanderone—
the original and the only
"Minnesota Fats"
who told me many years ago,
"If you want to write—write!"
That's what I did, Fats. I
wrote. . . .

Joseph R. Rosenberger
Mesa, Arizona

When a distinguished but elderly scientist says that something is possible, he is almost certainly right. When he says it's impossible, he is very probably wrong.

—Arthur C. Clarke
Omni

There are neither miracles nor mysteries—only undiscovered laws. . . .

—Richard J. Camellion

PROLOGUE

Doctor Yuri Mkrtchyan carefully placed his smelly pipe on the brass pipe holder and motioned for Colonel Anton Zimovniki to take a chair next to the desk. "I assume that Major Marleoff and his Hawaiian thugs succeeded in Honolulu, or has there been trouble? They couldn't have gone all the way to Honolulu, kidnapped half a dozen test subjects, and have returned so quickly." Mkrtchyan's voice was remarkably strong for a man so thin and frail looking.

"On the way to Honolulu, Comrade Marleoff and his men got lucky." Zimovniki pulled up his Cargo Jeans slightly and sat down. "They spotted a yacht 144 kilometers east of Oahu—the *Pearl of the Pacific*, a Tollycraft 40 motor yacht," Marleoff said. "Cecil Clarke, a well-to-do Englishman, owned the vessel."

Zimovniki deliberately paused and glanced up at the smooth stone ceiling 6.1 meters overhead. During the nine months he had been on the small island of Tukoatu, he had never fully adjusted to living and working in the vast complex of caves underneath the mountains that covered almost half of the island.

Doctor Mkrtchyan flicked a piece of lint from the left sleeve of his dark green laboratory smock and peered inquiringly at the KGB officer.

"Major Marleoff did capture the vessel, didn't he?"

"He faked engine trouble," Zimovniki said, ignoring the edge in the scientist's tone. "He and the Hawaiians moved along the side of the *Pearl* and boarded her before Clarke and his guests and the crew could realize they were faced with piracy. The entire operation went very smoothly."

Doctor Mkrtchyan moved the bony fingers of his two hands through his thick gray hair, and an expression of apprehension fell over his wrinkled face.

"How can Major Marleoff be certain that the other ves-

1

sel didn't manage to send out an SOS? And he did sink the yacht, I presume?"

Colonel Zimovniki, who disliked all six scientists and their assistants on Tukoatu, enjoyed seeing fear flash over the biochemist's face. Those damned know-it-all scientists! What did they know about security?

"The first thing Comrade Marleoff did was to shoot the antenna from the mast," he said mechanically. "Two of the crew resisted and were killed. Clarke and his guests—twelve in all—were taken aboard our cruiser. The *Pearl of the Pacific* was sunk by a small charge of explosive."

"You say the yacht was 144 kilometers east of Oahu," Mkrtchyan commented thoughtfully, showing widely spaced teeth as he spoke. "In that case the yacht was about 209 kilometers east of Honolulu, or in the middle of the Kaiwi Channel." A satisfied smile crossed his face. "The water is over 900 meters deep in that area, too deep for any recovery by divers. Give me your estimation of a U.S. Coast Guard search."

"The Americans will make a routine search. Finding nothing, they will have to conclude that the *Pearl of the Pacific* vanished, due to causes unknown. There isn't any way the Americans could even faintly connect its disappearance with this small island. Not only are we hundreds of kilometers east of where the yacht went down, but Mr. Nagai is a highly respected businessman in Honolulu. Furthermore, Major Marleoff is positive that no other ships were in the area. No one saw the test subjects being taken aboard the *Morning Star*. No one saw the sinking."

A sly glint crept into the Russian scientist's eyes. He leaned forward and placed his hands flat on the desk. "Yet, *Tovarishch* ("comrade"), you feel I was impatient, that we should have waited for the next submarine from the homeland?"

"Da, I do." Colonel Zimovniki was not surprised by the question or frustrated by it. "It was unfortunate that the supply submarine developed engine trouble and was forced to return to the Motherland. But the next submarine will arrive within a month. It will bring us not only vital supplies, but several dozen political prisoners and other *burzhuy* ("class enemy") types you can use as test subjects for your Bio-Memory Scanner."

"All the other subjects are hopelessly insane. Without test subjects we would lose a month's work, a month's ex-

2

perimentation. We could not afford such a loss; this project is too important."

"Exactly, Comrade Doctor. It's because the project is important that you should not have ordered me to send Major Marleoff and those Hawaiian trash to Honolulu to kidnap people. The risk was too great and the disadvantages far outweighed the advantages. It was only pure luck that Comrade Marleoff came acros the Britisher and his yacht."

For a long moment, Doctor Mkrtchyan studied the KGB officer, a large, square-faced man with steady eyes and short black hair brushed backward over his round dome of a head. The fact that Colonel Zimovniki had emphasized the *you*, making it clear that full responsibility lay on the shoulders of the scientist, did not go unnoticed by Mkrtchyan, who was in complete charge of the Soviet force on the island.

"I disagree with you, *Tovarishch* Zimovniki," Doctor Mkrtchyan said coldly, sitting very erect. "If Major Marleoff had gone to Honolulu and the kidnap attempts had failed, I, and I alone, would have taken full responsibility with the Chairman and the Central Committee of the Politburo." He paused, inhaled slightly and added smugly, "You need not have worried, *Tovarishch* Zimovniki. Your career would not have been jeopardized."

Always on his guard when the scientist used the formal *Tovarishch*, Anton Zimovniki barely smiled. "I was never worried about my career in the KGB, Doctor. I know my job and I do it very well, or I would not be following your orders. The test subjects are in the cells. Is there anything else, *Tovarishch* Doctor Mkrtchyan? I do have other duties."

"Since you and your people are monitoring regular *Amerikanski* radio traffic, keep me informed about the results of the search for the yacht of the Englishman."

"I would have done that without your instructing me to." Colonel Zimovniki's voice became harsh. "I will double security until the search is called off for the *Pearl of the Pacific*. "Any more orders?"

"*Nyet*. That is all."

The gazes of the two men collided and a silent understanding passed between them. Doctor Mkrtchyan took off his glasses and began to clean them with a tissue from a box on the desk. Colonel Zimovniki got to his feet and,

3

without a second look at Mkrtchyan, turned on his heel and left the tiny meeting room whose walls were fashioned from varnished plywood.

Once Zimovniki was in Corridor E, First Level West, he permitted his anger to show on his face. During his fourteen years in the *Kah Gay Beh*,[1] he had never felt so helpless, so degraded. To be forced to take orders from a chicken-necked, stork-legged scientist, a spit of a man who was a pure *soo-kyn syn* ("son of a bitch")! To Zimovniki's way of thinking, it would have been different if his record in the I.S.D. had been less than excellent. Such was not the case, however.

At the age of twenty-two, Anton Zimovniki had been asked by the government to join the *Napravleniye*, the Political Security of the Second Chief Directorate of *Kah Gay Beh*, commonly called the *Sluzhba* by the Russians. The request was based on his grades at the University of Moscow, where he had majored in political science. After preliminary training, Zimovniki had been assigned to the Industrial Service Division, which keeps close watch over critical production and special research projects.

He had risen steadily in rank and within a few years was considered a valuable asset to the I.S.D. During the middle of his ninth year of service—by then he was a Captain—the home office began to send Zimovniki abroad, first to some of the satellite nations, then to capitalist nations in Europe. Three times Zimovniki had gone to the United States, the first time as a legal, under diplomatic cover as an assistant to the Cultural Attaché at the Soviet Embassy in Washington, D.C. The other two times he had been an illegal. On one trip he had posed as a Portuguese paper salesman. The next time he had covered as a West German automotive engineer. In each case, he had been very successful, always returning to the Soviet Union with secrets involving American computer technology. Life had been pleasant for Anton Zimovniki, who was promoted to the rank of Major in 1978 . . . pleasant and very satisfying, his prospects excellent—

Until 11 months ago.

It had begun when no less than Comrade Lodiovtek, the Director General of the Second Chief Directorate, had sent

1. The KGB as pronounced in the Russian language.

4

for Zimovniki and had personally briefed him on his next assignment. After informing Major Zimovniki that he was being promoted to Colonel,[2] General Lodiovtek had informed him that he would be in charge of all security on Tukoatu, a tiny island in the Hawaiian chain which was privately owned by Hiromori Nagai, a Japanese-American millionaire who lived in Honolulu.

General Lodiovtek did not go into details of how the KGB was blackmailing Hiromori Nagai. Speaking in his nasal notched voice, Lodiovtek had only said, "We have enough on Nagai to put him in an American prison for the rest of his life, if he lived another three hundred years.

The Director General had explained that the top-priority Project *Mogilki* ("graves"), was one of the best-kept secrets of the Soviet Union. Because of the project's vital importance, all research would be conducted outside the vast confines of the USSR.

"There may be enemy eyes and ears even in Siberia," Lodiovtek had said, "but the *Amerikanskis* will never suspect a Soviet laboratory hidden in their own back yard."

There were other pluses for the Soviets, especially in regard to Tukoatu. Isolated, an emerald oasis in the vast stretches of the blue Pacific, Tukoatu was 104 nautical miles or 167 kilometers northeast of Molokai, one of the larger of the eight main islands in the Hawaiian group.[3] Furthermore, Tukoatu had a surface area of only 9.6 square miles. From 10,000 feet in the air, the island appeared to be one giant green-covered mountain protruding from the dark ocean floor. Closer to the ground, one could see that more than three-fourths of the island was a series of craggy mountains separated by gulches, water-carved gullies and deep valleys, all filled with *lauhala* trees[4], ferns that grew thirty feet tall, and fruit trees weighed down with

2. The KGB has ranks somewhat similar to the Soviet Army. There are three grades of Colonel.

3. Molokai is now covered with pineapple fields. It is most famous as the place where the Catholic priest, Father Damien, established a colony of lepers. Today, there are only 200 victims of Hansen's disease on the island.

4. A "screw pine." The leaves are used as a material for weaving.

breadfruit, mangoes, bananas, and coconuts. Everywhere were exotic flowers of vivid colors.

The only flat area was on the southeast side of the island, a few hundred acres that revealed the only signs of civilization—the hand of the two-legged savages called "men." Not too distant from the palm-fringed beach of dark volcanic sand was the rambling wooden house of Hiromori Nagai, who only visited the island two or three times a year. Farther back, to the west, not far from where the black volcanic cliffs, stopped their eastward movement, was a deserted Hawaiian village of *hales,* thatched huts resting on large poles. Except for the relatively small beach—the only section of the island off which a ship could safely drop anchor—the remainder of the oval-shaped island was battered by surf that thundered against bleak rocks and rolled violently into the openings of the numerous small caves dotting the west side of the island at the waterline.

Colonel Zimovniki turned the corner and instantly switched his face into an expressionless mask as he came to two security guards, who paused and saluted smartly. Returning the salute, Zimovniki continued on his way, anxious to meet with Major Amosov and Major Marleoff, his two assistants.

Once more he remembered the first bombshell that Josef Lodiovtek had dropped during the two-hour-long meeting. Zimovniki would follow the orders of Doctor Professor Yuri Mkrtchyan, the famed biochemist from the Lenin Institute. An unheard-of state of affairs! KGB officials did not take orders from civilian scientists.

General Lodiovtek, who was in full agreement, explained the reason for the unusual departure from protocol. Doctor Professor Mkrtchyan had close personal friends in very high places, both within the Council of Ministers and within the Central Committee of the Communist Party.

"But you, Comrade Colonel Zimovniki, will make your weekly radio reports directly to me," Lodiovtek had emphasized. He had then told an enraged (but not showing it) Zimovniki of other restrictions. There would be no contact of any kind with KGB deep-cover illegals, none of whom had any knowledge of Project *Mogilki,* who were a small part of a Pacific islands spy ring coded *Kabatskaya Melanholiya* ("Tavern Melancholy").

Bombshell number two! General Lodiovtek had then explained that Russian engineers and construction workers had been secretly working inside the higher levels of the caves for almost four years, making the complex habitable.

Supplies would not be a problem for the 300 men and several dozen women who would live and work in the labyrinth of caves buried deeply within the mountains. The technicians and workers had come by submarine. So would the supplies, every two months. The risk would be minimal. While the majority of caves, at the waterline on the west side of the island, came to a dead end after a quarter of a mile or more, there was one that did not, although no one would have suspected it from looking at the entrance from the outside. Only three feet of the entrance were above the water; yet there were 631 feet below the water, in a channel that was 284 feet wide and, moving inward for 3,986 feet, was 112 feet at its most narrow point. Any experienced sub skipper could navigate the channel and surface once he was 1,400 feet inside the mountain, through which the passage had been cut over the millions of years—1,400 feet because there was less than 8 feet of space from the ceiling to the surface of the water before that. Beyond the 1,400-foot mark, the ceiling rose suddenly to 40 feet and continued to rise until—at the end of the remaining 2,586 feet—the height was 86 feet.

Security? Only the most daring of on-the-water tourists ever entered the dead-end caverns. Once or twice a year, scuba teams from some passing pleasure boat would attempt to explore the long, wide channel, but few ever ventured more than a few hundred feet. Even if they swam to the 1,400-foot mark they could get no farther. A steel-mesh fence stretched across the width of the channel and rose from the rocky floor beneath the water to the ceiling. At every ten feet underwater a sign was welded to the fence: THIS ISLAND IS OWNED BY MR. HIROMORI NAGAI. TRESPASSERS WILL BE PROSECUTED TO THE FULLEST EXTENT OF THE LAW.

When the Soviet submarine approached, the fence could be raised on ball-runners concealed within the sides of the walls on each side of the channel.

Colonel Zimovniki hurried up the steel stairs to the next level, recalling how he had sat stunned when General Lodiovtek had explained the nature of Project Graves. For many years, Doctor Yuri Mkrtchyan had been convinced

7

that the 100,000 genes in every human cell carried far more than inheritable traits and the building blocks needed to create a complete human being. Already the scientists of the world, especially the Americans, had made vast strides in microbiology and in understanding the fantastically complex structure of the human cell. The key lay in the genes, composed of the chemical called deoxyribonucleic acid—better known as DNA—which provides the basis of all life from amoebas to human beings.

The genes are formed into two tightly intertwined strands—the famous "double helix"—each made up of four chemical links called nucleotides. The form and function of every living plant and animal are determined by molecules of DNA. Whenever cells divide, the DNA duplicates itself, passing on its genetic inheritance to the next generation of cells.

Scientists could also determine both the exact sequence of bases in a piece of DNA and the precise locations of genes within the chromosomes. Similarly, microbiologists can tell how the total of more than 100,000 genes fit into the forty-six chromosomes. To accomplish this, scientists clone a gene and mix it with chromosomes whose DNA spirals have been split down the middle.

Doctor Mkrtchyan was convinced that many of the genes in human beings contained and, therefore, transmitted to a newly conceived person ancestral memory—*racial memory!*

Race is a relative term and based—conveniently but falsely—not only on skin color but on divisions of language. An individual can be a Caucasian—a member of the "white race"—and speak perhaps *Plattdeutsch* (modern Low German). Culturally, he will have little in common with a member of the "yellow race" who speaks one of the Indo-Chinese languages. Yet the two will have everything in common, biologically, in that they are both members of one genetic race: MAN (genus *Homo*, family *Hominidae*, class *Mammalia*). One race: the human race.

With this premise as his foundation, Doctor Mkrtchyan's hypothesis stated that thousands of genes in every human being alive carried the memories of the hundreds and hundreds of millions who had lived but were now dead. Beginning with the first ape-man and moving upward through the long eons of time to Neanderthal and on to Cro-Magnon man (the same species as modern *Homo sapiens*), then Modern Man . . . every single memory was buried deeply in the mind circuits of every man and woman alive. It was all there, the memories, the hopes, the dreams, the aspirations, the joy, the sadness, the exaltations and ecstasies, the love, the hate and despair of all the dead—of the Roman emperors, the Greek philosophers, the scientific geniuses of the ages . . . the great poets, dramatists, musicians; the memories of great military leaders and statesmen, men such as Tiglath-pileser, Alexander the Great, Napoleon, Hitler, Stalin, Disraeli, Churchill, etc. Every single memory as well of the hundreds of millions whom history had ignored . . . the totally insignificant, those who had been born, had lived, and had died in total obscurity.[5]

The very concept was mind-boggling to the extreme and paradoxical to the nth degree. Imagine the humanistic thoughts of Christ, of Buddha, of Lao-tze, of Mohandas Gandhi, of Albert Schweitzer, thrown in with the insane, sadistic emotions of Tamerlane, Jenghiz Kahn, Hitler and Stalin. . . .

Those emotions, those thoughts, those trillions and trillions of memories were there, in the genes of every human being.

Suppose those trillions of memories could be sorted and the memories of each dead individual, of each person who had ever lived, made singular and traced back to any particular entity/personality, in a way similar to tuning in to a particular radio or television station? If this "tuning-in" process could be accomplished successfully, the Soviet Union would have at its disposal the combined knowledge of every scientific and military genius who had ever lived.

Even now, months later, Anton Zimovniki found the concept not only ridiculous but unbelievable. But certain men and women in the Soviet Government (the Council of Ministers) and the Communist Party (the Politburo of the

5. "Totally insignificant" is a relative phrase. To the Absolute no entity is insignificant or unimportant. It is worldly wealth and power that are actually insignificant. The spiritual development of a beggar might be ten times higher than that of an emperor, depending on whether one believes in Karma—"The Law of the Deed," or the ethical and moral consequences of an individual's acts.

Central Committee) had enough faith in the theory to give it a test, to give Dr. Mkrtchyan a chance to prove it.

During the meeting, General Lodiovtek had explained that Doctor Mkrtchyan, working with Doctor Anatoly A. Gavvda, had invented a device that he and Gavvda referred to as a "Bio-Memory Scanner." So far, the device was only on paper. "The machine will be built and tested on Tukoatu," Lodiovtek had said, lighting another American cigarette (it was rumored he smoked five packs a day).

Assisting Doctors Mkrtchyan and Gavvda would be scientists from some of the satellite nations—Doctor Todor Zhivkov, a leading Bulgarian geneticist; Doctor Paul Janos Ceausescu, a Romanian genetic engineer; Doctor Ludvik Svoboda, a Czech cytologist; and finally, another scientist from the Soviet Union, Doctor Sonya Zupik, an electrobiologist.

Only four months ago, Doctor Mkrtchyan and the rest of the scientists on Tukoatu had tested the Bio-Memory Scanner.

The device had half-worked . . . was half successful!

Memories of the long-dead and turned-to-dust had poured into the minds of the test subjects. During the tests the subjects were clamped rigidly to a special metal chair, laughingly referred to by the scientists as "the Throne," and verbalized the tidal wave of memories flooding their minds. They had no choice. The Scanner automatically stimulated the centers of the brain that controlled the vocal cords.

However, there were several very serious flaws. The minds of the test subjects (political prisoners brought from the USSR by submarine) could not withstand the tremendous tidal wave of memories flooding them. The subjects became stark raving mad, some within hours, others within days, depending on their age, and physical and mental health. Some of the subjects became catatonic, as mute and (seemingly) lifeless as stone. Others became lunatics who raved and raved—literally—spewing out a stream of nonsense gibberish for hours on end. Two subjects had actually died of exhaustion, from verbal fatigue. They had literally talked themselves to death! After that, Doctor Mkrtchyan ordered all the psychotic subjects drugged. Why not kill them? Because the chicken-necked *bzdoon* ("fart") hoped to eventually restore them to sanity!

The second bottleneck was that Doctor Mkrtchyan and his coworkers could not sort the spoken thoughts or tune in to the memories of any particular dead individual.

In the words of Doctor Mkrtchyan, "Further testing and research will be necessary."

Colonel Zimovniki felt like screaming curses, although he knew that his urge was only a primitive emotion that could bring only momentary release and solve nothing. He didn't give a damn whether Dr. Mkrtchyan and his crackpots succeeded or failed. His department was security. His job was to protect the island and to see that the 192 agents working under him functioned like a well-oiled machine.

Colonel Zimovniki quickened his pace. If only it weren't for the station monitoring six United States communications satellites that periodically passed overhead at various heights of thousands of kilometers. To the extremely cautious Anton Zimovniki that station, at the top of one of the higher mountains on Tukoatu, was a constant danger—an opinion he had voiced to General Lodiovtek, who had promptly told him that the parabola-shaped microwave dish could not be detected by either aircraft or any of the satellites themselves. The regular radar station, not far from Hiromori Nagai's house, was used to detect storms. The same radar with modifications could detect even high-flying aircraft. In addition, the dish would only probe a satellite after it had passed overhead and was only a few degrees of arc from the horizon. The dish could be raised and lowered from a shaft built straight down into the mountain. When not in use, the monitoring apparatus would be stored in the shaft and the opening covered with rock placed over a latticework of wood, just in case any satellite might probe the top of that particular mountain. One chance in ten thousand. But if that one chance did become reality, the probe would show rock, not metal. Everything would be analyzed as natural.

General Lodiovtek said so . . .

Top Level. Corridor B3. Zimovniki hurried down the narrow passage, opened a door to his right, and strode in. Major Sergei Amosov and Major Valery Marleoff, both of whom had previously worked with Zimovniki, looked up from the chairs in which they were sprawled.

"How did it go with him?" asked Amosov. Tall and on

11

the verge of being thin, he had deep-set dark eyes and, at only 38, hair that was a black-gray unruly shock.

"As usual, he was his sweet, charming self." Zimovniki went over to a small table and poured a glass of iced tea from a press-pump thermos dispenser. "As usual, he reminded me that he was boss. He even said that he would have taken full responsibility if Valery and the Hawaiians had gone to Honolulu and had been caught in one of the kidnap tries."

Major Amosov pulled in a ragged breath and looked at Major Marleoff.

"A lot of good that would have done you, Valery. Even with your forged identification, you'd have had a difficult time of it."

"I don't think we would have failed," Marleoff said firmly. "I'll admit the risk factor was the Hawaiians."

"They're all wanted criminals. That alone doubled the risk factor," Amosov said and directed his gaze toward Colonel Zimovniki, who was sitting down in a chrome and vinyl chair and wiping his face with a white handkerchief. "I know you're going to report Doctor Mkrtchyan's rash decision to the Center."

"Detail for detail, and take pleasure in it." Zimovniki bit off each word. "Not that it will do any good. We three are stuck here. Mkrtchyan has friends far more powerful than General Lodiovtek, even more powerful than Andropov. We must be careful. We don't want to make enemies of people who have more power than the Chairman of the *Kah Gay Beh*."

He took a sip of the unsweetened tea and smiled, relishing the report he would send to General Lodiovtek.

"Major, you had better tell him," Amosov said slowly.

Zimovniki was instantly alert. "Tell me what?" he said to Marleoff.

"We may have another problem," Marleoff said, sighing deeply. He leaned forward and put his elbows on his knees. "While you were reporting to Doctor Mkrtchyan, we listened in on the Englishman and the other captives. None suspected that the large cell was bugged. The four young women are prostitutes—call girls—that Clarke, the Englishman, had taken aboard for the enjoyment of his friends. One of the men is a Hawaiian banker. The other three are American businessmen. The middle-aged Hawaiian woman was the cook. The other two men are crew members."

"Pleasure cruisers do have accidents," Zimovniki reassured him. "A routine search will reveal nothing. The ship went down. There wasn't any floating wreckage. You said that yourself."

"We think that one of the crewmen escaped, or rather we can't account for him," Marleoff said hesitantly. "We found this out listening to the conversation of the captives. They keep talking about a Joe Kohalukai. They're wondering whether he escaped or went down with the yacht."

"Well, damn it! Didn't Aninin and Stashynsky search the yacht?" Zimovniki found it difficult not to break his rule of never raising his voice to subordinates. "You didn't see anyone swimming away as the boat was going down. Of course you didn't, or you'd have picked him up and he'd be in the cell with the others. So what's this all about?"

"The craft was searched from stem to stern, from port to starboard," Major Marleoff replied all too quickly. "After the charge blew a large hole in the hull, the yacht went down in less than a minute. No one could have survived. I'm certain."

Frowning, Zimovniki swallowed half of the tea, his quick mind racing for an answer. "But the Englishman and the rest of them aren't sure," he said coldly. "And we've got to be positive."

"What about Mkrtchyan?" Major Amosov worked at an imaginary speck of dirt under his thumbnail. "You'll have to tell him."

"To protect all of us!" Major Marleoff stared knowingly at Zimovniki. Well-muscled as a result of his hobby of lifting weights, he stood six feet two inches, had nice features and, although only in his early thirties, was half bald.

Colonel Zimovniki finished the rest of his tea, stood up, walked back to the thermos dispenser, put down the empty glass, then turned and faced his two assistants.

"I'll inform Mkrtchyan, but only after we get the facts. Let's go have a friendly talk with the people from the yacht."

Zimovniki went over to a counter-high steel storage cabinet, opened the double doors and took out a device known as a Variac. Designed to torture with electric shock, the Variac consisted of a small box which could be plugged into a light socket or any wall outlet, and a thick, foot-long rod attached to a length of cord. The controls in the rubber handle could be set from 40 volts to 500 volts.

13

"We'll start with one of the whores. Women are always the weakest," Zimovniki said as he and the two other KGB officers headed toward the lower level.

"I favor one of the crew," said Major Amosov. "The sluts might not know how many were in the crew."

"The old cook would." Marleoff uttered a low laugh. "What's the difference? No one can withstand high voltage for very long."

"I saw a Turk one time hold out for almost an hour," Amosov said. "It was at Vladimir."[6]

Thoughts tumbled around in Colonel Zimovniki's clever mind. Sergei and Anton were worried, but they were still missing the main point. Suppose one of the crew couldn't be accounted for? Good! It was Doctor Yuri Mkrtchyan who . . . *against my advice ordered me to have Valery take those six Hawaiian animals to Honolulu and kidnap subjects for his damned tests. If anyone will pay for such stupidity—nyet! it won't be Mkrtchyan. He has too many friends in powerful places. The blame would fall on poor Valery—and on Aninin and Stashynsky. Too bad. But I'm covered. I had to obey Mkrtchyan's orders. . . .*

An image of Mkrtchyan rose in Zimovniki's mind. Well, give the son of a bitch his due. He was a scientific wizard. No doubt about that. The egotistical old bastard was certain that the flaws to the racial memory experiments centered in the hippocampus, a very important part of the brain's emotion and memory circuits. It was fact that when the hippocampus was stimulated, the subject would be overwhelmed by stored images that he or she could not control. The subject would experience the worst kind of waking nightmares, a deep-pit hell of fear-inducing stimuli. . . .

Suppose Mkrtchyan and the other scientists succeeded. But it might take them years. *And I could be stuck here on this damned rock of an island for years!*

Colonel Mkrtchyan and the two men with him reached the lower level, turned into Corridor Ln-6 and soon were passing the "Chicken Coop," the individual holding cells where the test subjects, driven insane by the Bio-Memory Scanner, were kept in individual soundproof padded cells.

6. Vladimir Prison, about 100 miles north of Moscow. U-2 pilot Gary Powers and Josef Stalin's son, Vasily, were held at Vladimir.

Other than a small steel door (padded on the inside), the front of each cell was constructed of thick unbreakable glass, so that the subjects could be constantly watched by strolling guards, each of whom saluted when Zimovniki, Amosov, and Marleoff approached. However, the three KGB officers were more interested in the circus behind the glass fronts of the cells, intrigued by the men and women whose minds had been burned out by the billion-volt blast of memories from progenitors that extended all the way back in the past to half-human cave creatures.

All stark naked, some of the men and women shuffled aimlessly back and forth or in circles, each muttering unintelligible words. Others laughed or giggled. Many slobbered. Those who would have talked or shouted or raved themselves to death were drugged and suspended in leather cocoon-like hammocks. Those mindless creatures who could not feed themselves by reflex action, by the deeply buried instinct of self-preservation, were rendered unconscious by instantly acting tranquilizers and given shots of high-powered vitamins and minerals—a task the lab technicians hated, since they also had to force water down the throats of the living dead and do so without drowning the zombies. But Doctor Yuri Mkrtchyan's ordered had to be obeyed.

Colonel Zimovniki rounded the corner with his two aides and presently came to a steel door in Corridor Ln-7. Across from the door, in a room on the other side of the corridor, three guards sat at a table, their eyes on the TV screen that was picking up the images of the captives from the rotating camera monitoring the inside of the large cell.

All three guards rose, stood ramrod straight and saluted.

Zimovniki motioned to one of the guards. "Open the door. You other two cover him with your machine pistols."

Grinning, the guards moved toward the cell door.

The screaming would soon begin. . . .

CHAPTER ONE

His light-sensitive eyes protected by Ray-Ban Caravan sunglasses, Richard Camellion pushed open the glass door of Ogden's Tattoo Palace, all the while wishing he could be someplace other than in Honolulu. The Death Merchant's dislike of the Hawaiian Islands—the 50th State—had nothing to do with the people, who, as a group, were peaceful and friendly. Nor with the Islands themselves. Hawaii was truly the "paradise of the Pacific." *Even if the islands are a part of this ridiculous little planet!*

No land in the world has more gorgeous coloring—especially true of the mountains. In the morning, there are soft blues and greens, and as the sun climbs, the colors change to brilliant reds and oranges, deep green and bright copper.

Everywhere one could see flowering plants. Hibiscus as common as ordinary weeds. Brilliant red anthurium. Mysterious night-blooming cereus, shower trees with their big, bright blossoms spilling their flowers onto the street. Fragrant ginger . . . the yellow and purple bird-of-paradise, and the bright yellow Hau. Coconut palms lined the streets, their fruit—unwanted in this land of plenty—put out with the garbage for collectors to pick up.

The temperature, always around seventy-five degrees, was perfect; and when it rained, the shower was usually brief. Then the sky would clear. The air would sparkle, and a rainbow would curve over the mountains. In fact, it was not at all unusual to see half a dozen rainbows in a day, some of them double, repeating their colors in reverse from the center; and because the islands were still primarily agricultural, they were calm, clean, and beautiful . . . bright emeralds set in an endless ocean of heavenly blues.

Camellion had enjoyed coming into Honolulu International Airport that morning. Far below the aircraft, the

16

calm blue ocean seemed to breathe as it sparkled under a clear sky. As the Pan Am airliner had descended, Camellion had glimpsed a sight as familiar as Gibraltar—the craggy profile of Diamond Head, an ancient dead crater that was a National Natural Landmark and a State Monument.[1] And just beyond, the yellow-white sands and rolling white surf of Waikiki Beach. Far in the distance, on the curve of the horizon, near Schofield Barracks, was the 4,000-foot Kaala, the tallest mountain on the island of Oahu.

The sleek jet had dropped lower. There was Pearl Harbor, northwest of the airport, its waters shining like a mirror—not blue like the ocean, but silver. These were just some of the features that made Hawaii one of the most charming places in the world, in addition to the clear sky and blue ocean, steep green slopes and majestic mountains, brisk but mild breezes, and bright sun.[2]

It was the bright sun that the Death Merchant abhorred. The Islands themselves could be compared to a cheesecake baked by a master chef—with a dead rat in the center of it! The sun was the rat. By temperament and biorhythmically a night person, Camellion always felt exposed during the daylight hours, unless the sky was overcast—and the more rain and fog the better. Why, there was something obscene about killing in bright sunshine, in ridding the world of trash during the daytime. The days were meant for sleeping, the nights for work. . . .

He had felt totally exposed during the cab ride from the airport to the "Pink Palace," the Royal Hawaiian Hotel, a part of the huge Sheraton complex that included several hotels from central Kalakaua Avenue to Waikiki Beach— "naked" because he was unarmed.

How sweet it was after the bellhop had escorted him to his rooms on the seventh floor and the door was closed and locked. The Death Merchant had hurried to the bathroom,

1. Private homes nestle in a girdle of trees on the slopes of Diamond Head, and old gun emplacements are stepped down the 760-foot face. One can drive into the interior of the crater through a tunnel off Diamond Head Road.

2. There are actually eight main islands to "Hawaii." The largest island is Hawaii. It's called the "Big Island." Two other nicknames are the "Volcano Island" and the "Orchid Island."

lifted the top of the toilet's flushbox, reached into the water and pulled out two packages sealed in waterproof plastic. Quickly, he had replaced the top and opened the packages. In one pacakge had been two Jerry-Rigs and four spare magazines loaded with .380 ammo. The second package had contained two TDE auto pistols.

Camellion had strapped on only one of the J-R ankle holsters, shoved a TDE into the leather pocket, and carefully secured the strap over the rear of the small weapon. The spare clips he had put in the front pockets of his tropical suit. Dressed in a suit, he'd look like a *malihini* (a newcomer to the Islands), but he was not going to take the first chance, not until he knew the location of Banana Bread Box 1. Then, too, the suit was tailor-made in more ways than one. On the outside the suit was deep tan. But turn the coat completely inside out and the color was sky blue—complete with pocket flaps and breast pocket. Turn the pants inside out and—presto! A bright navy complete with belt loops.

He had not unpacked. He had not had the time. He had opened the attache case, reached into a special compartment and removed a small tube of spirit gum, a brown mustache of the shaggy dog type and a brown wig to match. He had distributed the gum, mustache and wig among his pockets. The second TDE autoloader he had placed in the left inside pocket of his coat.

He had put the leather suitcase and attache case in a closet, left the apartment, taken an elevator down to the lobby, walked out onto the street and was soon in a cab. Twenty-six minutes later he had sauntered leisurely into the Tattoo Palace on Kapiolani Boulevard, quickly noticing that the electric-needle art shop was in a block of cheap bars, massage parlors (Hawaiian massage is called *lomilomi*, and uses the knees and fists.), "adult" movie houses and cheap souvenir shops. The establishment to the left of the Tattoo Palace was a Chinese bakery, with a large sign that read: *Good people all—walk in and buy, Of Sam and Mow, Good cake and pie; Bread hard and soft, For land or sea, Celestial made; Come buy of we*. To the right was a photographer's place of business, where tourists could have their photographs taken while posing behind cardboard figures (minus the head) wearing Hawaiian native costumes—red and yellow *malos* for the men, *pa'us* for the women.

In the old days before the white man contaminated the Islands with "civilization," the Hawaiians wore simple garments. The *malo* was a strip of *tapa* (the inner bark of the paper mulberry) about a foot wide and three or four yards long, which the men wrapped around their waists and between their legs. The *pa'u* or skirt worn by the women was about thirty inches wide and also three or four yards long. This they wrapped around their waists, tucking the end in tightly to hold it in place. Both the *malo* and the *pa'u* were dyed and printed in many designs, the colors pressed into the material with wooden paddles which had been carved in various designs.

Came the contact with Eddie Ogden, the owner of the Tattoo Palace. A *hapa haole*, or part-white Hawaiian, Ogden—thirty-five at the most—was the son of an English physician and a *wahine*, a Hawaiian woman. He looked it, although his skin was lighter than the usual golden brown of the full-blooded Hawaiian. But he was well muscled, physically well formed, had wavy hair of a lustrous black, and eloquent dark eyes. His features were typical Hawaiian—thick lips, prominent cheek bones, broad nostrils, and a high forehead that slanted backward.

Camellion, recognizing Ogden from photographs he had studied at the U.S. Embassy in Bonn, got down to business as the man put down the *Science & Mechanics* magazine he was reading and looked up with bored eyes. "OK, what kind of tattoo do you want?"

"Mr. Charles Gambiers, a friend of mine, said you're the best tattoo man in the business," Camellion said pleasantly, watching and waiting for a reaction.

He got it, subtly, an alert, cautious gleam creeping into Ogden's eyes. "It seems I remember him. He had a French flag tattooed on his chest," Ogden said, getting slowly to his feet. All the while he looked at the Death Merchant. "I believe he lives on Bora Bora in French Polynesia."

"Yeah, French Polynesia, but he lives in Papeete, on Tahiti."[3]

"What does he do for a living?"

"He operates a sightseeing boat that docks at Moorea's

---

3. Three general regions of the South Pacific are Polynesia, Melanesia, and Micronesia. *Nesia* means island. Polynesia translates as *many islands*. Melanesia means *black islands*, and Micronesia, *tiny* or *small islands*.

Aimeo Hotel pier," Camellion replied, supplying the last of his part of the ID cipher to the CIA contract agent. "And the French flag is tattooed on his back."

Ogden took the unlit cigarette from behind his right ear and studied Camellion for a few moments. "Come over here, Mr. . . . Mr. . . . ? You didn't give me your name."

"Cosgrove. Albert Cosgrove."

Ogden moved to a display board to his right and lit his cigarette.

"Right here are over 750 designs you can choose from."

The Death Merchant followed Ogden to the board. Ogden stepped sideways, moved closer to Camellion, and reached into his shirt pocket. He took out a folded square of paper and, with his left hand, held it out to the Death Merchant. His back also to the door, Camellion opened the square of paper, read the name and address, then tore the paper into tiny bits and put them into one of his coat pockets.

"Anything you're supposed to transmit verbally?" asked Camellion.

"Nothing."

Camellion turned and started toward the door, not bothering to reply to Ogden's, "Aloha, Mr. Cosgrove."

Camellion pushed open the door, walked the few steps to the sidewalk, paused and, always cautious, let his eyes dart to his left. A Chinese was lounging against one of the windows of the photographer's shop, reading a newspaper. A warning bell tinkled in Camellion's mind. He glanced to his right. Another young dude—this one a Hawaiian—was in front of the bakery, in front of the window closest to the Tattoo Palace.

A setup! I've been fingered! While knowing he might be wrong, Camellion had more than enough instinct and experience to look carefully a second time into things that he was most certain of the first time. Should he be wrong about the two men, no harm would be done. They'd only think he was a loony and ready for a giggle jacket. They might even call him a few names. The hell with that—*Just as long as they call me for dinner.* On the other hand, should he be right and not take the proper measures—*I'll end up in a long icebox in the morgue, unless they intend a snatch and grab job.*

In that fraction of a second, Camellion saw that a Datsun station wagon, a Toyota, and a Jeep Wagoneer were parked at the curb in front of the tattoo joint.

I've walked into hell with the fire out! Fudge!

The Death Merchant took a step, made a motion as if to turn to his right, then did it—he dashed to the curb and was moving between the rear of the station wagon and the front of the Jeep Wagoneer as a surprised Tommy Lee Chong and a caught-off guard Duke Hahaninou were pulling weapons from underneath their gaudily colored shirts.

Tommy Chong got off the first shot, with a Charter Arms Bulldog revolver. But the .44 Special slug missed Camellion and, with a loud ringing sound, poked itself through the top left rear of the station wagon. A split second later, Duke Hahaninou triggered off a shot with his AMT auto-pistol, the big boom of his weapon mingling with the roar from Chong's Bulldog and creating more panic on the street. Although Hahaninou's .45 ACP projectile came within an inch of making contact with Camellion's right side, near hits were not acceptable in this kind of deadly game.

The Death Merchant's sudden, unexpected move—giving him seven seconds of lag time—placed the odds on his side. By the time the two would-be assassins had reshuffled their thinking, Camellion had pulled the TDE pistol from his left inside coat pocket and was crouched by the right front wheel of the station wagon.

A killer with a lot of pride, Tommy Chong did not like failure. He ran toward the rear of the station wagon while Duke Hahaninou, still trying to figure out what to do, put all his faith in Billy Puolani, the backup gunsel.

Not really certan if Eddie Ogden had fingered him, the Death Merchant reared up to the proper height and fired twice keeping one eye cocked toward the door of the Tattoo Palace. The first .380 full-metal-jacketed bullet buzzed into Chong's left side, sliced through his shirt and skin, passed through his pancreas, and came to rest against the inside of a rib on his right side. The second .380 FMJ projectile struck him in the outer left thigh, cut through the femoral artery and buried itself in the thick abductor group of muscles. More dead than alive, Chong jerked violently, let the Bulldog revolver slip from his fingers and wilted to the sidewalk.

Just for a moment, the sagging Chong was in Duke Hahaninou's line of fire. It really didn't matter. Compared to the Death Merchant, who was chain-lightning fast, Hahaninou was a crippled turtle.

The Hawaiian thug was about to swing the .45 AMT toward the Death Merchant when Camellion popped him twice in his broad chest with two more .380 slugs and at the same time heard glass shatter from a window above the bakery.

With a strangled cry of pain and fear, Duke Hahaninou spun, did a drunken sideways shuffle, fell against the plate glass window and slid dead to the concrete walk.

Instantly, Camellion dropped to the side of the wheel, made himself as small as possible, and pulled the second TDE auto-pistol from the J-R holster on his left ankle, all the while listening to the obnoxious roaring of a submachine gun and to the high velocity projectiles ripping into the left sides of the station wagon and the Jeep Wagoneer. By now the sidewalk had cleared of people, and passing cars were racing by wildly.

Camellion wasn't concerned about the halfwit firing the sub-gun. He knew the triggerman was a hot dog—*or he wouldn't have warned me inadvertently by first breaking the glass. The damn fool should have raised the window. If the window was stuck, tough. He should have checked it out in advance. And he's firing bursts that are far too long. A waste of good ammo.*

It was the passing cars that worried the Death Merchant. All he needed was for some rubbernecking driver to run into him.

As suddenly as the submachine gun had started, the firing stopped. Camellion stayed down. The gunman might be playing it cute. At the same time, Camellion knew he had to get to the alley behind the street and do a vanishing act. He was positive that the alley was there. He had thoroughly studied a map of modern Honolulu while on the plane. Then again, suppose the dummy with the music box had had only one magazine?

Camellion knew the gunman had reloaded when he again started firing and raking the already shot-to-pieces Datsun and the Jeep Wagoneer. By now, centering on the sound, Camellion had fixed the location of the triggerman in his mind. Still, he did not rear up. Instead, he waited until he heard the projectiles popping through the left rear of the Jeep Wagoneer. Only then did he jump up and begin

22

snap-firing both auto pistols. Four .380 bullets streaked through the window above the bakery and flooded all over Billy Puolani—one in the stomach, the other three slugs in his chest. Knocked unconscious in a microsecond, Billy Puolani dropped the 9-millimeter Spanish Parinco sub-gun, which fell to the windowsill, toppled off and hit the sidewalk below. The dying Puolani—skinny for a Hawaiian—toppled backward like a dead tree.

Two .380s from the right TDE broke the plate-glass window and the glass door of the Tattoo Palace. For good measure, as the Death Merchant left the station wagon and raced across the sidewalk, he tossed another slug through the shattered front window.

Aware that time was running out on him, Camellion jumped through the space where the glass of the front door had been, careful to avoid the numerous sharp slivers of glass protruding from the wooden frame, and careful not to slip on glass lying on the vinyl tiled floor.

Eddie Ogden was nowhere in sight. Glancing toward the closed door that opened to the rear room, Camellion raced to the end of the counter to his left and looked behind it. Ogden was crouched behind the counter, a Heckler and Koch PSP auto-loader in his right hand. Before the Hawaiian could swing around, Camellion dropped down beside him and jammed the muzzle of one of the TDEs against the left side of the man's neck.

"Drop it," he ordered in a coarse voice, "or I'll put a tunnel through your throat."

A stunned look on his face, Ogden placed the German pistol on the floor and froze, afraid to move because of the hot muzzle pressed against his neck. "You've got it all wrong," he said nervously, staring straight ahead. "I didn't know those gunmen were out there waiting for you."

"I don't have time to discuss it," Camellion said and removed the small auto-pistol from the Hawaiian's neck. "If you did finger me, the people who hired you will find out, and you couldn't hide from them if you went to the moon."

"Listen! I—"

The Death Merchant switched off Ogden by slamming one of the TDE pistols against the side of his head. Maybe Ogden was innocent, but Camellion wasn't going to take the chance of the Hawaiian's telling the police, or anyone else, that he had gone through the back room into the alley. And a lump the size of a small egg on Ogden's head would

23

convince the police that he had not been involved in the shootout.

Camellion shoved one of the TDEs in the ankle holster, dropped the other small weapon into a coat pocket, picked up the H&K PSP auto-loader and rushed into the back room, a small, dark cubbyhole whose rear door was locked and barred. Camellion removed the iron rod, shot the padlock from the hasp, and was soon moving down the narrow alley, headed in a northeast direction.

He had the address of Banana Bread Box 1. All he had to do now was get back to the Royal Hawaiian Hotel, grab his bags and clear out—and avoid the police and possibly other hit men in the process. He was positive that some sharp-eyed spectator, who had been a witness to the gun battle, would give his description to the cops. . . .

Suffering succotash! This is definitely not one of my better days!

CHAPTER TWO

In the world of clandestine intelligence operations, it is always more important to discover what one cannot do than what one can do. One must also be a coldblooded pragmatist and realize that any operation, no matter how well planned, always contains a murky X-Factor. That factor is always the unexpected and always involves Fate— "luck," "chance," or any name one wishes to give the X-component.

Luck did not frown on the Death Merchant. Half a block from the rear of the Tattoo Palace, he came to a narrow passage between the buildings, a four-foot-wide corridor that led from the alley to the other side of the block. Camellion hurried through the corridor and found himself on Kiuai Avenue. The passage was between a drug store and a Hawaiian restaurant where whole pigs were steamed in the old-fashioned way, together with salmon and other delicacies wrapped in taro leaves.

At an unhurried pace—to hurry would arouse suspicion—he walked a block and a half before he found a cab that was empty at the intersection of Kiuai and Hanapepe, its driver waiting for the light to turn green.

The light changed as Camellion was closing the rear door. "Take me to the International Market Place," Camellion said in an easy manner. "The Kalakaua entrance will do—and the faster you get me there the better." He faked a laugh. "If I make her wait, she might get out of the mood."

The driver—he looked like he had stepped out of a production of "Hawaii Five-O"—was as American in manner as Southern fried chicken. "I'll do my best, mac. But don't expect me to break any speed records. You just get off a ship or plane?"

Damn it! He's pegged me as a malihini, and from the way he's eyeballing me in the mirror, he'll be able to give a good description to the police.

"I've been in Honolulu a week," Camellion said pleasantly. "It's a nice city."

"But expensive. No one in his right mind would ever retire to these islands unless he's well off."

"Yeah, that's right." Camellion looked out the window. It occurred to him that Honolulu had grown more skyward since his last visit in 1970. Honolulu had always been a mixture of yesterday and today, of the Orient and the U.S. Around Honolulu Harbor, where the city began, buildings of Hawaii's missionaries and monarchs and Oriental immigrants stood beside sophisticated high-rise towers, parks, malls, plazas, sculptures, stores, and restaurants. *And it's a long city, a stretched-out city,* thought Camellion.

Honolulu's major business and residential sections stretched over some thirty miles of Oahu Island's leeward shore, from Hickam Air Force Base past Makapuu Lighthouse Ridge. From the water's edge, its ridges and valleys stretched up to cloud-wrapped peaks. At night, homes on the heights formed patchwork patterns of lights. Residential sections also extended from Diamond Head all the way to Koko Head. The constantly bustling tourist center of Waikiki and the business and industrial sections covered the central waterfront.

None of which helps me, except that it makes for a large area in which the police will have to search. Of course,

*after I get to Banana Bread Box 1 it won't make any dif-
ference.*

Ten minutes more and the driver turned onto Kalakaua
Avenue. At length, Camellion saw what he wanted.

"Pull up at that service station up ahead, to your left,"
he said lazily to the driver. "I'll get out there."

"You want me to wait?" The driver sounded surprised,
and Camellion could see the man's eyes searching him cu-
riously in the rearview mirror.

"I've got to go to the john, but don't wait," Camellion
said. "From the station—the next street is Royal Hawaiian
Avenue, isn't it?"

"That's it."

"Then from the station it's only a block to the market,"
Camellion said. "I'll walk. If she's really interested, she can
wait the ten to fifteen minutes. If she won't wait, then I
would have been wasting my time in the first place."

"Smart thinking," the driver said with a dry laugh. He
started to turn into the service station. Camellion leaned
forward and put his arm over the seat, a fifty-dollar bill
folded between his fingers.

The driver stopped the car not far from the first row of
gas pumps, took the fifty-buck bill from Camellion's hand,
then turned and looked at the Death Merchant. "Look,
haven't you got anything smaller?"

"Keep it." Camellion smiled and reached for the handle
of the door. "Buy your wife a new frock."

"Thanks, buddy," chuckled the driver. "But I'll buy myself a night on the town."

Camellion got out, slammed the door and the driver of
the cab pulled away. With long strides, Camellion walked
to the men's restroom on the side of the building.

Once the door of the restroom was locked, Camellion
quickly went to work. He first reloaded the two TDEs and
checked the West German PSP auto-loader. Next he
plugged the drain of the lavatory with its rubber stopper,
took everything out of his pockets and placed it in the
basin. The reversal of the suit came next. Three minutes
later, he was dressed in a sky-blue coat and pants of bright
navy. Everything then went back into his pockets—billfold,
keys, loose change, passport, pen and pencil, notebook,
penlight and other odds and ends, including a pocket
watch. Now the disguise, as slight as it was. Expertly he

used some of the spirit gum and attached the shaggy mustache to his upper lip. With the same swiftness, he slipped the wig over his own short brown crewcut and carefully adjusted the locks of genuine human hair. He looked at his work in the mirror above the lavatory. *Not bad!* The hair was moderately long, in keeping with modern style. Both the wig and the mustache had changed his appearance considerably. There were still problems, however.

The Death Merchant never overestimated his chances— one of the reasons why he was still alive. There was one chance in several hundred that someone had seen him enter the restroom and that the same person would see what appeared to be a different man coming out. He was not actually worried about the odds. Just as people seldom see the trees for the forest, so they never really see the individual. The input of sights and sounds pours into the sense receptors, but the mind registers the impressions with all the looseness of one trying to use chalk to write on water.

Going into the hotel was not a problem either. Many, many people went into Royal Hawaiian Hotel. Ah, but leaving the hotel might offer some difficulty—*if I continue to use this disguise.* His small suite of rooms was his for a solid month. The travel agency—a Company front— had been forced to take the rooms for four weeks in order to get a reservation at such short notice. The vinegar in the broth was the Royal Hawaiian's security people, especially the ones who were always in the lobby, posing as tourists or as guests. Those men (and a few women) did see the individual trees in the forest and did remember faces. One of them might wonder why a stranger was leaving the hotel with luggage, a man they had never before seen. Of course, if they took him into custody, he would be able to prove that he was Winston L. Cookhider, a citizen of the United Kingdom. His British passport "proved" he was Cookhider; he was registered at the hotel as Cookhider.

More vinegar in the broth! The security people would want to know why he was in disguise, why the wig and mustache. Only a slight search would reveal that he was wearing a special suit, a suit that could be reversed from tan to blue and navy or vice versa. From there, it would be only one short step to connecting him to the gun battle in front of the Tattoo Palace.

Camellion made a final check. None of the weapons created any noticeable bulges. Everything was in order. He left the restroom, didn't even glance at the service station, and began walking toward the International Market Place, one of the prime tourist attractions in Honolulu. It was a complex of open-front shops, vendors' carts, restaurants, and nightclubs set in a tropical garden setting shaded by huge banyans. Here one could watch craftsmen weaving coconut hats, painting portraits, and making jewelry, clothes, and sandals.

Finding a taxi at the International Market Place would be as easy as finding snow in Antarctica.

Another factor: Eddie Ogden. Camellion had only tapped the tattoo artist hard enough to lay him out for fifteen minutes or so. Ogden could be a double agent. Well, let him do anything he wanted. Ogden didn't know the hotel where "Albert Cosgrove" was registered. By the time the police checked every man of my description at each hotel, I could go around the world twice.

Twenty minutes later, Camellion had gotten out of a cab and was walking through the rather crowded lobby toward the bank of elevators, fully prepared for trouble of the worst kind. Seven minutes more and he was in his room. He had concluded that to try to leave the hotel in disguise would be too risky. The odds were only fifty-fifty that he could get away with it in disguise, or fifty-fifty that he wouldn't be stopped by one of the Royal Hawaiian's security people.

He went into the bathroom, removed the mustache and wig, brought them back to the sitting room and placed them on a chair. He walked to the closet, took out the suitcase and the attache case, sat down in an easy chair, put the attache case in his lap and unlocked and opened it. There wasn't anything of real value in the case, only magazines he had taken to read on the plane. The attache itself was an ordinary Samsonite three-inch VIP deal, its real value lying in its one special divider which appeared to be heavy vinyl but wasn't, not entirely. Half of the divider was composed of a special hardened mixture of certain chemicals that, when ignited, gave off a thick black smoke. The Death Merchant didn't think he would need the cover screen, but just in case he took out the penlight and removed the two batteries. He took the pocket watch from his coat pocket and from a compartment in the lid of the case removed a tiny spool of almost hair-thin wire, a roll of sealing tape, and a length of fishline. While the watch kept time, it contained a pinch of thermite and could also be used as a detonator.

When he had finished with his work, the watch and the two batteries were taped to the incendiary portion of the divider, and the length of fishline was stretched loosely from the stem of the watch to the handle of the case. The line was loose enough so that it would have to be pulled in order to ignite the thermite in the watch. Camellion carefully closed the case, making sure that the line was resting in the almost invisible notch in the prim of the larger portion of the attache case.

Another factor: the agent in the hotel—man or woman—who had placed the ammo and the TDEs in the flush box. No doubt the person was an "independent contractor," a contract agent. It was unlikely that he (or she) was in contact with Ogden. The Company was very cautious about never letting its right hand know how the fingers on the left hand were moving. On the other hand, Camellion didn't have any hard evidence that Ogden wasn't working with whoever had stashed the weapons in the bathroom. There was also the possibility that while Ogden was a double agent—*if he is!*—the other person wasn't. *Even if they do know each other, which I seriously doubt.*

With the Heckler and Koch PSP tucked in his belt, a 9×19 Parabellum cartridge in the firing chamber, the Death Merchant hung the key on the doorknob and left the apartment.

Down the thickly carpeted hall to the elevators. Five long minutes more and he was walking across the lobby, the suitcase in his left hand, the attache case in his right. With both hands full, he would be at a slight disadvantage until he was outside the hotel and in a taxi. He passed underneath the arch that opened to the huge lobby and waved off, with a shake of his head, a bellboy who offered to take his suitcase and attache case. He didn't intend for anyone to pull the string on the attache case.

Walking slowly, he analyzed the lobby. Clerks were busy at the long, curved desk. To his left, as he faced the street, were four glass-fronted gift shops, a coffee and soft-drink bar, and the dark entrance to the King Kamba Cocktail Lounge. To his right was the hotel restaurant, the *Aloha*

Nui Loa Room. A row of fearsome-featured Refuge gods, made of dark hardwood, stood in front of the restaurant on either side of the room's wide entrance.

Scattered out in the lobby, between gift shops and restaurant, were numerous lounging chairs and couches and potted plants. Watching over all this chrome and plastic elegance was a tremendous chandelier of sparkling crystal, suspended on a gold-plated chain from the center of the lobby's domed ceiling.

Still taking his time, Camellion let his eyes dart over the people he could see. Three nuns and a group of wide-eyed adolescent boys and girls were at the desk. A dozen other couples were also keeping the clerks busy, the youngest in their early twenties, the eldest in their seventies. The first trip to the Islands for many . . . the last trip for some.

The people sitting in the lobby looked normal enough, at least the ones facing the Death Merchant. Some were middle-aged couples, some men and women sitting alone, all ages. A woman with a baby. A man with two teenagers. Camellion was not a man to kid himself. Looks were always deceptive at close range. A man in a $500 suit or a gal in a $1,000 original could blow you away as easily as a dimbo in a $20 shirt and a 40-buck pair of slacks. The Death Merchant knew that there wasn't any way for him to know who might be waiting in the lobby to kill him—at least age and dress could not be utilized as an indication. And maybe no one was waiting at all.

Camellion kept to his right as he moved toward the entrance of the Royal Hawaiian. He was passing the entrance to the *Aloha Nui Loa Room* when he saw the man—a *haole*, a white man—standing by a potted miniature shower tree not far from the main entrance. Dressed in an expensive coral-colored suit and alligator shoes, the man wore dark aviator sunglasses with a gold frame and had a rolled-up newspaper in his left hand. Every now and then he would glance at the entrance, then look at the wristwatch on his right wrist. To anyone and everyone, it was obvious he was waiting for someone. At length, the man, in his thirties, made an angry face, took another long look at the entrance, glanced once more at his watch, then turned and started walking toward Camellion.

An amateur would have died without knowing how he had been killed, but Camellion could spot approaching death when he was asleep! The tipoff was the newspaper

30

and the way the man carried it. The paper was rolled too tightly. The man wore his watch on his right wrist. He should, therefore, be left-handed, the hand he would use to point a gun—a gun or a rolled-up newspaper!

The Death Merchant knew what was inside the newspaper—a finger-thick, ten-inch-long metal tube, consisting of three sections screwed together. In the bottom section was the battery-powered mechanism that would silently effect the firing. Pressure would cause a metal lever in the middle section to move and crush a glass ampule in the mouth of the tube containing concentrated prussic acid, the colorless and odorless liquid of cyanide, one of the deadliest poisons known to the human race. The poison would escape from the mouth of the tube in the form of vapor. *But the weapon has to be fired at a person's face at a distance no greater than two feet.* The victim would drop dead immediately, and since the vapor would leave no trace, it would be impossible to ascertain death by violence. The hit man would suffer no ill effects from the poisonous vapor. He would swallow three tablets of sodium thiosulfate beforehand as an antidote. Immediately after firing the tube, he would also crush an ampule of amyl nitrate, sewn in gauze, and inhale its vapor.

Camellion didn't bat an eyelash. *The mousetrap technique! Maybe he has a backup and maybe he hasn't. I haven't the time to turn around and look!*

The Death Merchant dropped the suitcase, raised the attache case in his right hand, pulled the string with his left, and flung the Samsonite case straight at the man sauntering toward him.

Still fifteen feet from Camellion, Karel Simunek was totally unprepared for the Death Merchant's sudden, unexpected move. One bottom corner of the case struck him in the chest, and he gasped from pain and staggered back, but did not release his hold on the newspaper. The case fell to the floor and began to hiss!

Simunek knew that he would never be able to get close enough to the target to use the gas. He dropped the *Moischensheiv* tube in the rolled-up newspaper, stepped back from the hissing case and reached quickly for a 9mm Sig-Sauer auto-pistol in a special holster built into the right side of his suit coat.

In the meanwhile, the Death Merchant darted behind one of the larger of the Refuge gods on display in front of the *Aloha Nui Loa Room* and pulled the HK PSP from his belt.

Toward the middle of the lobby, Reino Gutik and Tania Kabalof, Simunek's backup team, had been watching Simunek and Camellion. The two KGB *Mokryye Dela* ("bloodwet") assassination agents had assumed that the kill would go as planned. Such terminations always did. Gutik and Kabalof, posing as Swedish tourists, were as surprised as Simunek at Camellion's throwing of the attache case. They were even more startled as they heard Camellion's PSP crack sharply and saw Simunek, his left hand underneath his coat, stagger back from the impact of the two 9mm projectiles popping him in the stomach and lower chest. Almost at the same time, thick black smoke began pouring from the attache case.

The shots from Camellion's PSP pushed the emotional panic button. In an instant, the net of pandemonium dropped over the people in the lobby. Women screamed. The men who kept their heads grabbed their women and pulled them to the floor, or down on couches. Other men and women ran toward the elevators and toward the Hawaiian Palace, the bar and dance floor whose entrance was to the left of the main desk.

Snuggled down on a couch, Reino Gutik whispered to Tania Kabalof, "He's behind one of the wooden Hawaiian gods. We've got to kill him and get out of here."

This is one mell of a hess! Now, the Death Merchant had only one goal—to get to the main entrance and get out. Listening to people crying out in fear and terror, he pulled out one of the TDE pistols, thumbed off the safety, and thanked whoever had designed the hotel. The glass wall of the restaurant did not extend all the way to the floor. Four feet of the wall were built of colored glass brick . . . blue, green, pink, red. By keeping low, Camellion knew he could not be seen by anyone in the *Aloha Nui Loa Room*, where diners were crawling under tables or leaving by the side entrance that opened to a large mall.

Thrown off emotional balance in spite of their rigid training, Gutik and Kabalof fired too quickly, afraid that the tar-colored smoke would soon hide the target. If they had waited a few more seconds, they might have managed to effect a termination. As it turned out, Gutik's .45 ACP bullet and Kabalof's .32 ACP projectile missed the Death

Merchant's left side by several inches. Both slugs struck the thick glass wall of the restaurant and there was a loud cracking sound as large spider-web patterns of cracks appeared, spreading out from where each bullet had embedded itself in the five-inch-thick glass.

The Death Merchant didn't bother to return the fire, not from his present position. Every second counted and he didn't intend to get pinned down in a slug-duel. He waited until some of the thick smoke drifted across to him, then moved to the next tall wooden monstrosity of a Refuge god. He was weighing his chances of reaching the entrance when he heard a loud voice call out from the direction of the gift shops and bar across the lobby—"DROP THOSE WEAPONS, YOU TWO!"

Another surprise for Reino Gutik and Tania Kabalof, neither of whom had counted on one of the Royal Hawaiian's security guards drawing down on them. One had—Ralph Malahiie, one of the nonuniformed members of the hotel's security force. Malahiie had been in the King Kamba Cocktail Lounge. Hearing the rapid series of shots out in the lobby, he had rushed out of the bar and, seeing Gutik and Kabalof about to fire again through the drifting smoke, had assumed that the couple was the cause of all the trouble.

"I said drop those weapons, or I'll shoot," Malahiie called out again in a commanding voice.

From the corner of his eye, Gutik could see—thirty feet to his left—the young Hawaiian standing in the classic cop pose, his feet planted firmly on the floor, his left hand supporting his right wrist, his right hand around the butt of a Colt Detective Special.

Gutik and Kubalof knew that once they dropped their weapons the show would be over. The American Central Intelligence Agency would soon deduce that they were agents of the *Kah Gay Beh*. They'd spend years in jail. Sooner or later, they would be exchanged for Western prisoners of importance in some Soviet jail. They still would have failed this assignment. They still would go home in disgrace. Better to chance it and maybe die now.

Reino Gutik and Tania Kabalof spun and snap-fired together at Ralph Malahiie, who pulled the trigger of his short-barrelled revolver. His .38 hollow-point chopped into the Russian's chest at almost the same microsecond that

33

Gutik's big .45 bullet struck him high in the chest, shattered the left clavicle and sent him crashing backward.

Tania Kabalof's .32 slug missed Malahiie. The bullet shattered the window of the cocktail lounge, rocketed all the way down the length of the bar and slammed into the jukebox against the wall.

Unconscious and almost a corpse, Gutik let the Star PD pistol slip from his hand as he sank to the floor. Tania Kabalof, now all alone, didn't know what to do. She didn't have to. The Death Merchant did. He had added the *Drop those weapons, you two* with the three shots that followed, had come up with the right answer, and had moved out from behind the grotesque wooden statue of the Refuge god, positive that the attention of the two Russian agents would be elsewhere.

He spotted the blonde-haired Tania Kabalof and fired, the 9mm bullet hitting her just behind the right ear, its impact jerking her head as if it were attached to a large rubber band. The TKP pistol slid from her hand and she fell, her blonde hair streaked with blood.

"Freeze and drop those guns!" The gruff voice came at the same time the Death Merchant felt the muzzle of a handgun shoved against the small of his back.

The Death Merchant felt like an idiot! *I'll be damned if I haven't let some joker sneak up behind me. But he's an amateur or he would have shot and gotten it over with.*

From the way the gun in his back felt and from the sound of the man's voice, he was holding the weapon in his right hand. Most people would, since most are right-handed.

I had better be right. First, make him unsure of himself.

"You're talking to a Federal officer," Camellion said authoritatively. "I'm an FBI agent."

"Prove it after you drop those guns—and I mean drop them," the man said, a small note of hesitancy to his voice.

The Death Merchant let the two auto-loaders fall to the floor and moved with incredible speed. He twisted to the left, struck the man's wrist with his left elbow and brought his left arm behind the startled security man's right elbow so that the fellow's forearm rested against the Death Merchant's shoulder. The man's finger contracted against the trigger and the Smith & Wesson roared, but the muzzle was pointed away from Camellion, who grabbed his own left wrist with his right hand and pressed his left forearm against the man's right elbow. Camellion executed a swift twist to the front and, with a yell of fear and pain, the man—a white dude with a thick mustache—went flying to the floor, with the Death Merchant twisting the pistol from his hand as he fell. Before the hotel security man could recover, Camellion slammed him across the skull with the .38 S & W. A low groan. The man sagged.

Camellion picked up the .380 TDE and dropped it in his coat pocket. He picked up the 9-millimeter HK PSP and raced for the main entrance of the hotel, the thick smoke boiling around him.

Only ten feet from the series of doors (decorated too gaudily for his taste), Camellion found more bad luck rearing its head, this time in the form of two Honolulu patrolmen who had been driving by the hotel in a squad car and had been summoned by one of the frantic doormen. One cop was Hawaiian, the other a *haole*. Each had a Colt Lawman .357 Magnum revolver in his right hand.

The Death Merchant didn't hesitate. He didn't dare. He brought up the .38 S&W and the PSP and fired both weapons simultaneously, four times from the hip. He hated to kill innocent policemen, but there wasn't anything else he could do under the circumstances. It was either drop the two pistols and raise his hands, or blow up the cops before they could snuff him.

The Hawaiian went down with two .380 slugs in his body—first spinning all the way around, then falling sideways to the marble floor.

The white cop died on his feet. One .38 projectile struck him in the chest and made a messy mush of the aortic arch just above the heart. The second .38 bullet smacked him in the left shoulder and opened up the brachial artery. The dead man took two steps backward and fell, the front of his blue uniform coat gushing blood.

The Death Merchant tore out of the main entrance with all the speed of an express train, his sudden appearance almost giving the three doormen heart attacks. The two Hawaiians threw up their arms. The third, crouched to the left of the last door, threw up his arms and yelled, "D-Don't s-shoot!"

The first thing Camellion spotted was the blue-and-white patrol car parked out in the street in front of the hotel, *Honolulu Municipal Police Department* printed in gold (and trimmed in red) on its sea-blue door.

Ah . . . a chariot of the gods! Camellion raced from underneath the canopy, sprinted around to the driver's side of the police car, opened the door and looked in. The keys were in the ignition.

Several minutes later, Richard Camellion was roaring down Kalakaua Avenue, siren wide open, quadriflash lights flashing. . . .

CHAPTER THREE

Is all this that we see and seem perhaps a dream within a dream?

Although Samuel Coleridge, the English Romantic poet, wrote that line, it could have been composed by an Ivy League member of the CIA's clandestine service. Print Master Graphics, Inc. (*Creative Concepts to Finished Printing*) was not a dream, but neither was the printing concern what it seemed.

"Maintaining a Tradition of Quality Printing" in Honolulu "Since 1961," Print Master Graphics, Inc. was the second most important CIA station in the Hawaiian Islands. The main station was in Pearl City, just north of Pearl Harbor.

The printing establishment was housed in a long, low, white-painted Spanish-style building with a red tiled roof. Brilliant red and purple bougainvillea completely covered the south side of the building. On the north side was a parking lot. Palm trees were set in orderly patterns in front of the building, their fronds waving gently over the twisting drive made of carefully placed slabs of white rock.

Well established and with some of the largest firms in Honolulu as clients, Print Master Graphics, Inc. not only paid for itself but made a yearly profit of a couple of hundred grand. The printing concern often worked a second shift and sometimes even a third. After five o'clock in the afternoon, six watchmen were on duty. Each guard was paid $2,000 a month. All six were retired ex-Master Sergeants from the United States Marine Corps; all six were special contract agents of the Central Intelligence Agency.[1]

The actual Station was underground. Its two floors contained thirty-four rooms, twenty-one on the first level and thirteen on the second. None of the personnel ever referred to the underground complex as The Bunker, at least not around Floyd Keifer, the Chief of Station, who was more cautious than a one-legged man trying to hop on a tightrope.

Keifer always told a new man: "If you get into the habit of saying 'The Bunker,' you'll say it in public, and maybe around the wrong person. The Soviets have agents in these islands. Keep that in mind at all times."

There were even signs posted in the halls of both underground levels—DO NOT USE THE PHRASE, "THE BUNKER."

The station was reached from a small, windowless storage room in the rear of the printing establishment. Day and night a Company Case Officer was on duty in this room. It was his job to turn the dial on the old-fashioned safe that stood open in one corner of the room. Once the combination was set, a dust-covered paper cutter, resting on a wooden platform in the middle of the floor, moved silently to one side, exposing the entrance and a steel stairway whose steps were covered with thick, noise-absorbing rubber. This was the only entrance to The Bunker. There were, however, two emergency outlets. One opened in the floor of the garage to the rear of the printing company building. The second ended underneath the driveway in front of the building, the "hatch cover" being one of the white slabs in the drive.

The Death Merchant didn't know about these two emergency exits. But at least he knew that the station was at 14631 Pali Highway, almost five and one-half miles northwest of downtown Honolulu.

Which was more than Albert Gentry and Vancil Jourdan knew. The two FBI agents didn't have the faintest idea of where they were. All they knew was that they had gone to a private home in Makki Heights at 10:30 P.M. From there, two CIA men had driven Gentry and Jourdan to

1. Special contract agents are highly trusted and are required to sign loyalty oath statements, in accordance with the Official Secrets Act.

Pearl City. Outside of Pearl City, the Dodge Omni had stopped, and the two FBI agents had been ordered to lie down on the floor of the car. The Company man in the rear seat had then blindfolded the two resentful Feds, who felt they were being unjustly treated. It wasn't their fault that the CIA mistrusted the FBI and that a serious rivalry existed between the two organizations. It was J. Edgar Hoover's fault, who, when alive, had tried to hog the whole intelligence field. More than once in previous years, Hoover and his G-boys had seriously interfered with Company cases, especially phone watches and stakeouts.

More driving. The Dodge Omni had finally stopped, and Albert Gentry and Vancil Jourdan, still blindfolded, had been led from the car into a building. Down a hall and into a room. Down a flight of steps covered apparently with thick rubber. When the blindfolds were removed, Jourdan and Gentry found themselves in a small bare room containing only a long boat-shaped conference table and eight swivel-tilt executive chairs. Off to one side was a walnut vinyl-laminate coffee and snack center.

Six men sat around the table. Vancil Jourdan looked at his wristwatch and noticed that the time was 12:46 A.M.

Floyd Keifer, at the head of the table, introduced the other men to the FBI agents. To Keifer's right sat Albert Cosgrove, a lean, tough-muscled man with a firm jaw, off-blue eyes and a brown crewcut. Looking at him, the two agents were reminded of George Peppard, the motion picture actor. The lanky and long-faced man next to Cosgrove was Barney Krestell, a CIA Case Officer. The third man to the right was Olin Gammill, a member of the United States Office of Naval Intelligence. Gammill looked like a husky, sun-seasoned farmer from Kansas. Even his "Glad to know you" was as dry as a five-year drought.

The first man to Keifer's left was Simon Kirkland, another Company professional career officer. Big and deeply suntanned, he had dark shadows under his eyes and black curly hair.

Next to Kirkland was Wilfred Sims. He too was ONI. In his early forties, he wore horn-rimmed spectacles and had the face of a curious scholar.

Soft light radiated from the long opaque panel in the center of the ceiling. Fresh air poured in through ventilators set close to the floor. Two exhaust fans, one at each end of the ceiling, pulled out stale air.

Feeling uncomfortable, Gentry and Jourdan pulled out chairs and sat down next to Sims.

Floyd Keifer spoke rapidly, reiterating what the other men already knew. There were Soviet KGB agents in the Hawaiian Islands. Who they were was anyone's guess. So what else was new? Four and one-half months ago, COM-V-CON-2 began to detect very faint wave ducts that could only be the result of waveform-amplitude distortion. The CIA chief of station picked up the NSA report lying on the table in front of him and read directly from the top sheet. "Waveform-amplitude distortion, sometimes called amplitude distortion, refers to nonlinear waveform distortion caused by unequal attenuation or amplification between the input and the output of an analyzing device."

Keifer put down the report and almost smiled. "Gentlemen, don't ask me to explain what that means. For our purposes here, it means that the Soviet Union has set up a base somewhere in the Hawaiian Islands and is monitoring, or trying to monitor, our COM-V-CON-2 satellite that goes over once a day."

Albert Gentry, a strong-looking man of thirty-eight with a weather-beaten face, was a good Fed who never let pride interfere with his work. "Exactly what is COM-V-CON-2? Is it a civil corporation communications satellite or what?"

"It's a military satellite," Albert Cosgrove spoke up, his voice as cold and unfeeling as his icy eyes.

"COM-V-CON-2 means 'Communications for Vital Control,'" Keifer said. "It's one of our most vital satellites and helps coordinate communications between U.S. forces stationed all over the world. Once a day it passes over the Islands, between 0300 and 0400 hours. NSA has all the data; those electronic boys are on the track all right."

Olin Gammill asked, "What's the room for error margin? How can NSA be certain that the wave duct isn't a natural phenomenon being formed by atmospheric conditions?"

Keifer folded his hands and placed them on the NSA report. "The satellite has very sensitive X-band radio equipment that permits extremely sophisticated tracking. The equipment can differentiate between natural and artificial ducts. The one being picked up by COM-V-CON-2 is definitely coming from monitoring equipment. Only the Ruskies have the resources for such a setup."

Barney Krestell frowned and shifted in his chair. "Well now, surely the Russians would realize that we have the capability to detect their monitoring," he offered, playing the role of the devil's advocate. "All they would accomplish with their snooping would be to alert us that they have established a monitoring station somewhere in Hawaii. To me, there's something missing."

"I'm inclined to agree," Simon Kirkland said with that kind of slowness that comes with intense concentration. "The Soviets are anything but stupid. They plan well and never make a move without exploring all avenues of possibilities and probabilities." His gray eyes went from Keifer to Cosgrove and the two men on the other side of the table.

Floyd Keifer cleared his throat. He looked more like an aristocrat than a CIA Chief of Station. He wore an elegant dark-brown suit with a fine white pinstripe, a silver tie with a pearl tieclasp, and a white shirt with a soft collar. He kept his wavy brown hair, streaked with some gray, combed back above a broad face decorated with small eyebrows and a small mustache. His hands were slender, and always he was immaculate. The Death Merchant, when they met for the first time, had thought that Keifer must be running a race with Courtland Grojean for the best dressed spook!

"NSA has determined that the Soviets must be using a method called 'slant monitoring,'" Keifer explained. "Without resorting to all the technical terms, it means that the Soviets at their hidden base aren't targeting the satellite until it's almost to the horizon. It's a method that would have gone undetected if the satellite didn't contain the sensitive X-band radio system. As things stand, the radio system is barely able to detect the probe which has been lasting for only ten seconds.

"What can the Soviets learn in ten seconds? They wouldn't even have time to pick up the frequencies of the satellite." Vancil Jourdan, a cigarette between the fingers of his left hand, unbuttoned his white consort jacket with the fingers of his right.

Camellion—even Floyd Keifer assumed he was named "Albert Cosgrove"—answered for Keifer, who was lighting a cigar. "The satellite passes over the Islands every morning. By constantly monitoring the signals, day by day, Soviet scientists can eventually run them on a 'string-out' and gradually decipher the frequencies."

"And eventually devise an effective method of jamming," augmented Barney Krestell, a savage note to his low voice. He turned in his chair and looked at "Albert Cosgrove." "You're the hotshot that D.C. sent out here, and you're in charge. You're the guy who's supposed to make all the decisions. For my money, I think we had better do something damned fast—if not sooner."

The trace of a smile appeared on the Death Merchant's lips.

"What would you suggest?" he said mildly.

A man with a steel trap for a mind, Barney Krestell—nicknamed The Bomber because he was an expert with explosives—deduced at once that Camellion was baiting him, although not maliciously. His long face broke out in a lopsided grin. "Come off of it, Cosgrove. The way you shot yourself out of that trap at the Tattoo Palace and later, at the Royal Hawaiian, and you're asking me what I would do! I haven't time for these games. Neither have you."

Albert Gentry and Vancil Jourdan sat up straight in their chairs and stared at Camellion. They had read reports about the expert kill artist who had left bodies all over Honolulu, and now they found it difficult to believe that the man dressed in the neat antique white suit and black silk shirt, with the collar open, could be the master corpsemaker.

"You're the man? You did it?" Gentry stared hard at the Death Merchant. "You killed two policemen. That's murder, Cosgrove!"

Gentry's furious gaze swung to Floyd Keifer, and he pointed a finger at Camellion. "And he's in charge?" His tone was one of rage. "He shoots down two policemen in cold blood, and we're supposed to take orders from *him?*"

"It was necessary at the time," Camellion said calmly. "Unfortunate but necessary. I couldn't afford to be arrested."

"Necessary!" Thunderstruck, Gentry almost shouted the word.

"Mr. Gentry, Mr. Jourdan, these accidents often happen," intoned Keifer, as if speaking to children. "Sometimes a few must be sacrificed in order to save the many. I might add that you will follow orders because the director of the Federal Bureau of Investigation has maintained that you will. The Agent in Charge of your Honolulu office is aware of the task ahead of us. Of course, gentlemen, you don't have to participate. You can resign from the FBI. You are aware of the Official Secrets Act?"

Gentry, feeling Jourdan's foot press down on his as a warning to shut up, regained his composure. "I'm aware of the OS Act, and I have no intention of resigning from the Bureau."

"Nor have I," Vancil Jourdan said quickly.

"But there isn't anything in regulations that says I have to enjoy working with a murderer!" concluded Gentry.

The Death Merchant's voice was low but sharp. "Don't ever call me a murderer again, or I'll pull off your arms and tie them around your neck in a bow."

Gentry's mouth opened slightly, as if he were about to speak.

"Don't say it," the Death Merchant warned. "Quit while you're ahead, or you'll leave here with Satan sitting on your shoulder."

Stunned by the Death Merchant's frankness (Gentry considered the Death Merchant's words an open threat), both FBI agents stared briefly at Camellion, then averted their eyes.

The logical and orderly mind of Wilfred Sims prompted him to say, "Bickering is counterproductive. I suggest close cooperation and using any means available to achieve our objective, namely, to find and destroy the Soviet base." He shifted his eyes from Keifer to Camellion, took off his horn-rimmed glasses and began wiping the lenses with a green silk handkerchief.

"A very sensible suggestion," Barney Krestell said enthusiastically.

"Is there any hard evidence that it's the Soviets who are monitoring COM-V-CON-2?" From Gentry's tone of voice, his verbal clash with "Albert Cosgrove" might never have happened. "I feel we should have some foundation of fact that points to the Soviets or we might end up moving in the wrong direction."

Olin Gammill made a gesture of annoyance with one hand. "Who else but the damned ivans?" he said in his dry voice "The Chinese don't have the technology. I don't mean that they can't listen in to our hardware in space, but their technology is crude. There's no way they could pick up anything from COM-V-CON-2."

"Could I interpret that to mean that the equipment the Soviets are using isn't too large, too bulky?" Camellion asked in a polite voice.

The lines in Gammill's face deepened as he thought for a moment.

"It all depends what you mean by bulky," he answered. "The signal and frequency-deciphering equipment would fill a large room. It's the pickup dish—"

"Similar to a parabolic mike, right?" thrust in Vancil Jourdan.

"Yes, only to call it a directional microphone is an over-simplification," Gammill said. "The Soviets have to be using a dish with a diameter of at least twenty feet, and that dish has to be at least thirty feet in the air."

Al Gentry stuck to his guns. "I still say, where's the hard evidence that the Soviet Union is behind the monitoring?" he insisted.

There was a moment of silence, no one making any comments. Finally, Floyd Keifer tapped ash from his long cigar, the tip of his tongue moving slowly inside his lower lip.

"A federal prosecutor would call it evidence to the fact,'" he replied to Gentry. "We have that evidence."

The two FBI agents and the two ONI agents, becoming more attentive, shifted anxiously in their chairs.

Keifer went on. "Not quite a month ago, a very strange thing happened in Kaiwi Channel, the body of water between Oahu and Molokai. Pirates—and I use the word with tongue in cheek—boarded a sail and motor schooner named the *Pearl of the Pacific*. The pirates placed a small charge of explosives in the bilges, sank the ship, and kidnapped everyone on board. Of course, not in that order."

"How do you know this? Were the pirates captured?" inquired Gentry.

Keifer's frown was severe. "Mr. Gentry, listen and quit interrupting. What the pirates didn't know was that they had overlooked one man. He was on the lowest deck level doing a job of caulking when he heard gunshots from the main deck. His name was Joe Kohalukai, and he used common sense. He assumed an act of piracy was taking place. Accordingly, he put on scuba gear, hid in a bench locker and waited, all on the assumption that the ship would either be sunk or taken in tow. If the latter, he didn't know what he would do. He next heard several men below deck. They were speaking to each other in Russian. Kohalukai estimates that the explosion took place about fifteen minutes after he heard the two men talking, after they passed through the captain's cabin. When the *Pearl of the Pacific* started to go down, Kohalukai got out of the locker, waited until the doomed vessel was about 100 feet down, then swam clear of the ship."

"I assume he had air tanks?" said Wilfred Sims.

"You assume right. Kohalukai stayed under water for twenty minutes, scared stiff because he knew the depth below was 900 meters, or almost 3,000 feet. And he had no way of knowing if the pirate vessel was still around. Finally, he had to surface. There wasn't a ship in sight. There wasn't any wreckage, anything. Fortunately for Kohalukai, his scuba suit had a built-in lifejacket, which he activated.

"He floated in the water the remainder of the day and all that night. All the while he was afraid that sharks might be around. It was 11:30 the morning of the next day when a low-flying Coast Guard plane spotted him bobbing around in the water. The aircraft was an amphibious job, and the plane landed and picked him up at once. As far as the Coast Guard was concerned, the *Pearl of the Pacific* had been boarded by pirates. On that basis, they would keep the story under wraps. If the pirates thought Kohalukai was dead they might get careless and make future mistakes." Floyd Keifer turned his head slightly and looked at Wilfred Sims, the senior ONI agent. "As you people in ONI might have already deduced, the Agency has its ways of finding out about such things. The night—"

"Uh huh, how many godamn agents have you got in the Coast Guard?" Olin Gammill said, some mockery in his voice.

"The night of the same day that the Coast Guard found Joe Kohalukai, we took him under our wing and ordered the Coast Guard to keep silent. To be sure, the Coast Guard conducted a routine search for the *Pearl of the Pacific* when she didn't put into her port of call. The ship is listed as missing." Keifer placed his hands flat on the table. "Questions, gentlemen?"

The unpleasant look on Olin Gammill's face deepened. Wilfred Sims's eyebrows knitted into a displeased frown. The Death Merchant didn't blame the two ONI agents for being annoyed at the CIA's quick grab of Joe Kohalukai and the Company's not reporting the incident to ONI until

44

now. Keifer had told him the entire story after he had arrived at Banana Bread Box 1 during the late afternoon of the previous day. Thinking about it, the Death Merchant inwardly sighed. Escaping the police after he had fled from the Royal Hawaiian had not been an easy task. With siren wide open, he had driven the police car east for several blocks, then had turned off the siren and turned north for several blocks. Next he had turned off into an alley, parked, walked off to the next street and had gotten in the front seat with a man who had just started his Celica. He had shoved a gun into the man's ribs and had told him to either drive or " . . . have your head blown off." He had forced the man, a portly individual in his fifties, to drive him two blocks from the address on Paki Street, had put him to sleep with a *Sangdan Chirugi* high punch to the side of the chin, and had walked the rest of the way to the mortuary on Paki Street. Several hours later, while the regular police of Honolulu searched the city for him, he had been driven to Print Master Graphics, Inc. On Grojean's orders to the covert boys in Honolulu, he had not been blindfolded.

Wilfred Sims gave Keifer a long searching look. "All right, Floyd. You scored one on us with Kohalukai." He finished good-naturedly. "But there'll be another time. ONI will have its pound of flesh."

Kirkland's laugh was as large as his body. "That will be the day," he chided Sims. "ONI couldn't catch up with the Agency if we gave you an extra ten years."

Sims only smiled and rubbed his fingers across his high forehead.

"I'd like to know how Kohalukai knew the two men were speaking Russian?" Olin Gammill's question was direct. "Hell, Floyd, you'll be telling us next that he's a language expert!"

"No, Kohalukai is not an expert in linguistics." Keifer sounded cross as he snubbed out his cigar. Gently he adjusted the knot of his four-in-hand tie. "He has worked on ships for all of his adult life and has heard people speak a lot of languages. He knows the Russian language when he hears it. He did recognize the word 'da.' Furthermore Kohalukai has a smattering of Polish which he picked up while working for five years as a cook's helper on an ocean-going steamer. Need I remind you that in root structure Polish and Russian are similar?"

45

Barney Krestell said coolly, "It all falls into place, considering that we know there's a Soviet intelligence network operating in the Pacific. We must assume, based on what we have, that the *Pearl of the Pacific* was pirated not by the Soviet Union, but by a boarding party that included Russian nationals. Those two Russians might very well have been from the secret Soviet base that's somewhere in the Islands."

The news of a KGB *apparat* ("network") operating in the Pacific islands—including Japan?—brought a flare of interest to the Death Merchant's eyes, although he wasn't unduly surprised. Like the CIA, the KGB operated worldwide, and Camellion had not expected Keifer to put all his cards on the table at one sitting.

Vancil Jourdan said bluntly, "Perhaps Al and I missed something, but what does an act of piracy—whether or not the Russians were responsible—have to do with finding the station that's locking in on the satellite every morning? What's the connection?"

It's time I get into this ball game! "We don't know," Camellion stated with his usual tell-it-like-it-is style. "Kohalukai didn't see any bodies sinking into the depths, and the boarding party didn't have time to conduct any real search of the vessel. They didn't want the schooner. They sank her. Kidnapping seems to have been their only motive. Why is the unknown factor. We'll probably find the answer when we find the Soviet base."

Camellion leaned forward and turned his attention to Keifer.

"How long have the Company and ONI been searching for the Soviet base?"

"Three months." Keifer again adjusted the knot of his tie. "In order not to tip our hand, we used high-flying planes with infrared cameras. We've scouted every island. Results, negative. I assume you know why. Of course, we discussed the situation yesterday."

He glanced at Gammill, then let his gaze wander to Sims, Gentry, and Jourdan. "I'd appreciate theories from you gentlemen."

"Hell, Floyd, quit insulting our intelligence." Vancil Jourdan pushed back his chair and got to his feet. He was a nice-looking man, clean-cut and well built, who looked younger than his thirty-four years. However, his features

46

were marred by his teeth. They were large and uneven. "The Russians wouldn't operate the dish without radar. They couldn't take the chance. Your planes get halfway close and the Soviet's radar detects them. Excuse me for a moment."

Jourdan turned and walked over to the coffee bar. Earlier he had noted that the bar had not only a "Mr. Coffee," but also a continental coffeemaker whose bottom globe was full.

"Give the man a gold A," Camellion complimented Jourdan. "The logical place for a dish would be on a mountain top, say on some privately owned island. No doubt—"

"Such an installation would stand out like a twelve-inch erection on a midget!" interrupted Albert Gentry. "I can't buy that theory."

"But only if the dish were stationary," corrected Camellion. "I don't think it is. I think the dish, or antenna, is being raised and lowered each morning. Maybe it's the same with the radar. But I doubt it. I think the radar station is a permanently fixed structure. All the islands have storm watch radar."

"It's only your own theory," commented Wilfred Sims.

"Based on what Floyd has told me, my theory makes sense. There are mornings when COM-V-CON-2 doesn't detect any probes. We checked back on flight search records, and each time planes were in the air, ONI search planes."

"Isn't there any way that the satellite can trace the signal and find its point of origin?" Gentry slipped in the question quickly.

"Forget it," Barney Krestell answered. "First of all the signals are too faint, and even if they were loud and clear, there isn't time to triangulate."

Vancil Jourdan called from the coffee bar. "Al, the usual two cubes?"

Gentry turned around in his chair. "Black. I'm still on a diet."

Olin Gammill, looking at Gentry, said casually. "You don't look fat to me—nothing personal, understand."

"I'm not, but I've cut out all sweets and fats," Gentry explained. "My cholesterol is up."

A loud, deliberate sigh came from Barney The Bomber Krestell.

"This is all very interesting, what we've been saying. To me, it's all academic and adds up only to the power of positive pessimism. We need a definte plan of action."

"I don't believe in the theory of avoidism anymore than you do," Camellion said, sounding casual. "What leads you to believe that I don't have a definite plan?"

Krestell brightened. "Where do we begin?"

"At the beginning." Camellion smiled. "Why should we hitchhike when we can take a jet?"

Simon Kirkland frowned in annoyance. "Stop the riddles and get to the point, Mr. Cosgrove."

"The point is that the KGB sent non-Russian hit men after me," Camellion said and fixed his eyes on the two FBI agents. "What does the Bureau have on those three? They must have had rap sheets from here to next year."

Al Gentry completed his long sip of coffee, put down the stoneware cup and reached into his right-side coat pocket. He took out a long brown envelope and would have passed it along to the Death Merchant if Camellion hadn't said, "Read it. Just the bare essentials."

Gentry took the sheets out of the envelope and unfolded them. He cleared his throat and began to read. "The Chinese you blew up was named Thomas Chong. He was born in Manila in 1954 and came to Hawaii with his mother. His father was killed in a construction accident. Arrested for car theft, assault with a deadly weapon, malicious mischief and for indecent exposure."

"A real sweetheart," muttered Simon Kirkland. "He probably stuffed dumdum shells up children's noses for a pastime."

"One of the Hawaiians was Leo Hahaninou, nicknamed Duke," continued Gentry. "One conviction for armed robbery. He drew ten to fifteen and was paroled in 1978. He was an alcoholic, but didn't have a drop in his body when you snuffed him, Cosgrove.

"The third louse was Billy Puolani. A true psycho. Born and raised in Hono. He first got into trouble when he was only eight. He almost beat a little girl to death with a board. He's been in and out of jail most of his twenty-eight years. He was snorting nose candy[2] when you snuffed him, Cosgrove." Gentry glanced up and over at the Death

2. Cocaine.

48

Merchant. "You did the world a favor when you killed that piece of trash."

"And the couple in the lobby who tried to massage me with slugs?" Camellion said. "They were too professional to be turkeys."

"Well, there we have an odd situation," Gentry said, a deliberately sly note in his voice. "The police took the bodies to the morgue, but somehow the corpses revived and walked off. When the Bureau made inquiries, we were told by the Hono police that a 'higher authority' in the U.S. Government had—and I quote—'taken possession of the bodies.' We all know who that higher authority is."

Simon Kirkland chuckled. "Hell, it's not our fault if the FBI is too slow to catch up."

Richard Camellion was not in the mood for any form of good-humored frivolousness. "Floyd, what did the Company learn from the corpses?"

"Two things," Keifer responded promptly. "The woman had been operated on for appendicitis. From the way the stump of the appendix was tied off, the technique used was Russian. Fillings in the teeth of the man and the woman were typical Russian. We're certain that both were 'bloodwet' assassins. The gas tube the man carried proves as much."

"You gave the papers a good cover story," sighed Vancil Jourdan. "I'll give you credit for that."

"We instructed the Honolulu police to give out that story to the press," Keifer said. "You all read it in the papers. Mr. and Mrs. Harvey Willbeck were undercover police officers from the States." A self-satisfied smile crossed Keifer's mouth. "We made Cosgrove here the bad guy—a Syndicate hit man from the mainland."

Barney Krestell pushed back his chair, an anxious expression on his face. "So far no one has mentioned Eddie Ogden. We haven't any actual proof that he didn't sell us out."

"He was your man, wasn't he?" Wilfred Sims inquired of Keifer.

"For almost three years. We could tell you what his grandparents ate for breakfast before they died. We are almost positive that it wasn't he who fingered Cosgrove. He would have been committing suicide. He knows that when the stink dies down, we'd use a polygraph, voice analysis and drugs to get the truth out of him, to ascertain any possible part he might have played in the ambush."

Olin Gammill said, "We could hardly call it coincidence the way the two KGB hit artists were waiting for him at the hotel. How could they know his name or even the hotel at which he was staying?" he swung his head toward Camellion. "You sure as hell didn't give him your name and where you were staying—did you?"

"I told him my name was 'Albert Cosgrove,'" Camellion said. "You see, 'Albert Cosgrove' was simply a name I made up for Ogden, on the spur of the moment. I was registered at the Hawaiian hotel as 'Winston Cookhider,' a British subject."

Enjoying the look of surprise on even Floyd Keifer's face, Camellion gave the men another start when he said, "The logical conclusion is that the KGB has been onto Ogden for sometime and planted a bug, or bugs, in his place of business. Whoever was listening at the other end heard me give him the name 'Cosgrove.'"

"I can't buy it; it's too farfetched," Simon Kirkland scoffed, squirming about in his chair. A skeptical look flowed over his sunbaked face. "Even if the Russian 'in deep black' agents in Honolulu had had the time to phone every hotel and resort in the city, they wouldn't have found any 'Albert Cosgrove' registered. Somewhere between Hono and The Center, there's been a leak."

A leak in Grojean's section—a mole? Possible. Not probable! Yet the fact that the Covert Section might have been penetrated made Camellion's spine crawl.

"There is another answer," Camellion said. "We know that the two *Mokryye Dela* gunmen in the lobby were specialists. I believe they were stationed somewhere on Hotel Row and were on call. I also think—"

"Hell, none of what you're saying makes sense," began Krestell fiercely.

"Zipper your mouth and listen. I believe the KGB had agents stationed in front of the Tattoo Palace—maybe across the street in another building—and that those agents took photographs of me when I came out of the shop. I believe that somehow those agents managed to tail me back to the Royal Hawaiian. Between the time I entered the hotel and came back down, twenty minutes had elapsed. That gave the KGB time to move in the blood-wet team into the lobby."

"Oh shit! The KGB's not that good." Albert Gentry dismissed Camellion's words with a short wave of his hand. "That theory is like a bucket full of holes."

Neither concern, anger, nor resentment crossed Camellion's face as he said to Floyd Keifer, "Floyd, I assume your people found the passports of the two dead *Mokryye Delas?*"

Keifer looked perplexed. "Naturally. Why do you ask?"

"Was the great seal in the paper?"

"Yes. You know, or should, that KGB cobblers are experts.[3] The State Department has been trying for years to find a paper that the KGB can't impregnate with the Seal."[4]

The Death Merchant shot an acid look at Gentry. "See what I mean about the KGB being good? Don't ever underestimate those pigsty boys. It wouldn't have been all that difficult to trail me if trained KGB officers were stationed in back and in front of the Tattoo Palace and had cars stationed in strategic positions."

"Then why didn't one of them try to kill you?" said Sims, his face grave and intense.

"Who knows?" Camellion shrugged a shoulder. "Maybe I wasn't in the right position and they didn't want to further warn me by risking a miss. Besides, after the three hoods failed to do the job, the KGB then counted on its kill specialists to complete the hit—the two goofs in the hotel. *Mokryye Dela* people almost never miss."

"Well, Cosgrove—or whatever your name is—you were damned lucky at the Royal Hawaiian," commented Barney Krestell. Camellion had analyzed Krestell as a man who had the blunt attitude that made him face reality, no matter how unpleasant.

"Cosgrove's as good a name as any," Camellion said, "but leave out luck. Ninety percent of it was experience. I've fought the KGB too many years not to recognize an

3. Soviet experts who specialize in forging passports are known as "cobblers." This is a Russian term. As with any jargon, that of the KGB changes, yet some phrases are constant. For years, the GRU—Soviet Military Intelligence—has referred to the KGB as "The Neighbors."

4. Most tourists don't realize it, but watermarks of the Great Seal of the United States are invisibly embedded on every page of an American passport. These watermarks can only be seen when held up to a strong light.

ambush. It's also experience that tells me that the KGB illegals[5] here in Hawaii had a go-between who hired those three scumballs who tried to terminate me at the tattoo joint."

Olin Gammill spoke thoughtfully, "It would be of some help if we had a way to ascertain if the KGB illegals in Hono are part of the personnel at the Soviet base doing the monitoring of the satellite."

Floyd Keifer shook his head. "I doubt if the two factions are even aware of each other's existence. The KGB is every bit as cautious as we are."

"I'd say the Russians weren't half as vigilant as the CIA," Vancil Jourdan remarked coolly. "I doubt if the KGB blindfolds GRU agents when they set up a meet."

"No doubt because the GRU people don't have big mouths!" Keifer's voice was even more frigid than Jourdan's.

For a very long moment there was a palpable silence in the room, finally broken by Simon Kirkland, who said, "A month ago we did trap one illegal. The son of a bitch committed suicide before we could stop him. He used cyanide. We did find a code book buried inside a sack of fertilizer in a tin shed on the side of his house, but we haven't been able to crack the code, not yet."

"What about that bird Ogden?" Looking down at his cigarette, Gentry did his best to sound pleasant. He didn't like any of the Company men or the ONI boys and felt inferior in their presence. "I don't think he's any lily of the valley."

Krestell gave a tiny laugh. "Hell, you feds don't think any independent contractor is fit to breathe the same air as you saints." He paused, as if reflecting. "Come to think of it, most of them aren't—present company excluded." He turned and grinned at Camellion. "The way we got from the Home Office, you're a specialist among specialists."

"Yeah and I can tell you two hundred and seven different ways to serve buffalo chips. Buffdung is my speciality. It's the breakfast of pioneers."

5. An "illegal" is an agent who does not have official cover and diplomatic immunity. A "legal" agent normally has a cover job with a Soviet diplomatic mission, but his real duties are spying/espionage. In 1980, the Soviet Union had 482 people in the U.S. as "legals," people with diplomatic immunity.

Olin Gammill put his hands on the open collar of his white long-sleeved jacket and said, "This is one piss-poor time to make jokes."

Keifer responded to Gentry's earlier question. "Ogden's not going anywhere. When the stink dies down and the local police stop snooping around, we'll check his house and place of business for hidden transmitters. We'll take him apart with a polygraph and truth drugs."

"Someone in Hono had to hire the three gunsels who came after me," Camellion said curtly. "Right there"—he turned and stared at Krestell—"is where we're going to start. That's the beginning."

"If it means anything, Duke Hahaninou was reputed to be a strong-arm man for the Renton mob, but we could never prove it," offered Vancil Jourdan. "The Renton mob controls all the major rackets in Honolulu."

"Go on. I'm listening," Camellion said patiently. "I want to know all about the Renton mob. How big is it? I know that the Mafia isn't strong in the Islands."

"Archie Renton—he's half Hawaiian and in his late fifties—controls the Hono underworld," Jourdan said in disgust. "He's supposed to be a businessman. He owns a sugar plantation on Kauai and has an importing and exporting business in Honolulu. His big take is in narcotics. The Bureau knows it and the Drug Enforcement boys know it. The hell of it is, we can't prove it. We don't have anything that will stand up in court."

Gentry interjected, "Several years ago, the Justice Department thought it could nail him on an income tax evasion rap. Renton beat the case. We have his home under constant surveillance. We have a tap on his phone. The P.I. boys[6] keep a watch on his mail. Hell, we even go through his garbage twice a week after it's picked up, in the hope that he might slip and throw something incriminating in a wastebasket."

"You're wasting your time, Cosgrove," Olin Gammill said. "Renton's not working for or with the KGB. He has the mind of a snake. He's not about to get mixed up in something he can't handle. For Christ sake, he hates the Reds as much as we do. Organized crime can only take roots in a free society. Can you imagine Renton helping the

6. The Postal Inspectors of the U.S. Postal Inspection Service.

53

very people who would put him up in front of a firing squad if they had their way?"

"Olin's right, Cosgrove," Simon Kirkland said. "Renton wouldn't work for the KGB anymore than a cobra would attack a dozen mongooses."

Camellion locked his fingers together, put his elbows on the arms of the chair and held his folded hands in front of his chest. "I don't expect him to welcome us with open arms, but he might be able to give us a lead that will help us find the traitor who is working for the Soviets. Whoever that man is, he had contacts in the underworld. Renton knows what's going on in the Hono underworld. Or does anyone have a better suggestion?"

For a short while no one said anything. At length Wilfred Sims spoke. "Personally, I would first subject Eddie Ogden to intensive interrogation. Renton won't give us the time of day or the day of the month."

The Death Merchant's blue eyes glittered strangely. "By the time I'm finished with Renton, he'll talk so much you'll think he's been given a triple vaccination with a phonograph needle."

"Now hold on, Cosgrove!" Jourdan raised a restraining hand. "We can't drive over to Renton's beach estate at Diamond Head and start shoving him around. He has one of the best law firms in Honolulu on retainer. If we deviate from standing legal procedure, the Bureau will be defending itself in Federal Court against a lawsuit—invasion of privacy and only God knows what else."

Divert from standing legal procedure! Camellion laughed deeply. And the American people wonder why organized crime exists!

"We," he begin, "are not going to do anything. I am. I'm going to kidnap Renton and make him talk. I'm going to make it appear as though a rival mob did the job. I have to. I don't want the KGB to get wise to what we're really doing. And don't tell me there aren't gangsters in Honolulu who'd like to see Archie Renton in hell with his back and both legs broken!"

"The Sammy Fong outfit would like to see Renton in a dozen hells," Barney Krestell said with a hearty laugh. "Kidnapping Renton though . . ." He made a sound with his mouth. "It won't be easy. We can get the layout of his place down to the inch, but that bird is well guarded, well protected."

"Damn it! The Federal Bureau of Investigation can't be a party to such lunacy!" Gentry bridled with disbelief, so agitated that he grabbed the arms of his chair and tightened his fingers, as though he might jump to his feet. "Why damn it, man! You're making us accessories to violating a federal law. They still remember Watergate in the States. Do you know how the Bureau would look if *this* became public? Congress would start an investigation that wouldn't end until the year 2000."

A stunned Vancil Jourdan leaned sideways and touched Gentry on the arm. "Al, Floyd has already explained that the Director is aware of this operation," he said tiredly. "We don't have any choice in the matter."

"Unless you resign," the Death Merchant said in a quiet voice.

Jourdan looked down at the polished table top.

Gentry squinted at Camellion, his face rock hard, anger boiling in his big eyes.

"How many other agents in the Bureau will be in on this madness?" he demanded of the Death Merchant.

"Ask Keifer," shrugged Camellion. "He's the head of this Station."

Floyd Keifer met Gentry's eyes squarely, and there was a warning in them. "The two of you, James Bell, the Agent in Charge of the FBI Hono office, and six other agents. You and Jourdan will function as liaison between us and them. All reports and contacts at the funeral parlor on Paki Street. We'll give you the name of the place and the address before you leave. One more thing, none of you FBI men will be asked to participate in anything that is not legal. You can quit waging a war with your ethics."

"Now that we've separated the saints from the sinners, the saved from the damned, how and when do we grab Archie Renton?" Twisting a heavy silver skull ring on the middle finger of his right hand, Barney Krestell snickered slightly. A realist of the first order who believed that any means justified outmaneuvering the KGB, he didn't even try to conceal his contempt of other U.S. government employees whom he called "morality idiots"—people who permitted ethics to color their judgment.

"As soon as we study the layout of Renton's estate and know all his habits and where we can grab him the easiest, we'll put together a plan," the Death Merchant said. He gave Gentry and Jourdan an earnest look. "Your job for now is to bring me what the Bureau has on Renton. You should have a file on him as thick as the Yellow Pages. I'll also want photographs and a scale drawing of his estate. Have it all at the funeral parlor by ten tomorrow morning. No, make it noon tomorrow. That will give you more time to do a better job."

Grimacing, Gentry nodded slowly. "You have it. But I'm curious about something no one has mentioned." His dark eyes waltzed to Floyd Keifer. "If there's not a mole in your network and not any connection between the Russian monitoring base and the KGB Pacific spy ring, why should the KGB go to all that trouble to knock off Cosgrove? He's only one man. Hell, our intelligence agents travel back and forth all the time to the Islands. Why single him out?"

The Death Merchant's face did not show any emotion. "Ogden's a trusted contract man. A Company man had to inform him that a specialist would arrive in Honolulu. It was a Company man who had to give Ogden the correct ID phrase for him to memorize and the date on which I would arrive, even the hour. Conclusion: either Ogden is playing both ends against the middle or else his place is full of hidden transmitters. The rest is simple. The KGB doesn't want specialists around any more than we want their blood-wet people running loose in our backyard."

Camellion leaned back in his chair and locked his hands behind his head. In a lazy manner he stretched out his legs. "Floyd, I want a list of every privately owned island in the Hawaiian chain. I want the size of each island and its general terrain."

"The computer can give us that information in an hour," Keifer said. He adjusted his gold rimmed eye glasses with thumb and forefinger. "Understand that there are several hundred islands that are privately owned. Some are nothing more than specks in the Pacific. Others are ten times the size of an aircraft carrier. Picking the right island is going to be one big job. And I don't believe in crystal balls."

"First things first" Camellion said. "You have to crawl before you can walk and walk before you can run. Most of us can do more than we think we can, but usually do less than we think we can."

"Meaning we grab Renton first and pick it up from there," Simon Kirkland said. "Grabbing that creep is not going to be easy."

The Death Merchant merely smiled.

CHAPTER FOUR

The slight hiss of air circulating through the ducts in the wall was a constant sound in the small room of the Bunker, the only sound Richard Camellion could hear. No larger than a cell in a federal penitentiary, the room in Banana Bread Box 1 contained a folding bed, a table and chair, a chest of drawers, a small refrigerator, a hot plate, a lavatory and a toilet stool. A curtain at one end of the room opened to a shower stall. There wasn't any closet.

The room and its contents were all that the Death Merchant needed. Dressed in a dull black nylon jumpsuit and house slippers with extra-heavy felt soles, he studied his face in the large mirror above the lavatory basin. Yeah, there were times when the Company made mistakes, serious mistakes. But more often than not, the organizational procedures functioned with 101-percent efficiency. A special messenger from the U.S. Embassy in West Germany had brought his two steel footlockers and aluminum Jensen case, filled with special Auto Mags, to the Company complex beneath Print Master Graphics, Inc. The same messenger had also flown in his other two suitcases.

Camellion smiled when he thought of how the Hono police must be tearing their hair over the contents of the suitcase he had left in the lobby of the Royal Hawaiian Hotel. Other than ten pairs of undershorts (of which there were only three pairs that fit his 36-inch waist), the suitcase had contained two child's toys, an "electronic laser gun" and a "Galaxy" walkie-talkie "to contact your spaceship in outer space." Having foreseen the possibility of having to leave the suitcase, he had also included a "space map," a hand-drawn map of the solar system, marking Io, one of Jupiter's moons, as *"Base Z-LLL2y. Invasion fleet stationed here."*

No doubt some of the cops will be seeing UFOs within a week!

Archie Renton. Camellion was convinced that his plan would work. Since the general meeting several days ago, not a lot of water had passed under the bridge. Just the same, the thin trickle had changed to a small stream. *By 0500 hours tomorrow morning, that stream will be a raging river. We'll have Renton right here in Banana Bread Box 1. Or we'll be stone dead in the market place, with only the wind to mourn us. . . .*

He was satisfied with the makeup job. A middle-aged Chinese stared at him from the mirror. He had built up his cheeks with plastic putty, had changed the shape of his nose and mouth and had used collodion and liners to add wrinkles to his skin. The eyes had taken more time and expertise. They had been changed to slant in the same way that skin fixation was used. The inner corners of the eyes had been partly covered with the skin duplication of the upper lids. The lower lids had been shortened and the edge lines made parallel with the lines of the upper lids, the strips of gauze glued to the temples at the hairline and drawn above the ears to the back of the head where they had been firmly tied together. A securely fitted wig of black hair helped to hold the lifted skin in such a way that the shape of the slanting eyes remained unchanged.

Camellion put on a pair of old khaki pants and a faded blue cotton shirt, decorated with red and orange flowers and as worn as the rest of the garment. He tucked the shirt into the pants and was buttoning the pants over the jump-suit when the tiny buzzer on the door sounded.

He opened the door and motioned for Barney Krestell to come in. Camellion had also applied his makeup artistry to The Bomber and had changed the Company street man to a Hawaiian. He had widened Krestell's long face, had used hollow tooth "fronts" over the man's teeth and had turned his skin to a rich brown with liquid powder. A touch here and there with a liner, a tight-fitting wig of curly black hair, and an ugly red scar, and the changeover had been complete. Barney's own mother wouldn't have recognized him. His own mother would have sworn that he was a *hapa haole,* a part-white Hawaiian—and that Camellion was a *Pake-kanaka,* or China-man.

"Everything's all set. The boat's ready as soon as we get there," Krestell said. Like Camellion, he wore old clothes over his black jump-suit. Open-toe sandals were on his feet.

58

"All we have to do is drive to Kewalo Basin, get on the *Lady Luck* and pull off for Diamond Head. It's a slick scheme, even if I didn't think it up."

"Don't get overconfident," warned Camellion, who had sat down on the bed and was strapping on sandals. "We have to take out a dozen of Renton's goons before we even get to the main house—and all of it without noise one."

"I didn't mean to imply that it was going to be easy," Krestell said, his voice and face serious. "At least nobody will remember us when we get on the *Lady Luck*. We're just a couple of worthless deckhands going aboard to help the skipper take out some tourists who want to get an early start on some deep-sea fishing."

"It will be one o'clock in the morning by the time we get there." The Death Merchant stood up. "I doubt if anyone will notice us. You have your phony identification?"

"Not to worry." Krestell cocked an eye at the Death Merchant. "Should the police stop us for any reason, I can prove I'm Jasper Liholiho. By the way, who are you, Fu Manchu the Second?"

"Ling Da-hoi, in case anyone asks," Camellion said. "Let's get going. Better to get there too early than on time."

They left the room, walked down the thickly carpeted hallway, and in a short while were walking up the padded stairs that led to the storeroom. The Case Officer on duty in the storeroom might have been a robot. He neither moved from his chair nor spoke.

Once, while Camellion and Krestell were moving through the printing company's building, they met one of the watchman carrying his time clock. He looked right past them and kept on going. Nor was the watchman at the side door a chatterbox. He only handed Camellion a set of keys, said "The green '78 Dodge Aspen," pushed down on the bar and opened the door.

A few minutes more and Camellion and Krestell were pulling out of the parking lot, Krestell driving. The night was a pleasant 70 degrees, the midnight moon a big white-yellow tub in a clear, star-bright sky.

Expertly, Krestell drove the Dodge Aspen over the white rock-slab driveway and onto Pali Highway. Due east, right across the highway, was the National Memorial Cemetery of the Pacific, this quiet home of the dead spread over the vast bowl of Punchbowl Crater, which native Hawaiians and *kamaaina-haoles*—oldtimer white people—called *Puowaina,* the Hill of Sacrifice. Tablets in seemingly endless rows marked the 21,000 graves of the dead from World Wars I and II, the Korean War, and the Vietnam War. Toward the center of *Puowaina* was a massive monument, the "Courts of the Missing," on which were listed, on marble slabs, the names of 26,280 missing servicemen.

They drove in silence. It wasn't until Barney Krestell turned east onto Lunalio Freeway that he said, "I shouldn't ask you, Cosgrove, but if I don't it will bother me for the rest of my life. Why did you pick me to go in with you to Archie Renton's estate? You must have had access to my Blue File."

"No, I didn't read your bib on the B-F." The Death Merchant, with the aid of a penlight, looked down at the car's registration he had taken from the glove compartment. "Mr. G. gave me a rundown on the more active personnel at Banana Bread Box One. You're an expert in *Te,* Okinawan karate, and in *Kuntaw,* the Filipino art of hand and foot fighting. In short, my friend, you're 'Well versed in pen and sword.' Tell me, where did you learn those two little-known forms?" Satisfied that the car's registration was made out to Mr. Ling Da-hoi, he returned the registration form to the glove compartment.

Krestell glanced at the speedometer and pressed down on the gas pedal. "My father was in the Marines, in World War II. He taught me Okinawan *Te,* or *Karate Do* as it's called today. From Te it was only a short step to *Kuntaw.* I assume you're familiar with the martial arts."

"I have a black belt, third dan, in *Tae Kwon Do* and a bleck belt, second dan in *Goju-Ryu* karate, and I've a smattering in other forms. Let's hope that tonight we won't have to use any of the techniques we know. . . ."

The *Lady Luck* was a Hatteras 48-foot long-range cruiser, all glistening white in the moonlight. Even the polished rails around her foredeck sparkled in the soft mellow rays of the bright moon. Yes, sir . . . a better-class fishing boat for tourists who could afford her.

Camellion and Krestell stepped up from the boardwalk pier onto the short ladder on the port side of the vessel and were met by a fat but tough-faced Hawaiian wearing red beach trunks and a red-stripes-on navy cotton shirt.

"Captain Norward's astern," the man said. "Mr. and Mrs. Hollinger ain't here yet."

Krestell glanced at Camellion and smiled. So realistically had the man spoken that one could almost believe that this was to be a genuine fishing trip.

The Death Merchant and The Bomber made their way to the stern.

Captain Stan Norward—Olin Gammill—looked up from the bosun's chair at the approach of the two. "You're early. The Hollinger's aren't due for another ten minutes." He took off his navy fisherman's cap and placed it on the top knee of his crossed legs. "Kirkland's down below, asleep."

The Death Merchant and Barney Krestell sat down close to the closed stern railing. "How far out will we meet the Coast Guard cutter with the SDV?"

"Forty miles," Gammill said and flipped his cigarette over the side into the water. "The cutter will be there. Don't worry."

Presently, Mr. and Mrs. Hollinger arrived. The outdoor type, in his early thirties, Roger Hollinger was a tight-faced man with rounded shoulders. He wore tan cargo jeans and a tan poplin shirt, the ends of the shirt tied over around his narrow waist, over a belt that had a brass snap-hook for a buckle, the kind of snap-hook found on any ship.

Mrs. Hollinger (who was actually an ONI agent named Valerie Kohrn) wore the women's version of cargo jeans and tan shirt to match, only the ends of her shirt were neatly tucked into her pants. She carried a large Breton red cotton duck shoulder bag and, like her "husband," wore moccasin-style heavyweight canvas deck shoes. She was pretty, too, young, not over twenty-two, and slender, with blonde hair cascading in gentle waves down her back.

Ten minutes later, her super diesels throbbing, *Lady Luck* pulled slowly out of Kewalo Basin, the Death Merchant on the stern deck, watcing the lights of the marina recede. The smell of paradise was not in his nostrils, and he could detect an invisible presence on the cruiser, an essence that always walked silently with him—

Death. . . .

CHAPTER FIVE

The Death Merchant steered the "Slim Jim" Swimmer Delivery Vehicle toward the beach fronting Archibald Renton's estate in Diamond Head. In back of Camellion sat Barney Krestell. In the third seat, behind Krestell, sat Simon Kirkland. In the fourth and last seat was a rounded waterproof plastic drum. There were two more plastic drums on the sides of the vehicle, one on the port side, one on the starboard side.

There are different kinds of SDVs, yet all have the same basic characteristics and major components—a propulsion unit consisting of motor, propeller and shaft, and various gauges to indicate depth, direction, time, and status of the vehicle.

The Slim Jim was of the wet type, this meaning that the Death Merchant and the two men with him, all dressed in closed-circuit-breathing scuba gear, were in direct contact with the water of the Pacific Ocean.

The craft was not without its disadvantages. There was always the danger of severe shock should something go wrong with the electrical system. Another hindrance was that, since the Death Merchant and the other two men were using closed breathing systems, Camellion had to be careful to maintain proper depth control—not really a problem in this case. Camellion was going in at only four fathoms, or twenty-four feet.

When the mileage marker revealed to the Death Merchant that the Slim Jim was nine nautical miles from the *Lady Luck,* which was ten and a half nautical miles south of the Renton estate, he filled the SAC—the surfacing air chamber—with air and began the trim procedure. Slowly the SDV rose to the surface and began to bob gently in the water.

Camellion opened a watertight compartment to his left and took out an LEA 1000 hand-held passive night vision viewer, a device that increased the background starlight 50,000 times. He unscrewed the rounded face plate of his scuba suit, lifted the night vision device to his right eye and began to study the sea and the shore. There were no vessels in the vicinity, neither to port nor starboard. A mile and one-half ahead the stretch of private beach was empty, the surf rolling gently over the sand. There were a dozen cabanas on Renton's private beach and these striped tents posed a definite threat. There could be a bodyguard or two in these cabanas.

Archie Renton's $450,000 mansion, a two-story white stucco house, rested in the middle of fifty-three acres. The well-manicured front lawn was decorated with palms and with tall, skinny kiawe trees. Bird of Paradise, yellow hau flowers, and white carnations bloomed in flowerbeds. Three hundred feet in front of the mansion was a nine-foot-high decorative wall constructed of pink-colored bricks. The only openings were two gates, the narrow gate of wrought iron (seven feet tall) and the two-section gate that sealed off the end of the driveway (concrete of a deep pink color) from Puueo Avenue. These double gates were electrically controlled from the house and would silently swing inward at the touch of a button.

East of the mansion was a Japanese garden with a fish pond, a small bridge, carefully trimmed bushes of a dozen varieties and a small Shinto shrine. Further east, at the end of Renton's property was another wall—concrete blocks painted to blend in with the rows of palms. To the west, at the end of Renton's property, was another wall. Both walls stretched down to the beach, almost to where the surf lapped constantly at the sand.

Archie Renton, born in a slum section of Honolulu, had not risen to the top because he lacked intelligence. To the contrary, his cleverness had earned him the nickname of "The Owl." The Death Merchant was not going to make the serious mistake of underestimating such a man. Camellion automatically assumed that Renton would realize that the weakest link in his chain of defense around his home was the beach. Guards would be watching the beach day and night; and while The Owl might have anticipated assassins coming ashore in scuba gear, it wasn't likely that there would be any underwater protective devices, other than the usual shark fence. Renton had a daughter whom he dearly loved. She and her friends often used the beach.

The Owl wouldn't do anything to endanger the girl. But there would be guards, some of them stationed in the cabanas, others just north of the rocks at the southwest corner of The Owl's property. Many of these rocks were huge boulders the size of automobiles. The end of the west side wall ended at the boulder farthest from the water, 90 to 100 feet from the surf.

The Death Merchant returned the night vision instrument to its watertight compartment, secured his face plate, made sure the closed-circuit breathing system was working perfectly, and went about working the controls of the SDV, flooding the ballast tank with water. Gradually the vehicle submerged, Camellion levelling off at ten feet. He pushed the motor switch to the first speed forward and began watching the compass and the mileage gauge. A tiny green light glowed in the cockpit, and every now and then he consulted the small topographic map which showed the area's ocean floor. One mistake now . . . just one . . . *and we can all go home!*

Thirteen minutes later, the Death Merchant concluded that he had reached the proper coordinates. He stopped the engine and took the SDV to the sea floor, gratified that the depth gauge showed only twenty-two feet.

Camellion unfastened his seat belt, pushed with his legs and freed himself from the vehicle's metal seat. He started upward and his head soon cleared the water. Quickly he looked around. The water sparkled with moonlight. Not quite a hundred and thirty feet ahead, the surf broke over the rocks. Good! He had dropped the SDV right on target. The mass of boulders was only a short distance away.

He swam back down to the SDV and nodded to Barney Krestell and Simon Kirkland. The two unfastened their seat belts, pushed themselves from the vehicle and, with Camellion, began unstrapping the three plastic drums, each of which was four feet long and a foot and a half in diameter.

With each pulling a plastic drum by a length of rope and carrying a spear-gun, the three men began swimming underwater toward the shore, but not without some difficulty. Each drum was heavily weighted so that it would not float to the surface and pull the man with it.

The three stopped swimming when the surface was only a foot above their heads when they were standing. They weren't worried about anyone's seeing them in the water.

The moonlight penetrated less than a foot of the water, and the surf breaking over the rocks scattered the bright moonlight between the water and anyone waiting at the end of the west wall.

A keen judge of human nature, the Death Merchant was counting on another factor to help him: the fact that none of Renton's enemies had ever tried to attack his home from the sea. If guards were waiting by the wall, they would not be alert. At 2:30 in the morning, they would probably be dozing.

Camellion handed the end of his rope to Simon Kirkland. Barney Krestell pulled a special watertight Vertex signal transceiver from a rubberized bag attached to his scuba suit, extended the long telescoping antenna and held the device so that only the tip of the antenna was above the water.

The Death Merchant swam only ten feet, then started to walk along the sloping sandy bottom, his splashing lost in the sound of the surf ahead. Once the water was splashing around his thighs, he pulled a standard sheath knife from his belt and carefully slit the rubberized material of the bulge on the front thigh of his left leg. The water was breaking around his ankles when he shoved the knife back into its holder, then reached into the slit and pulled a 9-millimeter High Power Browning auto-pistol from the now-open pocket. A six-inch noise suppressor was attached to the muzzle of the Browning. He could have removed the weapon from the inside of the suit, but that would have necessitated his waiting until the entire suit had been removed.

Camellion hurried across the water-washed beach, glancing every now and then at the cabanas 350 feet to his right. His feet sinking into the wet sand, he finally came to the nearest boulder whose sea-side had been made as smooth as glass by the action of the water. Slightly to his right—*it can't be more than twenty feet!*—was the end of the west side wall. *Eighty feet from where I'm standing.* He unfastened his face plate and opened it. For a few moments he listened to the surf breaking over the small rocks, splashing against the boulder and, east of him, rolling in over the white sand of the beach. He looked around the west side of the large boulder—more rocks, some as small as a baseball, others the size of a barrel and bigger. Half a dozen were larger than a small pickup truck. Growing here and there among the rocks were ruhoii ferns and any number of a

65

variety of weeds. But nowhere was the vegetation thick enough to conceal a man.

For a second or two, Camellion considered sending the signal to Krestell and Kirkland. No. He would first investigate. Why get them killed needlessly?

There wasn't any way for him to know what lay ahead until he investigated. Therein lay the danger—that an enemy would spot him, alert the other guards, then open fire. So be it. What is, IS. This was the kind of life, the kind of deadly danger, that Richard Camellion loved—sailing with a tide that knew no ebb. Better to be a wolf for only an hour than a sheep for an entire century.

Now he applied all his training in *Ninjitsu*. He moved low and very quickly, sure of his footing, breathing evenly. Very alert, he ignored the weight of the air tanks on his back.

Cigarette smoke! Again he got a whiff of cigarette smoke. He stopped and smiled. The breeze was blowing from the northeast. *I can't be more than forty feet from the end of the wall. Now the question is, how many? Where? Almost certainly by the wall.*

Carefully he placed the spear gun on the ground and crept forward very slowly. All the while he listened, every cell, every nerve of his body ready for instant action.

Low voices! He could barely hear the voices. He stopped, cocked his head and strained his ears. *Fifty feet to my right and thirty feet in front. I've got 'em!*

Again he moved forward, very slowly, yet at three times the speed of the average man. At thirty feet he could catch parts of the conversation between the two men—"We'll . . . about eight." " . . . yeah, but if we . . ." " . . . a good lay. We'll take them. . . ."

Step by step, crouched low, the Death Merchant closed in on the targets. He stopped when he could no longer be shielded by the larger rocks. No problem. He was only twenty feet from the two men. He thumbed off the safety catch of the Browning auto-loader and listened.

"First voice: "You know how the boss feels about young chippies. Hell, that one's only sixteen. Man, that's cradle-robbin'!"

Second voice: "Yeah but she looks twenty-five and has plenty of know-how."

First voice: "That's the hell of it. She's been giving it

away like a fire sale. Sluts like that ain't too careful. No tellin' what a man could pick up from a bitch like that."

Second voice: "Hell, why all this talk? Shit, Dave. You know you're going with me."

First voice, slightly angry: "Stop tellin' me what I'm goin' to do. I don't know whether I'm goin! I gotta think about it."

A satisfied look crossed Camellion's lean mean features. *You're going, all right, but not to shack up with any teen-age whore. Do it!*

He stepped out from the side of the mass of granite and raised the Browning auto-pistol. In that split second he saw that one man was sitting on a folding canvas camp cot, his back against the brick wall. The second man, a fat slob in this thirties, was lying down on his back on a camp-type mattress, his hands underneath his head, his legs raised at the knees and crossed. He was lying perpendicular to Camellion. Two Colts AR-15 semiautomatic sporter rifles were leaning against the brick wall.

Feeling embarrassed over two such easy hits, Camellion pulled the trigger. *BBaazitttt*. The first 9mm round-nosed bullet hit the man leaning against the wall in the right temple. He was jerking from the impact of the slug when the Death Merchant's second full-metal-jacketed projectile stabbed into the left rib cage of the man on the mattress. The man did not even have time to rear up. The low cry of pain and shock, crawling up through his throat, was cut off by the second 9mm bullet that struck him in the left side of the head, just above his ear. He fell back and lay still.

NEVER does a wise technician leave anything to chance, not unless he is forced to. The Death Merchant ran to the two corpses and very quickly put a bullet into the back of the man who had fallen forward and now lay on his face, and a slug into the forehead of the man who had flopped on his back. Positive now, he moved back to the side of the large slab-rock and looked toward the mansion, hundreds of feet to his right, to the east. The house was dark, the early morning air cool and quiet. A night for sleeping. A night for Death. Some 400 feet to his right and slightly to the southeast of his position, the cabanas stood lonesome on the beach.

Possibility analysis: Assume that one or more of the cabanas sheltered guards. If so, the guard or guards were asleep or not on alert, not watching the seashore. No matter, nothing was happening. *Or could the FBI report be wrong?* Six to eight guards the report had read. Two were now dead. Where were the other six? One thing was certain: Death was always like a whore—taking everything and never giving anything in return.

Comfortable on one knee, the Death Merchant opened the waterproof container fastened to his chest and took out a Vertex code signaler. He extended the antenna and began to send a message in Morse code, his finger jingling the button: *Two guards by wall terminated. All clear. Come ashore. I'll meet you at the beach. Acknowledge.*

Barney Krestell answered at once, the tiny light blinking on Camellion's Vertex, which was no larger than a standard pocket radio.

Message received and understood. Meet you on the beach. Be careful and don't step on your shoelaces. Out.

Camellion put away the Vertex device, thinking that the Company technicians were among the best in the world. The instrument was so simple. Then again, it was complicated in that the broadcast frequency could not be picked up by ham operators. Only a Vertex could pick up a signal from a Vertex.

Camellion picked up the silenced Browning automatic and made his way to the shore, keeping to the side of the tall limestone rock once he was thirty feet north of the breaking surf. In a short while, The Bomber and Simon Kirkland emerged from the water, in their black scuba suits looking like strange aliens coming ashore from the depths of the sea. Kirkland pulled two plastic drums, Krestell one. With difficulty, the two managed to drag the three drums through the surf, over the smaller rocks and across the shore, the plastic containers leaving long, wide paths in the sand, indentations that the water, forever rolling in and out, gradually erased.

The three men dragged the plastic drums past the wet sand to where the ground was fairly dry and went to work.

"Open the A-3 container, too," Camellion whispered to Simon Kirkland, "and get the spare suit ready. Preparing it now will save a lot of time once we get back here with 'The Owl.'"

A-1 and A-2 drums contained three extra tanks of air, three Ingram Model 10 submachine guns, Sionics suppressors for the three chatterboxes, fifteen spare magazines—five magazines to an ammo bag—a Heckler & Koch G3 SGI sniper's rifle, three spare magazines for the rifle, and a night vision scope and MAW-A1 Sionics silencer for the weapon.

Silencers were attached to the Ingrams. Bags of spare ammo went over shoulders, Camellion and company of two working so quietly one could hear the grass grow!

Kirkland mounted the night vision scope on the HK sniper's rifle and slipped a 7.62-millimeter shell into the firing chamber. It would be the ONI agent's job to remain by the end of the west wall and take out any gate crashers, such as the local police, should something go wrong and an alarm go off or gunfire start popping. Or should the feds, parked in two cars in front of the mansion, on Puueo Avenue, try to intervene. It wasn't likely that the four FBI agents would dare enter the grounds of Archie Renton. An ordinary shootout wasn't under federal jurisdiction. But in case the agents were foolish enough to get involved—blooie! Kirkland would put them to sleep forever.

"Si, Barney, set your Ingrams on three-round bursts," whispered the Death Merchant. "We'll save ammo that way."

Krestell pulled back the knob on top of the Ingram and cocked the weapon, then pushed the firing lever to "S." "What about the cabanas?" He placed the Ingram on the ground and started to unbuckle the straps securing the two tanks of air to his back. "We can't sneak in from the rear with those cabanas at our backs, not knowing who or what might be in them."

Kirkland, who was climbing out of the legs of his own scuba suit, suggested, "Those cabanas aren't all that much of a problem. You two can go in closer and riddle them with slugs. With two full magazines, you could terminate a dozen men."

The Death Merchant pulled a belt and a holster filled with another Hi Power Browning from the A-1 drum. "We will, maybe. But not now. We'd lose too much time. We're going in from the front, through the shadows made by the trees and bushes."

Krestell gave Camellion a bitter look, as though the Death Merchant had been a test-tube baby and the experiment had failed. "The front? What the hell! Why take the long way?"

"It's the safest," Camellion said. "Being the safest, it will also be the swiftest route."

"OK, you're the boss. But if it were up to me, I'd go in from the beach and first riddle the cabanas." protested Krestell.

"Yeah, if you were the boss," Camellion said, all the while knowing he could count on The Bomber. The man always spoke his mind, and Camellion was always suspicious of an associate who never found fault with him.

Camellion glanced at Kirkland, who appeared to be remarkably cool.

"Si, you know what to do. But make damned sure you have to pull the trigger before you do."

"You and Barney do your jobs. I'll do mine." Kirkland was matter-of-fact, his face showing no concern.

Freed of their scuba suits, Camellion and Krestell moved north along the inner side of the west end wall, the shadows cast by the palm trees and by the wall concealing them in their jet-black jump suits.

Halfway up the wall, or a hundred and fifty feet from the front pink brick wall, they got down behind a clump of *'ohi'a* ferns. From a long case on the right side of his belt, he pulled a Javelin Electronics Model 22 night-viewing scope, with a 75mm f/1.4 objective lens, held the rubber cup against his right eye and started to study the large front yard.

"We're lucky that Renton doesn't have any dogs prowling the grounds," whispered Krestell.

"He did have until a year ago," Camellion said. "Dobermans. One bit one of his daughter's friends. Bye-bye went the whole lot."

There they are! Two of them. Camellion handed the night vision scope to Krestell. "Fifty feet in front of the house."

Krestell put the scope to his eye and soon found the two hoods.

"Yeah. They're squatting in front of a couple of those skinny, twisted trees. One crud's a real creep. The nitwit is spinning a revolver on his finger. He must think he's a *paniolo!* [1] Hey! Two more have just come around from the other side of the house. They're both carrying rifles.

1. An Hawaiian cowboy.

See for yourself." He handed the night sight scope to Camellion.

The Death Merchant saw the newcomers walk over to the men in front of the kiawe trees, speak briefly, then turn and continue on their way. The two men came to the northwest corner of the house, turned and walked on the flagstones on the west side. They came to the door of a glassed-in porch, opened the door, went inside and sat down on lounge chairs.

The Death Merchant shoved the Javelin night sight scope into its case and secured the flap. "We'll cross over and go in behind the two in front of the house. We'll take them out first."

Eighty percent concealed by the palm trees, they moved east. Sixty feet to the driveway. They made it. Another four seconds in crossing the drive. There was some danger, due to the moonlight that filtered in through the openings in the palms and in the kiawe trees; however, the odds were against any of the guards seeing them—*unless they were expecting us and knew where to look.*

The fragrant odor of hibiscus filling their nostrils, Camellion and Krestell got down behind a mass of hibiscus bushes and began crawling along on their hands and knees. They inched along on their stomachs, like two giant slugs, past a circular flower bed of haus and Bird of Paradise; and when they stopped, they were only thirty feet north of Wayne Sherill and Lyman "The Mouth" Kane, the two hoods in front of the kiawe trees. Their Ingrams ready to fire, Camellion and Krestell got to their feet and crept forward on the well-trimmed lawn.

It could have been instinct on the part of Lyman Kane, a tall, heavy-lidded gunsel. Or maybe he just wanted to get up and stretch his legs. What mattered is that he stood up, took several steps outward, turned and saw two dark figures racing toward him. For only a second, surprise made him freeze, a natural enough reflex. Another tick in time and he was dead, and a low *bbaazitttttt* was echoing from the noise suppressor on the Death Merchant's Ingram.

Wayne Sherill, the gunman who had been spinning an RG .44 Magnum revolver on his finger, also froze for a few seconds in surprise at seeing Kane's corpse sag to the grass. He attempted to raise the RG, not realizing what and who he was up against.

During that slice of a second that Camellion had terminated Kane, he had also deduced that the odds were that reflex action would cause Sherill to turn in Kane's direction. For that reason, the Death Merchant came in from the other side, to his left, and to Sherill's left. Barney The Bomber also came in from the left.

The next thing that the startled Sherill felt was the large muzzle of the Sionics suppressor pressing against his back between his shoulder blades.

"Drop the piece or you're dead," Camellion hissed out.

Sherill, finding it difficult to accept what was happening, let the .44 mag revolver fall to the grass.

"Sit down, stupid, and put your hands behind you," Camellion ordered. "If you even breathe hard I'll make your heart and lungs look as if they've been washed in a washing machine filled with red paint." And to Krestell, he said, "Drag the other dummy to a tree and prop him up."

Sherill tried to brave his way out of the situation. "You guys can't get away with this. The Owl will mail your heads back to you in a basket."

Camellion jammed Sherill so hard in the small of the back with the muzzle of the noise suppressor that the man cried out in pain. "Listen, you stupid piece of trash, we blew up the guards by the west wall. We saw the two others that were here and know they're on the sun porch. How many more guards are on the grounds and in the house? Lie once and I'll shoot twice." Camellion watched Krestell pick up the RG revolver, jam it in his belt, then go over to the dead Kane and start to drag him toward the tree by both arms.

"Only four," Sherill said, his voice betraying fear. "Two outside and two inside."

The Death Merchant, standing over the man, jabbed the muzzle of the noise suppressor into the man's left shoulder with such force that Sherill groaned and flinched. "You're a damned liar. I'll ask you just once more. How many guards? Where are they?"

"S-Six," Sherill muttered. "Four are outside. Harvey and Hanapepe are on the sun porch. There a-aren't any guards inside the house."

"What's the color scheme inside? What color are the walls?"

"Color—what do you mean?"

"Never mind." Camellion didn't even bother to call the gunman a liar. He merely touched the trigger of the Ingram. *Bazzziittttttt*. Three 9mm round-nosed slugs zipped through Sherill's left clavicle, shot perpendicularly through his left lung, tore through the end of his liver and the upper portion of his stomach, bored through a section of the taenia coli and came to a bloody, skidding halt in the sartorius muscle of his left leg. Sherill's chin dropped to his chest. His body went limp. He was dead.

"Do you believe him?" Krestell whispered.

"He could have been telling the truth. I doubt it," Camellion said. "Tell you what: you go up the east side of the house and stop at the southeast corner. Come back the same way and meet me at the northwest corner. I'll wait for you. We'll take out the two guards on the sun porch and go inside the house."

In the moonlight. Camellion could see Krestell's eyes give a start.

"The glass falling will make a racket," he said. "Hell, that's doing it the hard way."

"We know the layout of the interior from the drawing we got from the feds. The sun porch is right off the living room. East of the living room is the hall and the stairs to the second floor. We can be up those stairs before the people in the house know what's happening. Get going and keep an eye on that garden east of the house."

Why argue? Krestell nodded and began to creep east. The Death Merchant moved west.

Born to live a life of stealth and violence, Krestell moved as silently as a drifting shadow along the front of the house, keeping to the shadows of the palms and the kiawe trees, his mind jumping to the map of the estate which he had committed to memory. There was a long hedge of mokihana berry bushes between the flower garden and the east side of the house. The bushes would shield him from the garden. He was almost certain that there weren't any guards in the garden. The garden was too far away from the house.

He reached the northeast corner and looked around the edge. Nothing but black shadows. His Ingram in the firing position, he moved ahead. The hell with Cosgrove and his orders about those cabanas. There was something very coldblooded about that bird and the way he operated. He had an approach like a jackhammer and could make a rock nervous.

73

Feeling acid sweat trickling from his armpits and soaking his jumpsuit, Krestell quickened his pace. Very soon he came to the southeast corner of the mansion. He looked up. All the windows were dark. Carefully he looked around the corner and studied the rear of the house. Moonlight and shadows. Wooden lawn furniture on a patio covered with a green awning. There they were, the cabanas, all lined up in a row, 150 feet to the southwest. Yeah, the hell with Cosgrove and his orders. Krestell looked at the cabanas for a long moment, then raised the Ingram and raked the dozen square tents, placing the projectiles a foot and a half from the ground. A long *bazittttttttttttttt* flowed from the noise suppressor as fifty five nine-millimeter slugs, from the extra-long magazine, tore into the canvas.

Not a single sound from the cabanas.

Krestell took off the empty magazine, put it into his ammo bag, pulled out a full magazine and reloaded the Ingram. Again he fired. Again a long *baaazittttttttttttt* from the Ingram's silencer, this time the slugs ripping through the canvas at a four-foot level. By God! The tents had to be empty—or else he had killed them all with the first blast of lead.

On full alert, ears and eyes working at full capacity, The Bomber reloaded and began retracing his steps.

The Death Merchant, standing in a flower bed of pandanus fringed with *kukui*, looked around the northwest corner of the large two-story mansion—and instantly felt like pulling his hair. One of the men who had been sitting on the sun porch was halfway between the door of the sun porch and where Camellion was standing, a .45 Commando Arms Carbine in his left hand.

This is worse than being an octopus with all his arms tied in knots!

With the conviction that the Fates had it in for him this morning, the Death Merchant fired, the little Ingram buckling slightly in his hand as three 9mm projectiles stabbed through the short barrel and the long noise suppressor and chopped into Will Harvey's chest, the slam of the impact knocking the gunman off his feet. The carbine fell from his hand and hit the flagstones with a loud clanging sound.

Fate spit again in Camellion's direction. Harvey was still falling when the glass door to the sun porch opened and

Big George Hanapepe started to step out. His foot had not touched the first step when he saw Harvey start to wilt to the ground. At practically the same moment the Death Merchant fired, most of his view obstructed by tall hauui bushes close to the house. Two bullets missed. The third projectile struck Hanapepe in the right forearm and shattered the ulna bone. Hanapepe let out a yell of pain, threw himself backward from the doorway, stumbled and fell on his back.

An old pro and a quick thinker, Hanapepe, who was a mixture of Irish, German, French, and Tahitian, knew that he was severely handicapped by his broken arm and that the man with the machine gun was not alone. Awkwardly pulling a .45 Colt Commander from a left shoulder holster with his left hand, he knew that his only chance for life was to warn the other guards and, to prevent the man with the machine gun from rushing him, put half a dozen slugs through the door. Almost trembling with fear, he placed the auto-pistol on the floor, held it down with his right knee, pushed off the safety with his left thumb, then picked up the weapon with his left hand and pulled the trigger six times, the heavy weapon roaring as the big flat-nosed bullet shattered the glass of the door and shot upward into the wild blue yonder.

A disgusted Camellion had never been in any danger of getting iced by Hanapepe. Not knowing how badly he had wounded the man, the Death Merchant rushed along the side of the house until he came to the edge of the sun porch. Only after Hanapepe had fired the last round from the Colt Commander did Camellion, who had switched the Ingram to full automatic, take several steps outward, swing the Ingram to the three-foot-wide glass section between the door and the edge of the house, and open fire. The instant the glass was shattered, he moved the weapon sideways and up and down, hosing down the sun porch and the furniture with a full magazine of projectiles. Copper-jacketed slugs stabbed all over George Hanapepe. His nose dissolved. His right ear was torn off. A third 9mm bullet zipped into his right side. Another caught him in the chest below the left nipple. Two more in the gut. One in the stomach. Thud! Thud! Thud! Slugs buried themselves in the furniture. A tall cobalt-blue vase exploded and then the glass of a living room window dissolved like smoke in a high wind.

The Death Merchant's main worry was that The

Bomber might have gone all the way around the house and come back up the west side and . . . *mistake me for one of the enemy. No. He will not come back from the south. He's too professional. He knows if he came in a direction facing me, I might accidentally blow him away.* . . .

Camellion was correct. Krestell rounded the northwest corner of the house and was soon beside Camellion, whispering loudly, "We're going to have to work faster than a hound dog scratching fleas. They must have heard those damned shots all the way back to Hono!"

"Our friend out in front said four guards were on the outside," growled Camellion. "That means four or more are inside." He pulled back the cocking knob on the freshly loaded Ingram. "I'll go first. Don't slip on blood or glass."

Both men were charging past the dead Hanapepe, who resembled a bucket of red paint shot full of holes, as the lights in all fifteen rooms of the house went on and a 114-dB siren on the roof began screaming. Not for a second did Camellion and Krestell hesitate. Now, more than ever, every instant counted. They raced through the wide entrance of the sun porch into the living room.

Archie Renton lived well and was a man who could afford what he wanted in life. The walls of the living room were paneled in solid jacaranda wood and decorated with valuable Hawaiian objects of art, with cloaks and capes made from hundreds of thousands of tiny feathers from forest birds, worn by ancient Hawaiians of high rank. On a highly polished table were bone and whale-tooth ornaments, several woven basketry images of war gods and beautifully carved wooden bowls, irregular in their polished silkiness, from which the Hawaiians ate their *poi,* a tropical paste made of taro roots.

It was the Death Merchant's highly honed instinct of self-preservation that saved him. He spotted the short man with the lava-hard face coming through the doorway to Camellion's right, getting ready to fire a Universal Enforcer semiautomatic carbine. With a terrific jerk of his body, Camellion twisted to his left and forward at the same moment that Jerome Sadamocky fired. The three 9mm Para slugs from the UEC missed, burned air between Camellion and Krestell, missing the Death Merchant by only an inch and Krestell by a good foot. Thud, thud, thud! All three projectiles buried themselves in the jacaranda wood wall.

Even as Camellion was twisting himself to the side and

forward, he was swinging the Ingram submachine gun to his right. Now he fired before Sadamocky could realign the carbine to either target. *Bazaaazitttttt!* The blast of 9mm Ingram slugs turned Sadamocky's chest into bloody chopped meat and rib bones and knocked him back through the door, the dying man's inner scream colliding with its own echo.

Camellion and Krestell raced across the room to the opposite entrance, beyond which was a large hallway which also served as the vestibule. Across the hall was the long dining room.

If the chandelier over the table had not been lit up like a Christmas tree in Times Square, Stacy Brookes might have lived and might even have succeeded in whacking out Camellion and Krestell. But the light, his luck, and his stupidity were against him. He attempted to dive under the cherrywood dining table before firing. The only thing he accomplished was getting himself killed by Krestell, who stitched his left side with six projectiles.

The Death Merchant's long legs ate up the steps of the stairs, his eyes watching the four-foot-wide open hallway to his left at the top of the stairs, and the ten-foot open stretch to his right. Halfway up the stairs, Camellion sent splinters of wood and blue-flowered wallpaper flying from the left corner of the hall with seven slugs, then raked the right corner with a dozen more high velocity projectiles—just in time to prevent Gary Poe, one of Renton's personal bodyguards, from cutting down on him with two Colt Diamondback revolvers. Wooden slivers stung Poe's slat-lean face, forcing him to throw up a protective arm and to jump back from the corner. A tall man with thin blond hair and a thick blond mustache, the stone killer was well aware that his longevity would take a very sudden drop once the attackers—how many of the bastards were there?—reached the upstairs. Poe decided to return to the master bedroom where Vernie Grafway, Archie Renton's second personal bodyguard, was waiting with Mr. and Mrs. Denton and their daughter Delora.

Poe and Grafway occupied a bedroom across from the Rentons. Upon hearing the shots from Big George Hanapepe's auto-pistol, the two bodyguards had jumped out of bed and, only in their undershorts, had rushed into Renton's bedroom to do what Renton was paying them $3,000 a month to do. They found that Renton was already out of bed, naked fury on his freckled face and an AMT .45 Hardballer pistol in his hand. Mrs. Renton was trying to comfort her terrified daughter. Delora had been in the adjoining bedroom and had rushed hysterically into her father and mother's room.

Renton had ordered Poe back into the hallway, snarling, "Get the hell out there and try to find out how many they are. It has to be the Fong mob. I'll hang Sammy Fong on a meat hook for this!"

Poe, backing toward the doorway of the master bedroom, almost succeeded in getting inside. He would have if Richard Camellion had not reached the top of the stairs, dropped as Poe triggered both Diamondbacks. The big revolvers roared, the two slugs stabbing several feet over the Death Merchant and going through the door of a linen closet at the end of the hall. The echoes from the Diamondbacks were getting off to a nice rolling reverberation as the Death Merchant stitched Poe with the last three slugs of the Ingram. With a sharp cry, Poe felt stabs of pain and an instant of regret. Darkness started to squeeze his consciousness and he fell heavily against the door of the master bedroom and slid to the floor, eyes wide open, mouth twisted in a cadaverous snarl.

Barney Krestell reached the top of the stairs. The Death Merchant got up from the floor and looked at the fallen gunman.

Krestell watched the hallway below. "Getting into that bedroom won't be easy," he said. "And damn it, every light in this shack is on and that damned siren is still going."

"Getting in would be a snap, if we didn't have to take The Owl alive," Camellion said calmly. "But I have an idea I think will work."

"It had better—and fast. The police are on their way. They have to be."

In the master bedroom, Mr. and Mrs. Renton, their daughter Delora, and Vernie Grafway heard Poe cry out and his body fall heavily against the door.

"God damn it! The sons of bitches got Gary!" Grafway said, enraged.

"Stop your cursing in front of my family," Renton ordered. He was a man of medium height and build and, due to daily exercise and careful eating habits, had a thirty-six-inch waist. His muscles were solid. As bald as a tombstone, he had several hairpieces of brown hair, these resting on wig stands on the dresser.

Outwardly remarkably calm for a man tiptoeing on a tightrope between life and death, Renton looked down at his wife and his daughter crouched by the side of the bed. "Get in the closet and keep as low as possible," he said, his nervous tone betraying his fear. "Hurry. Do as I say!"

A pretty woman in her forties, but only in a hard sort of way, Norma Renton looked at her husband for a moment but didn't speak. "Come, dear," she said to her daughter, trying hard not to lose control of her own voice. Together, mother and daughter crawled on their hands and knees to the closet. Norma Renton pulled open the folding doors. The two crawled inside. The doors closed.

Archie Renton ran across the room and got down to one side of a cherrywood chest of drawers. Grafway hurried over to the side of the dresser, the end closest to the closet in which Mrs. Renton and her daughter were hiding. There was no need for words between Archie Renton and his top gun. There were only two doors through which the attackers could charge.

Several minutes passed, minutes that seemed like an hour. Even though they expected the double-pronged attack, Renton and Grafway jumped slightly when the bedroom door to the hall was thrown open. Both men fired, Renton's .45 Hardballer pistol and Grafway's Smith & Wesson .44 mag revolver filling the bedroom with crashing sound. They had fired needlessly. The doorway was empty. Renton and Grafway were staggered by another surprise in the form of several dozen 9mm projectiles that ripped apart the door connecting Delora's bedroom with her parents' room. The mirror on the dresser dissolved into a thousand fragments of glass. A Queen Anne chair, covered in blue velvet, was ruined when four slugs ripped through its back. A bracket clock, the case of solid hand-decorated black-lacquered hardwood, exploded. An original Victorian bellpull, woven in floral pattern, did a double flipflop from the impact of several slugs. Afraid for their lives, Renton and Grafway ducked down to the ends of the dresser and the chest of drawers, their eyes widening when Camellion's voice came from the hall.

"We know you're in there, Renton. You can't drop from the balcony. It's too high. Even if you could, our man outside would kill you. We want only you, Renton. You and whoever is with you toss out your iron, or we'll throw in grenades. And if the grenades don't kill your wife and kid, we will. You've got to the count of ten to surrender. One . . . two . . . three . . ."

"Hell, we can't surrender," whispered Vernie Grafway angrily. "They'll blow us away if we do."

"They'll blow us up with grenades if we don't, you idiot!" said Renton, his mind racing. And he thought, *You're as good as dead anyhow, Vernie. They don't need you.*

A man's past is a kaleidoscope of many fractured events and fragmentary emotions, all stacked in a mishmash of recall. Renton had lost track of the men and women he had ordered hit. He was a son of a bitch and knew it. Yet he had one chink in his armor. He dearly loved his wife and daughter. The button man in the hall was no doubt telling the truth. Fong wanted him.

". . . four . . . five . . . six . . ."

Without even blinking, Renton turned and shot Grafway three times with the Hardballer auto-pistol. As Grafway sank to the rug, a look of stark disbelief forever frozen on his double-chinned face, Renton yelled, "This is Renton. I just killed my bodyguard. He wouldn't give up his gun. Don't fire. I'm tossing out my gun."

"The clip first," Camellion yelled back. "Then the weapon. Walk out backward with your hands above your head. Don't turn around until we tell you to. Try anything cute—if you're lying and there's a goon in there with you—and you'll get it first."

Renton removed the magazine from the Hardballer and tossed it through the door. Next he threw out the Hardballer auto-pistol. With a shuddering sigh, he raised his arms, turned around and started backing toward the doorway, desperately hoping that his wife and daughter wouldn't panic.

His heart pounding, Renton backed out through the door, keeping his head rigid, his eyes straight ahead.

"Turn toward me," a voice said.

Renton turned and saw a tall Chinese staring at him.

The Death Merchant first tapped out a short coded message to Simon Kirkland: *We have the prize and are heading for the beach. Respond.*

Kirkland tapped back on the Vertex: *The gates to the*

driveway are open and the cops will be here any minute. I'd better take out the first couple of cars. The other fuzz will hesitate and proceed slowly—more time that way for us to get to the beach and in the water.

Right—do it, the Death Merchant replied.

Camellion, Krestell, and their captive moved down the stairs, crossed the vestibule, raced down the length of the living room and retreated from the mansion through the wrecked door of the shot-apart sun porch. All the while they could hear police sirens wailing, getting closer and closer.

"Renton, don't try to escape," snarled Camellion, "or you'll get the business right here. To get even, we'll get to your wife and kid later. You'll be breaking bread with the dead, but they'll get a beauty treatment with sulfuric acid."

They raced across the yard and within a minute reached the shadows of the palm trees, Krestell gritting through clenched teeth, "I'd like to know who in hell opened those gates? You, Renton?"

"The gates opened automatically when the alarm went off," panted Renton. "The cook and our houseman sleep downstairs. They have rooms off the kitchen. One of them must have pressed the alarm button when they heard Big George fire."

The three men turned south and started through the rocks toward the beach. Camellion had slung his Ingram over his back on its sling strap and, the fingers of his left hand wrapped around the neck of Renton's pajama top, was prodding the racketeer along by poking him in the small of the back with the Browning fitted with a silencer. Every so often Renton would let out a grunt, if not of actual pain, of acute discomfort, but not from the slight pokes that the Death Merchant was giving him. In his bare feet, Renton was having a miserable time walking on pebbles and, once beyond the yard, on weeds and sharp-bladed wild *pili* grass.

Barney The Bomber Krestell led the way. The Death Merchant and his captive followed. The three were almost to the desolate spot where they had left the scuba gear and the plastic containers when the first police car—siren screaming, top strobe lights flashing—turned through the gates onto the driveway.

Simon Kirkland was not a cruel man. He was, however,

dedicated. It was the final result that counted, the success of the mission, and the mission would only be a success when the Soviet monitoring station was found and put out of commission. To help accomplish that, he would have— had he been ordered to—cut his own mother's throat with a dull knife.

An expert shot, Kirkland was ready with the HK G3 SG1 sniper's rifle many minutes before the first police car turned into the driveway from Puueo Avenue. Thinking how easy it was to take life from another human being, he sighted through the night-vision scope and began to squeeze the trigger, the 7.62mm (X51 NATO [2]) projectiles burning through the special MAW-A1 Sionics silencer.

Ping. Ping. Two holes appeared in the windshield of the police car, the impacts of the spitzer-shaped projectiles slamming the driver and his partner against the seat. Both men had holes in their heads. Both men were as dead as they would ever be. Out of control, the dead driver's foot still on the gas, the car swerved to the left. It plowed through a flowerbed of *haus* and crashed against a kiawe tree as a second patrol car turned and came through the gates, the driver slamming on the brakes when he saw what had happened to the first car. Instantly he knew there was a hidden sniper with a silenced rifle. Too late! Kirkland fired five more times, the fourth and the fifth projectiles killing the driver and the cop sitting next to him. One of the bullets had also cut through the front seat and had struck a third officer in the lower stomach; yet he was not severely wounded. The bullet had lost much of its power in going through the back of the seat and the Sam Browne belt of the cop.

Kirkland studied the inside of the pink brick wall in front, seeing everything clearly through the night vision scope which turned the darkness into medium twilight. The rounded circle of light—the field of vision through the scope—came to the narrow gate that was meant to admit people. Three SWAT boys had just come through the gate and were creeping toward the bushes and the trees. They carried Armalite automatic rifles and wore TAC vests and riot helmets. One SWAT man also carried a riot shield of transparent polycarbonate.

Calmly, Kirkland fired the last six rounds of the SG1

---

2. The same as a .308 Winchester cartridge.

sniper's rifle, aiming for the legs of the three SWAT men. All went down with howls of agony. His hands sweaty in the flesh-colored surgical gloves, Kirkland pulled out the empty magazine, reloaded and sent five slugs at a third police car coming to a halt parallel with the open gates between the drive and Puueo Avenue, its tires screeching. The projectiles chopped into the right side of the car, but Kirkland could not be sure that he had hit anyone. Nor did he have time to find out. It was time to get the hell out. Considering the kills he had scored, it would be half an hour before the cautious police would get to the beach—if then.

Putting down the rifle, Kirkland pulled out the Vertex signal device, extended the antenna and began pressing the large button. *I'm coming to the beach. Watch for me.* He put away the Vertex device, picked up the rifle and began hurrying to the beach, moving as quickly as he could without making a noise in the brush. In the distance, to the northwest, he heard the *thump-thump-thump-thump* of a helicopter's rotor.

By the time Kirkland reached the area where he and the others had removed their scuba gear and had opened the plastic containers, he found that "Cosgrove," Krestell, and Archie Renton were waiting, minus their rubberized scuba suits but wearing air tanks strapped securely to their backs, the mouthpieces of the air hoses ready to be taken into their mouths, the clamps ready to be placed over their noses, the rounded glass face masks, on thick elastic bands, hanging around their necks.

"We didn't want to take the time to put on the suits." The Death Merchant answered Kirkland's silent inquiry. "We don't need them. We won't have to submerge in the vehicle for more than twenty feet, and the water is not all that chilly. With the closed breathing system, there will be no telltale air bubbles, even if the police could get a boat here in time."

"I'll help you with the tanks," Krestell said. Stooping, he picked up the tanks on their harness.

Nine minutes later, after Camellion had made certain that Renton was breathing properly through the mouthpiece of the twin hoses, the four men were fighting their way through the splashing surf. Their face masks were in place, their noses sealed off; the vital mouthpieces in their mouths. When the swirling water was almost up to their chests, they submerged and began swimming underwater to the SDV.

Far behind them the police helicopter had stopped directly over the mansion and was raking the ground with two powerful spotlights.

The Death Merchant had only one worry, one that he had not voiced to either Krestell or Kirkland: that the baralyme, which absorbed CO_2 in the closed breathing system, would give out. . . .

CHAPTER SIX

1000 hours. Blue sky above. Blue water below. The *Lady Luck,* her engine silent, bobbed gently in the water. On the Beaufort Scale, the wind was force 3, its speed seven to ten knots. Wavelets were only a foot and a half high, with their crests here and there breaking to give a few small "sea horses."

Captain "Stan Norward" was on the stern deck with "Roger" and "Joan" "Hollinger." Joan Hollinger was in the fisherman's seat, a large rod and reel in the chair harness in front of her. Any idiot could see that she was fishing. . . .

Joseph Luther Samson Hukimula, the hard-faced deckhand, who was a Company contract agent, was at the wheel on the bridge. In the forward cabin below decks, Richard Camellion went over a mental checklist while Barney Krestell, Simon Kirkland, and Archie Renton ate a midmorning snack of pork and beans, canned biscuits and fried Spam.

All is in order, Camellion told himself. As the SDV had been returning to the *Lady Luck,* all the weapons used in the raid on Renton's mansion had been dropped in 900 feet of water.

All the ballistics experts in the world can't pull slugs from dead men and match them to weapons that can't be found.

The SDV had reached *Lady Luck* and had then been sunk in 1,210 feet of water. It would be recovered by the U.S. Navy the next morning at 0300 hours. A dozen recovery lift bags were attached to the underwater vehicle and a timer mechanism geared to a larve cylinder of air inside the SDV. At 0300 hours the timer would release air into the lift bags, which would carry the SDV to the surface.

Camellion had removed all makeup from his own face and from the faces of Kirkland and Krestell. The three "Chinese" had vanished.

We're eighty-one nautical miles southwest of Renton's estate and fourteen miles from shore. It isn't likely that any police boats will stop and search us. But should a police boat stop—Archie Renton would be drugged and stashed in a secret compartment built into the bilges.

PLAN CHERRY TREE was right on the mark. At 1400 hours that same afternoon, Renton would be transferred to the *Mary Ann*, a second cabin cruiser. By then, the Death Merchant would have changed Renton's features and the mobster would appear twenty years younger. Heavily drugged, Renton would be taken ashore, supported by other "drunken" merrymakers on "vacation."

By 1800 hours Renton would be in a small, hidden room in the Chapel of the Roses Mortuary on Paki Street in Honolulu.

"You're not a bad cook," Kirkland complimented Krestell. "You'd make a good wife for some lucky man."

Krestell's long horse-like face broke out in a mock smile. "I use a secret formula for frying Spam. I fry it well, serve it hot and pray a lot."

Kirkland wiped his fingers on a handkerchief. "You know what the Chinese say about cooking," he said. "Many men can cook, but Fu Manchu." He looked across the table at Archie Renton, who now was dressed in a flowered sports shirt and beach shorts, and who looked as though he were eating his last meal. "Cheer up, Renton. You have your health and I'm sure your bills are paid."

"You men aren't part of the Fong mob," Renton said, "or any other mob in the Hono area. The disguises you used and the way you operated! Who in hell are you and what do you want with me?"

"All in due time, Renton," Kirkland said. "Before midnight you'll be singing like a prima donna, and it won't be Country and Western!"

"You're feds!" Renton lashed out. He shifted on the chair, the chain of the extra large handcuffs, securing his left ankle to a leg of the table, rattling. "You're feds and what you've done is illegal. I demand to see my attorneys when we dock."

The Bomber laughed in Renton's face. "You're slipping, Owl. Do you really think the feds would raid your place like we did and kill half a dozen cops? Screw you, stupid. The FBI wouldn't use the methods we're going to use to make you sing. You're going to talk your head off and thank us for the privilege of letting you."

"It takes two to make a dialogue," Kirkland laughed, "but in your case, Archie, we're going to make an exception. You're going to blab enough for half a dozen people."

"Two to make a dialogue, but five like him to pop popcorn," the Death Merchant said. He was lying on a bunk and looking up at the low ceiling.

Kirkland turned and looked at him. "Five?"

"Yeah. Five. One to hold the popper and four to shake the stove."

CHAPTER SEVEN

The entire day had been a hideous nightmare for Archie Renton. The tall man with the strange blue eyes—the one called Cosgrove—had given him a shot in the arm. Immediately, Renton had felt lightheaded. He couldn't speak intelligibly. He found it impossible to coordinate his movements. His ears began to ring. His vision became distorted, as if the world had become a hall of mirrors, the kind of mirrors used in sideshows, mirrors that grossly distort images. The man called Cosgrove became two feet tall and six feet wide. The man with the long, narrow face had become straw-thin, his feet as tiny as thimbles, his head as large as a mountain. The boat had turned to rubber, the floor and ceiling rippling like waves on a stormy sea. Helpless in his horrifying dream world, Renton recalled being taken to another ship, another cabin cruiser. More distorted people. Much later, men had put his arms over their shoulders and had led him from the boat to the dock; and all the time he remembered that "Cosgrove," after giving him the shot in the arm, had done something to his face—but what? There had not been any pain. A long ride in a car. Transfer to another car . . . a long black limousine. Another ride. A slight prick in the arm as a hypodermic discharged its small cargo of drug.

Blackness.

Renton awoke with tiny devils hitting the inside of his skull with hammers. He tried to sit up, looked around— and screamed in horror. He was lying in a casket, his head on a satin pillow, the lower part of the casket lid closed over his body. The long black automobile! It had not been a limo. It had been a hearse!

Cosgrove and one of the men who had been on the first cabin cruiser unfastened the lower part of the casket's lid, threw it back, and helped an unsteady Renton out of the burial box. They led him to a chair, pushed him down, handcuffed his hands behind his back, then sat down close by.

Renton saw that, besides the two men who had lifted him out of the casket, four other men were in the room whose walls and ceiling were painted an off-white. At one end of the room were four other caskets and two bronze burial vaults.

A funeral parlor! The thought screamed in Renton's mind. I'm in a goddamned funeral parlor!

Floyd Keifer, dressed in a navy blazer and light blue slacks, flicked ash from his cigar and looked at Renton, who found that, in spite of a headache, his mind was clear. His vision was no longer distorted and unreality had become reality. People and objects had resumed their normal sizes and shapes.

Keifer said, "Renton, there isn't much that goes on in the Islands that you don't know about, especially in Honolulu. We want to know who's been hiring cheap hoods as hit men for special jobs."

The mobster stared back at Keifer, trying to part the cobwebs of confusion. They had raided his home, had gunned down his guards, and had brought him—to where?—to ask him such a ridiculous question? It didn't make sense.

Renton also found that he could speak coherently. "I demand that you let me call my attorneys," he said and discovered that his mouth was very dry and that his throat hurt when he spoke. "I demand to know where I am and who you are."

Keifer didn't speak; his face didn't change its expression.

Olin Gammill sighed loudly, dropped his cigarette on the concrete floor and crushed it out with the toe of his left foot. "He 'demands,'" he said in disgust. "Gutsy bastard, isn't he?"

The Death Merchant sat spread-legged on a chair, its wooden back facing him. He motioned to Wilfred Sims and Olin Gammill. "OK. We have to do it the hard way. Get on with it."

Sims, Gammill, and Barney Krestell got up, The Bomber and Gammill going over to Renton, Sims walking over to a long porcelain-topped table. Sims picked up the small leather case on the table, unzipped it and took out a hypodermic. He turned, held up the small glass piston, pushed down slightly on the plunger and, in the light of the single bulb hanging from the ceiling on a twisted cord, saw a tiny drop of fluid ooze from the hollow needle. Then he turned and smiled at a wide-eyed Archie Renton. "Get ready to take a trip to hell, Renton."

The mobster tried to rise, a nameless panic stabbing at his brain. Krestell was too fast for him. Stepping behind the gangster, he applied a forearm hold over Renton's neck, forcing him back down to the chair. Olin Gammill pushed down on Renton's shoulders and Sims deftly slipped the needle of the hypodermic into the subcutaneous tissues of the racketeer's right forearm, close to the ulnar artery—an uncertain effort since the mobster's arms were handcuffed behind his back. Sims pushed down on the plunger and thirty milligrams of Succinylcholine chloride found its way into Renton's body.

Sims pulled out the needle and walked back to the case on the table. He put down the empty hypodermic and pulled another one from its elastic band in the leather kit.

Known py the trade name of *Anectine*, succinylcholine chloride is one of the worst horror drugs in existence. Archie Renton very quickly felt the drug's effects. At first there was a growing numbness in his fingers and toes, a creeping paralysis that soon reached his arms and legs. He could not support himself. He fell sideways from the chair and was caught by Olin Gammill, preventing his head from hitting the concrete floor. Renton's arms, legs, stomach, and chest became dead lead. Very suddenly he couldn't breathe. He tried to scream, but no sound came from his throat. Realization pounded in his brain. These men were going to kill him. Air! AIR! He had to have air.

As easily as he would take a Sunday stroll, Wilfred Sims walked over to Renton, bent down and injected him with the contents of the second hypodermic, muttering, "We should let the son of a bitch die."

Gradually the paralysis left the terrified Renton and he could feel life-giving air rushing into his tortured lungs. He lay on his right side, panting, staring at Gammill's legs.

Barney Krestell nudged Renton with his foot. "You came within twenty seconds of dying, Renton," he smirked. "Next time you might not be so lucky."

"Who is hiring the hit men, Renton?" Floyd Keifer asked again.

Barney The Bomber looked at the Death Merchant, who had put his hands on the back of the chair and was resting his chin on his fingers.

"Should we sit him up?" Barney asked.

"He might as well die on the floor," Camellion said, all the while knowing that the Anectine only made the victim think he couldn't breathe. The drug in no way interfered with the autonomic nervous system, which controlled such functions as breathing and the beating of the heart.

"I'm waiting," Keifer said again, this time impatient. "Or do you want another shot, Renton?"

"I—I can only tell you what I've heard," panted Renton. A pathetic figure of a man, he was not a pleasant sight to look at.

"Put him on the chair," the Death Merchant ordered. "The first time he stalls, give him a full dose and kill him."

"You're the boss," grunted Krestell. He and Olin Gammill picked up the frightened mobster by the armpits and shoved him down on the wooden chair. In the meanwhile, Sims had refilled the first hypodermic; now he moved to the side of Renton, who glanced up fearfully at the ONI agent.

"You're only sixty minutes from fire and brimstone, stupid," Camellion said pleasantly to Renton. "You had better blab like you have never blabbed before. We'd just as soon kill you as step on a cockroach."

Krestell laughed. "Yeah, like Kirkland said, make like a prima donna. You won't get any applause, but you won't have to make a final curtain call."

In a desperate tone of voice, Archie Renton said that he honestly did not know the name of the man, or men, or group, hiring gunmen for "special hits." He very hurriedly explained that some months ago there had been rumors in the Honolulu underworld that gunsels were being hired for "special hits." Renton, talking as if he expected each word to be his last, said that he and his boys had been trying to find out who was doing the recruiting and why.

"W—We were thinking that maybe the Mafia from the States were going to try and move in on us," he said. "When we got the word that Tommy Chong was hired as a mechanic,[1] we were going to grab him and make him tell us what was going on, who hired him and why. But some creep gave him the business before we could get to him— that shootout at the tattoo joint."

Richard Camellion smiled. "I'm the 'creep' who did it. But go on. You said you got the word about Tommy Chong. How? From whom?"

Renton's throat felt like sandpaper dipped in acid. "Please," he muttered. "Could I have a glass of water?"

"No!" Camellion's tone was sharp. "You're even lucky to be alive. Don't push your luck."

"Chong's girlfriend," croaked Renton, his head hanging down. "A prostitute. She told a girlfriend. We got the story through a bartender. He said that foreigners hired Chong. He heard that foreigners were hiring gunmen at fabulous prices. We tried to find Lucy Chimonk, the girl Chong was shacking up with. We couldn't. She disappeared. I guess she's hiding out since Tommy got killed." Renton's voice became more frantic. "What else can I tell you?"

Olin Gammill tapped his cigarette. Ash fell on Renton's bald head.

"I don't think he's said enough to keep on living." Gammill looked at a calm-faced Floyd Keifer, then at the Death Merchant, neither of whom revealed how the word *foreigners* excited them. "Let's kill this rotten son of a bitch and get it over with."

"Wait! For God's sake, wait!" Archie Renton, straining at the handcuffs, tried to get to his feet. Krestell and Gam-

1. Underworld slang for gunman, or "hit man."

mill roughly shoved him back down, The Bomber snarling, "What makes you—you of all people—think there's a God?"

Richard Camellion got to his feet, turned the chair around and sat down. "Like one goldfish said to the other goldfish, 'There must be a God. If there's not, who changes the water?' "

"I remember something that might be of interest," Renton almost shouted. Sweat flowed down his face. His eyes were wild and wide.

"We're listening," Floyd Keifer said.

"It's o-only a rumor." Renton's voice trembled. "But we've been hearing that something's not right on the island of Tukoatu. It's an island up north."

If Renton had been watching Hugh Hale Gamberkrone, the National Security Agency (NSA) man sitting next to Floyd Keifer, he would have noticed Gamberkrone's eyes light up briefly with intense excitement.

"What about Tukoatu?" Pretending disinterest, the Death Merchant thought of the computer readouts. *Tukoatu has got to be the objective!*

"Like I said, there's something funny going on. The way we heard it, Hiromori Nagai, the Jap millionaire who owns the island, fired his two Hawaiian houseboys and the two men—*hapa haoles*—who took care of the grounds around his house on the island."

Sneered Wilfred Sims, "So what's mysterious about four guys getting canned?"

"Nagai didn't give any reason for firing the four," Renton said nervously. He hesitated. "The way we found out . . ." The mobster paused again. "Henry Liholihoi—one of the house boys—was mad as hell about getting canned for no good reason. He had been employed at the island house for six years. Liholihoi swiped three valuable pieces from Nagai's art collection before he left the island. He stole three *pililaakas* that were over three hundred years old— three heads woven from vine roots, with the mouths outlined in dogs' teeth and the scalps made of human hair. Liholihoi—"

"He fenced the three heads to you," the Death Merchant, guessing the rest, finished. "The three *pililaakas* are worth about twenty-five grand each. What did you give Henry Liholihoi for them?"

"Three G's apiece," stammered Renton.

Olin Gammill offered. "We can have the FBI pick up Liholihoi and question him."

"There's m-more," Renton said desperately, "and that's what's so odd. Hiromori Nagai never reported the theft. In all these months, he—"

"How many months?" Camellion asked.

"Liholihoi stole the heads . . . oh . . . it's been maybe twelve or thirteen months ago," Renton said. "In all that time, Nagai hasn't reported the theft to the police, not even to the insurance company. If he had, I'd know about it. I mean. I m-mean . . ." Renton searched for words.

"You mean your contacts in the Honolulu Police Department would have tipped you off if Nagai had reported the loss," Keifer said flatly. "Isn't that what you're afraid to say? Out with it!"

"Yes-ss." Archie Renton's hoarse voice and watery eyes literally begged for life. Yet he knew. From the beginning of the beginning he had known. These men called each other by name. How could they let him live?

"Will, give our guest a sedative." The Death Merchant spoke in a voice of authority and very clearly. "He looks tired. Put him to sleep."

"NO!" Renton yelled the word. "Don't k-kill m-me, p-please!" He felt the powerful hands of Gammill and Krestell on his shoulders, preventing him from getting up from the chair.

"We're not going to kill you, Renton," the Death Merchant said. "There's still a lot of talking you have to do. There are names and dates and places you have to give . . . the names of policemen and public officials and politicians you and your mob are paying off . . . the routes you're using to bring H and coke[2] and other drugs into the Islands.

Renton gaped dumbly at Camellion. He was finished and knew it. All he hoped for now was to remain alive.

Wilfred Sims questioned the Death Merchant with his eyes. "Cosgrove, are you serious? Do you really mean a tranquilizer?"

"I mean 1,200 milligrams of meclizine hydrochloride." When Camellion saw puzzlement bloom on Sims' face, he added, "Thorazine, if you prefer the trade name. I know

2. Heroine and cocaine.

92

you have it in the kit. I put it in myself. It's in the pink vial."

Archie Renton, feeling that he wasn't going to be killed on the spot, watched Sims go back to the kit, take out an empty hypodermic and fill it to the 1,200 mg mark.

"What . . . w-what are you going to do with me?" Renton asked, staring at the Death Merchant. "I know you're not going to let me go. At least you can tell me who you are. . . ."

"All you need to know is that you're going to spend the rest of your life in a federal prison in the States," lied Floyd Keifer.

Sims walked back to Renton and, with Krestell and Gammill holding the mobster by the shoulders, injected him with the powerful drug. Sims was pulling the needle from Renton's flesh when Renton's head dropped. He would be unconscious for hours. When he awoke he would be in Banana Bread Box One, but he wouldn't know it.

Barney Krestell put his hands on his hips, looked down at the unconscious Renton and made a face. "I don't know about the rest of you, but I'm getting tired of hauling Renton around in a goddamn hearse. It's downright spooky."

Sims, Keifer, and Camellion burst out laughing. Gammill gave a series of little chuckles. For the Bomber to say that anything was "spooky" was downright ridiculous. In contrast to the men who were amused, Hugh Hale Gamberkrone appeared to be vaguely annoyed. A man in his late thirties, he had aquiline features, black bushy eyebrows and thick black hair combed back and parted to the right. A hearty eater, he was right on the edge of being corpulent.

H.H. Gamberkrone had not come to Honolulu to attend a luau. He had flown from Washington, D.C., because of his talents in spectrophotometry. For the past four mornings, COM-V-CON-2's cameras had been photographing the Hawaiian Islands as it passed overhead, using two cameras that responded to infrared rays. The photographs from the satellite had been radioed to NASA in the United States and, enhanced by computer processing methods, changed into colored mosaics resembling synthesized radio maps. By analyzing the spectrum picked up by the spectrometer a split second before the cameras in COM-V-CON-2 took the photographs, an expert spectroscopist like Gamberkrone could separate man-made objects from natural objects.

Earlier in the day, the computer people at Banana Bread Box One had ascertained that of the 162 privately owned islands in the Hawaiian chain, only one had all the features necessary to house a Soviet base. That island was Molokai. The island was 9.6 square miles in surface area. Most of the island was mountainous, with some of the peaks being 4,000 and 5,000 feet high—just perfect for radio telemetry analysis of a satellite. Just perfect for a "dish."

"We can't haul Renton out of here at this hour," Olin Gammill said. "It's almost eleven o'clock. How would it look if a hearse went driving about in the suburbs?"

"We'll take him back to the base tomorrow," Floyd Keifer said, "when there's plenty of traffic on the roads. But we'll use the bakery truck." He finished lighting a cigar, dropped the gold butane lighter into his coat pocket, and turned toward the Death Merchant. "Cosgrove, what was all that nonsense you were giving Renton about his giving us names and dates, etcetera? The Agency couldn't care less about Renton's gangland activities. Anyhow, we already have a pretty good idea of the rackets he's into and whom he's paying off here in Hono."

Dressed in a light blue two-piece blazer suit, Camellion turned and grinned crookedly at the CIA Chief of Station. "Think ahead, Floyd. Once the FBI has the information we get from Renton, the Bureau will be a part of the operation in every way, an accomplice if you will. There's no way the Bureau could ever reveal the operation, unless it wanted to convict itself."

A slow smile spread across Keifer's mouth. "Hmmmmmm. A good idea. We'll tape everything Renton confesses to and turn copies over to Gentry and Jourdan, after we've deleted any references that might hint at the operation."

"We'll do Renton a favor." Sims pushed his eyeglasses higher on his nose. "When we're done with the son of a bitch, we can put a microgram of AP-Seven in his food. Why hell, he'll never know he's dead. And the best medical examiner in the world can't detect AP-Seven."

"We'll do no such thing," Camellion said flatly. "Renton's death has to look like a mob hit. We'll blow him up with a sawed-off shotgun and stick him in the trunk of a car and leave the vehicle in downtown Hono. Or have you

94

forgotten that it's supposed to be the Fong mob who grabbed him?"

"Cosgrove is right," broke in Krestell admonishingly. "You've read the papers and heard the TV news. Everyone, including the police, think it was the Fong mob who did the job." He snickered loudly. "I almost feel sorry for Sammy Fong. The police are really giving him a difficult time."

"Don't get overconfident," warned Olin Gammill. "One feature writer in *The Express* questioned the theory that it was the Fong mob. His thesis was that the snatch was carried out too smoothly; and even the Hono police are sure that some kind of underwater craft was used. Like he said—I believe the writer's name was Himby—the job was too well executed for the Fong boys to have been involved."

AP-Seven! The thought rolled around in the Death Merchant's mind. It was a poison closely related to botulinus toxin. A pint of AP-Seven would wipe out half the population of the world. The U.S. had it all in germ-virus weapons: plague, meningitis and a dozen more of the "fever" diseases—at least 170 deadly diseases. The Soviet Union had the same diseases in its G-V arsenal. Think of it. Just thirty-one grams of Q-Fever virus would be enough to kill twenty-six BILLION people. Then there were the C-Weapons—chemical warfare. The U.S.—and the Soviet Union—had enough to destroy the poulation of the world ten million times over. One drop of B-Wilfrin-6, a nerve gas, could kill 250,000 people. A one-pound container, filled with B-W-6 and exploded over New York City—or Moscow—would kill every human being within a radius of fifty miles—provided the day was halfway windy.

And fools worry about nuclear warfare!

There were problems. Already certain concerned people in the United States were stirring up a stink about the U.S. Government's germ warfare and nerve gas program. *It's unfortunate. Peace-loving men and idealists have always been naive fools who will never learn that peace can only come through strength of the military. . . . And wait and see the result when the public learns that UFOs are top secret U.S. military craft, begun by the Nazis and perfected after the war by German and American scientists. Or if the American public ever learns that cattle multilations are the result of nerve gas experiments. But so far the public have been fools. The Company's "disinformation" peo-*

95

*ple have seen to that. Damned clever, too. By cutting out
the tongues and sex organs of the cattle, the technicians
have made the public believe that the mutilations are the
work of cults, devil worshippers and other kooks. . . .*

H.H. Gamberkrone spoke up. "Mr. Keifer, what time
will the special courier arrive tomorrow?"

Keifer blew out a cloud of cigar smoke and looked at his
wristwatch. "On the two-o'clock afternoon Pan Am flight.
It will take him three hours to get to the station, though.
He'll have to come a round-about way.

"I was informed that your base has all the facilities necessary for enlarging the photographs." Gamberkrone's
voice was gentle, almost ingratiating.

"Don't concern yourself. We have all the equipment
you'll need," Keifer said. "I'll tell you though, we're all
confident that Tukoatu is the right island. The information
we got from Renton is more evidence."

"But not hard, conclusive evidence," Camellion, forever
the realist, said. His blue eyes stabbed at Gamberkrone.
"That confirmation will have to come from you."

"I can only tell you what the spectrum reveals," Gamberkrone said stiffly. "Are you gentlemen certain that your
computer hasn't made a mistake?"

"The computer didn't," Camellion said.

"We're positive that the computer was accurate," Keifer
said quickly. "We programmed the Hensen-L-6 with all the
pertinent data in reference to the islands—size, terrain, the
works. Three different times the computer picked Tukoatu. Tukoatu has to be the target, or we're up against one
big, dead end."

The Death Merchant said casually, "Maps from the
Hawaiian Geological Survey Department reveal that the
west end of Tukoatu is riddled with giant caves. A lot of
the entrances are right at the waterline, some below. It's
our theory that the Russians built the base inside the caves
by bringing in workers by submarine, from Mother Russia
herself."

"The irony is why Mr. Nagai would assist the Soviet
Union," Keifer said. "It can't be for the money. He's worth
at least twenty million—made it in banking and in real
estate. His family has been in Hawaii for over a hundred
years. His maternal grandparents came here from Japan in
the 1870s."

"Blackmail," said Wilfred Sims who was pouring a cup

of coffee from an aluminum pot on a hotplate on a crate next to a $12,000 solid-bronze casket. "The ivans have to be blackmailing him. What other answer is there?"

"We may never know," the Death Merchant said with the certainty of intimate knowledge. "The world is fighting a new kind of war, a war that really hasn't gotten into full swing yet."

"Terrorism." Krestell gave Camellion a long thoughtful look. "You're referring to terrorism."

"I mean a war in which terrorists, glamorized as 'young idealists' will destabilize nations from within while the threats from the Russians immobilize our allies from without."

"I'm inclined to agree," Keifer said bitterly. "The Israelis haven't helped the overall situation any. Their colonization of the occupied territories and of all of Jerusalem has served as a crystalizing agent for the movement which Moscow is riding, while at the same time practicing genocide against Moslems in Afghanistan."

"Yeah, plus the fact that the Arabs are calling for a jehad—a holy war—against the U.S.," Olin Gammill said.

"Not all the Arabs," Camellion said. "Only the rug-flying Iranians want a jehad. Sadat and the Saudis are on our side, even if they don't like the $1,785 billion we've given Israel since 1977."

"Fuck'em and their stupid holy war," growled Krestell, walking over to the coffee pot. "There isn't anything those sand fleas can do."

"Wrong," Camellion said evenly. "There are some six million Moslems employed in the Common Market nations in Europe. For the most part they are of Turkish, Arab, Pakistani, and North African origin. Turkey herself—our front line of defense against the pig farmers—is gripped by a wave of terrorism, and the military takeover by the generals hasn't changed anything."

"Terrorism isn't a 'holy war,' " insisted Krestell.

"Next to Catholicism, the second most powerful religion in France is Islam," Camellion said. "Over two million rug kneelers are working in French industry. The Moslem population of Britain has doubled in the past two years. Some 200 Imams of a resurgent Islam have been brought into West Germany to educate the children of Moslem workers in schools and social centers. And those idiots in Washington, by destroying files and weakening security organiza-

97

tions, have made it all but impossible for subversive movements to be watched. Add the threat of a terrorist war within Western countries to the threat of Russian maneuvers turning into a drive north or south of Aden, westward from Afghanistan, or from East Germany across the Rhine, and you've got bad bad trouble."

"You're absolutely correct, Cosgrove," Floyd Keifer said. "In the end it is likely that hundreds of millions of people will pay for the 'human rights' delusions of a halfwit from a little town in Georgia. . . ."

CHAPTER EIGHT

Banana Bread Box One.
The next day. 2000 hours. 8:00 P.M. civilian time.

During the twenty-one hours that had passed since the meeting in the Chapel of the Roses on Paki Street, progress had been made. Not until Hugh Hale Gamberkrone was safely inside B.B.B. # 1 did he remove a "mole" from his right knee and a Xanthelasma, or yellow nodule, from his right eyelid and explain that the mole contained seven microdots for "the Station" and that the yellow nodule (ordinarily a tiny lump of fat under the surface of the skin, from a deposit of hard fat) harbored a speck of a message for Albert Cosgrove.

Company technicians within the station at once enlarged the microdots. The seven sheets of paper, enlarged from the seven microdots, were from NSA's cryptanalysts. With the help of an I.B.M. 7148 computer and an Atlas 660, NSA's experts had broken the code found in the book hidden in a sack of fertilizer. The code was a music cipher, based on the common element of all music, what physicists call $1/f$ noise. The KGB had evolved the code on the premise that time correlations found in music are the same as $1/f$ noise and that the structure of music is fractal. From that point on, it had only been a short but complicated step to transforming notes—specific noise—into letters. All one needed to read the code was a piano. Or a flute. NSA boys had even found out the code name of the Soviet Pacific network—*Kabatskaya Melanholiya* in Russian. "Tavern Melancholy" in English.

The message for Albert Cosgrove was in a code that only Camellion could decipher. He did not reveal the contents of the short message.

The messenger from NSA arrived on schedule, on the two-o'clock Pan Am flight from the United States. The "messenger" turned out to be two fortyish women traveling as Franciscan nuns—Sister Sethrida and Sister Encratis. The two nuns took a cab from the airport to Our Lady of Peace Cathedral, on the corner of Bretania Street and Fort Street Mall. The two nuns walked into the cathedral, went to a pew and knelt down to pray, Sister Encratis taking a large Catholic prayer book from her pocketbook. The two nuns didn't even glance at the man in the same pew; he too was kneeling, a rosary in his hands. After ten minutes, the Sisters left the pew, genuflected and left the cathedral. Sister Encratis, however, had forgotten her prayer book. Wilfred Sims slipped the book into his pocket and left the church. Simon Kirkland, seven pews behind Sims, also left the cathedral. After changing cars five different times, Sims and Kirkland finally arrived at Banana Bread Box One.

CIA technicians quietly and quickly went to work. They slit the heavy covers of the prayer book, took out the strips of film containing hundreds of microdots and went about the business of enlarging them, a task that was not only technical but lengthy. It was seven o'clock that night by the time the spectrophotometric photographs had been enlarged to 15″ by 20″. All 842 of them!

Hugh Hale Gamberkrone went to work. With scores of charts made with the aid of a spectrometer and a spectrophotometer, he began to compare the radiations frozen in the photographs with the charts, explaining the procedure as he worked, first placing illuminated magnifier lamps around the "Z" folding tables that had been placed end to end.

He explained that a spectrometer was an instrument for measuring spectra and/or to determine the wavelengths of the various radiations. Similar but more complicated, the spectrophotometer measured the relative amounts of radiant energy or radiant flux as a function of wavelength.

None of the men, including Richard Camellion, fully understood Gamberkrone's explanation.

In his characteristic manner, Krestell said, "OK, so what's the difference between the two?"

"A spectrophotometer does a better job of analysis," Gamberkrone said happily, spreading out another chart. "You see, a spectrophotometer has a monochromator which isolates narrow bands of radiant energy from its source. The spectrophotometer does this by means of photovoltaic and photoemissive cells. My charts cover the energy radiated from 1,100 to 13,500 angstroms. The spectroscope attached to the infrared camera on the satellite covered the same range."

Krestell winked at Camellion. "Oh yeah, sure. You've made it as clear as fresh rain water."

Gamberkrone, a pleased expression on his face, looked over the charts spread on the tables, then at the stack of large photographs at one end.

"Never mind those," the Death Merchant said to the NSA expert. He held out a batch of photographs an inch thick. "These are the photographs of Tukoatu. Analyze them first, please."

"It will save you a lot of time," Simon Kirkland said heartily to the expert.

"Provided Tukoatu is the right island," Albert Gentry said. He glanced down at the gray attache case next to the chair on which he was sitting. There were four large tapes in the case, tapes that contained a four-hour-long confession by Archie Renton—names, dates, everything. Gentry had not asked Keifer, who had given him the tapes, how the CIA would dispose of Renton—"nullify" him in Company language. Gentry didn't want to know. No doubt Renton would be found dead in the trunk of some car in Hono, riddled with slugs. A gangland hit. The Company killers were always damned clever about such things.

H.H. Gamberkrone went to work and began comparing his charts of spectographs with the spectographic radiations in the colored infrared photographs of the island of Tukoatu. An hour passed. Gamberkrone found nothing unusual in the photographs. All spectra revealed only natural vegetable and mineral formations.

The men relaxed around the large room. Gammill and Krestell stood at the office refrigerator bar, drinking Scotch, and yodka and orange juice on the rocks. Wilfred Sims and Simon Kirkland sat talking shop with Ralph Muldance, a CIA man who specialized in exotic weapons and communications. Albert Gentry sat reading a newspaper while Floyd Keifer and Richard Camellion leaned back on easy chairs close to a table on which rested an automatic Cappuccino Expresso Maker which Keifer—a non-drinker but a connoisseur of Italian coffee—had bought with his own money. Next to the table with the expresso maker was a metal serving cart on which rested a Freedom 35 dialer telephone, a Swedish-designed Ericofon (takes less space than any other phone) and a deluxe portable telephone with an operating range of 5,420 feet. On the second tray of the serving cart was an old-fashioned-type phone, a tiny palm-size French style instrument, "The Lady Belle," a gold-clad baroque *objet d'art*. Keifer had paid for the phone, which was used for inter-station communications only.

Pure luck fell over the station at 7:45 P.M. Gamberkrone sat up straight on the high stool, turned around and looked at Camellion and Keifer.

"I've found something," he said excitedly. "I definitely have detected something that is most unusual."

It was as if all the men had been jabbed in their butts with a sharp needle—that quickly did they gather around the tables and bend their heads over the charts and numerous photographs while Gamberkrone explained that he had detected abnormal radiation from the top of one of the mountains in the central west section of Tukoatu. With precise movements, he used the end of a slide rule to point to a small area of the large photograph.

"At this position, please note the greenish-purple and blue lines interlaced with the red and yellow and lines of various orange hues." Gamberkrone sounded like a professor speaking to his class. He raised his head and looked from face to face. "Gentlemen, those greenish purple and blue lines indicate something that is not a natural part of the mountain." He looked down at the map again, then quickly consulted his charts of spectrum lines. "What is confusing is the mingling of the lines. It seems that a natural formation is a part of a man-made structure. Here,"—he tapped the yellow, orange and magenta—"is rock. The greenish purple and faint blue lines indicate wood, but dead wood."

"Are you saying there's a difference between a tree that's not been cut down and . . . say, a two-by-four piece of wood?" asked Olin Gammill.

"Oh, definitely," the NSA specialist said. "As much difference as between you and a corpse. A tree is alive. A piece of wood that's been cut and aged is dead. But you didn't let me finish. As you can see, some of the blue lines are of various hues. They indicate metal of strong molecular density. Steel, I should say. But like I said, the blue radiation is intermingled with the radiation of the dead wood. The wood is probably lumber.

"What peak is it?" asked Keifer.

"The lines could indicate a covering over the shaft that contains the dish," offered the Death Merchant. He watched Gamberkrone superimpose a clear plastic map over the large colored photograph with the hundreds of spectrum wave radiation lines.

Gamberkrone looked down at the plastic map whose various features fitted exactly over the photograph. He moved the magnifying glass slightly. "It's Mount Haleatimu. I think the name means 'The House of the Moon.' "

"I've heard that name before," Barney Krestell said, staring down thoughtfully at the two maps.

"You're thinking of Haleakala, the House of the Sun," Floyd Keifer said "Haleakala is the name of the giant mountain that forms the larger half of the island of Maui."

The Death Merchant added, "The entire top of Haleakala is a natural park. It seems that Haleakala is the world's largest dormant volcano."

It was then that the message from Courtland Grojean slid once more into his consciousness. The possibilities were so staggering as to be beyond belief, as to numb the imagination.

Within the next six months there might be 5,000 more active volcanoes in the world. All of them within the Rim of Fire. A dozen or more in the Western part of the United States. If the Russian scientists succeed. . . .

Forcing his mind into another channel, Camellion put his right hand lightly on Gamberkrone's shoulder. "Is there any method you can use to determine the size of the area from which the abnormal radiations emanate?"

"I can only give you a rough idea." Gamberkrone picked up a 15X magnetic comparator with an E-13 B2 reticle, then turned and looked at Camellion. "I don't have the necessary equipment to do an exact job. Both the photograph and the transparency are scaled 1:378,838 and are enlargements magnified over 400 times. This magnification was due to the extreme height of the satellite. Any figure I arrive at will have a fifty percent possibility of being incorrect."

"All we ask is that you do your best," Camellion said. "We don't expect you to be an Einstein."

"Very well." With slide rule, triangle and protractor, Gamberkrone began to calculate the measurements of the abnormal spectrum lines. He didn't seem to mind the numerous eyes watching his every move, watching him work.

Five minutes passed, during which time Gamberkrone measured, remeasured, mumbled to himself, consulted his spectrum charts, and made numerous calculations on paper. Another 300 seconds ticked into the past. The men shifted impatiently from foot to foot. Everyone was relieved when the NSA analyst picked up a red pencil and wrote on a pad: *A round opening. 75' in D. at max. 25' in D. at min.*

Gamberkrone sounded sad. "It's the best I can do, gentlemen."

"Your best is more than better," the Death Merchant said, smiling. "I'm convinced the abnormal lines indicate the mouth of the shaft that holds the dish. The Russians have camouflaged the opening with rocks placed over and fastened to a wooden framework. Or maybe the Russians made the mistake of using nails in the framework, or perhaps the tips of the steel girders in the shaft are protruding in some manner."

"Could Cosgrove be right?" Keifer asked Gamberkrone. "Could the wavelengths from steel below penetrate through rock and wood?"

"No. Whatever the metal is, the radiation is showing between the rocks," explained Gamberkrone. "I don't think it's from nails. More likely, the emanations are coming from large metal bolts."

Simon Kirkland, his big hands flat on the table, grinned, "Either way, we have the proof we need—at least enough hard evidence to proceed."

"We can get some of the Navy boys and go in," said Barney Krestell with a lot of enthusiasm. "We can make a two-pronged attack. Land on the east-end beach and blow up the cave entrances on the west side. Troops in choppers can land on top of Mount Haleatimu. According to the map, there's plenty of room on top of the mountain."

Floyd Keifer backed a few feet from the side of the table and gave Krestell a look of disapproval. "You know better than that, Barney. We're not the Marines. And we must be sure. Mr. Nagai has a lot of power in Hawaii and knows a lot of people in high places." Keifer glanced at the Death Merchant. "If we're wrong and there isn't any Soviet base on Tukoatu, Nagai could sue the hell out of Uncle Sam. Worse, the Company would look like idiots and our careers would go down the drain. Think about it!" He turned and walked to one of the easy chairs by the expresso machine, sat down and let the other men have a hard look.

Olin Gammill and Ralph Muldane started toward the bar, Muldane commenting, "We haven't considered the possibility that there may be a perfectly innocent explanation for the covering, or whatever it is, on top of Mount Haleatimu. Floyd does have a valid point."

Vancil Jourdan blinked at Hugh Hale Gamberkrone, who was folding his spectrum charts. "Mr. Gamberkrone, would you say you are positive in your findings?"

"We could tap Nagai's phone and get bugs into his mansion here in Hono," Wilfred Sims suggested to Keifer.

Gamberkrone looked insulted. "Of course I'm positive. Spectrum analysis is an exact science. The only thing I'm not sure about is the diameter of the opening." He held up a forefinger. "I told all of you there would be a fifty-percent margin of error in the measurement of the opening."

Keifer shook his head at Sims. "No, we can't bug Nagai's phone or home. We don't have the time. And if Nagai is involved with the Soviets, the KGB will be checking for transmitters at least twice a week. All they'd have to do is find one and they'd know we're onto them." Keifer looked up smugly at the Death Merchant, who was pouring a cup of expresso and who didn't seem to be at all concerned. "You're in charge, Cosgrove. I suggest that you tell us how we're going to proceed—and whatever we do, the responsibility will be yours."

The rest of the men in the meeting room looked at "Albert Cosgrove," looked and waited.

Holding the cup and saucer, the Death Merchant sat down next to Keifer. "I was thinking that a chameleon's tongue is as long as its body," he said with mock serious-

ness. "And did you know that the term *bootlegger* originated on Indian reservations of the West? Since it was un-
lawful to sell booze to the Indians, ingenious peddlers often
carried flasks of firewater in their boots to conceal them
from government agents."

Krestell turned his head so that Keifer wouldn't see him
smile. Days earlier he had gleaned that the man called
"Cosgrove" was, like himself, a fatalist who was neither in
awe of God nor afraid of the Devil, a dispassionate pragmatist who could realize that there were situations which
only a Final Solution could solve.

"Cosgrove, I'm not in any mood for your brand of hu-
mor," Keifer said darkly, "or should I have said your
brand of sarcasm? The goddamn Russians are sitting in
our back yard and you make jokes!"

The Death Merchant, having decided that he was going
to buy a Cappuccino Espresso Maker when and if he got
back to the States, took a sip of coffee. Ignoring Keifer's
remark, he held the cup and saucer in his hands and let his
gaze wander over the curious, interested faces.

"Floyd is right," he said in a serious tone. "We can't go
steamrolling in and make like gangbusters. We'll have an
attack force standing by, say twenty miles west of the island, but first two or three of us will do a recon job. We
can use a large SDV to scout the caves on the west side."

"What about the house and the beach on the east side?"
asked Simon Kirkland. "We can't pretend they don't exist."

"I don't intend to." Camellion's tone became very ur-
gent. "But it's the west side of the island that counts. The
Russians couldn't have possibly used surface ships to bring
in equipment. The island doesn't have any natural deep-
water harbors, and I'm sure the ivans didn't stop a cargo
vessel five miles out and unload equipment. The U.S.
Coast Guard or our Navy would have noticed."

"They used submarines," Wilfred Sims said. "Subs that
used one of the underwater entrances on the west side of
Tukoatu."

"If any man here has a better answer, now is the time
for him to speak up," the Death Merchant said.

Silence. From their expressions, while the men were interested, they still entertained serious doubts as to the feasi-
bility of what Albert Cosgrove was proposing, unless he
was excluding them from the actual attack. Somehow they
sensed that he wasn't. Well now . . . gathering intelligence

and evidence was one thing. Doing a John-Wayne-Landing-On-The-Beach number was quite another.

Ralph Muldane turned from the bar, a glass of white wine in his right hand. As dark-skinned as an American Indian, although he was of English-Irish heritage, he had high cheekbones and a crookbilled nose that emphasized his strong profile. "You can forget any secret reconnaissance. How do you think we could snoop around those caves without the Russians not knowing about it? The KGB is certain to have transponders[1] and maybe sonar placed at strategic positions on the ocean floor all around the island."

"You're forgetting that this is Hawaii," Camellion countered. "All kinds of ships pass Tukoatu. A lot of those ships come close to the island. Skindivers from those ships come close to the island. Some of the cave openings on the west side can be seen. It's only natural that passing scuba and skindiver boys should explore those caves. Don't forget all the U.S. Navy men at Pearl who are skindiving enthusiasts. No, my friend, the Russians don't have any warning system. They don't because first, they don't need them. They can watch the shores from inland observation posts. Second, it would be too dangerous to put warning devices in the water. Some diver might accidentally find one and report it to the Coast Guard or the Navy. That alone would blow the whole show for the Russians."

"I think Cosgrove is right," Wilfred Sims opined. "It all fits together. The maps of the Hawaii Geological Survey show that there is only one mammoth cavern on the west side of Tukoatu and that all the other numerous caves amount to nothing more than long tunnels that come to a dead end. All the KGB guards have to do is make sure no one gets into the main cave. It has to be that cave their sub is using."

"That would be an easy enough job," cut in Krestell. He was decisive, without any doubt or hesitation. "The island is private property. No one from a passing ship would simply ignore the signs that have to be posted. What could they do or say if someone popped up with a gun and told them to get the hell out of the cave?"

---

1. A radio transmitter-receiver that transmits identifiable signals automatically when the proper interrogation—"pulse" time—is received.

"We're going to invade the island; that much has been settled." There was almost a tranquility about Simon Kirkland's voice. "So now what we have is actually a 'Command and Control' situation. The only thing that remains to be settled is the logistics of the operation."

" 'Command and Control'—hell! We're not going to use any nuclear weapons," Sims said with a laugh too loud to maintain the pretense that he was totally calm. Suddenly his face became grave and he became consumed with concern. "On the other hand, who knows what the Soviets might have in their complex on the island."

"They don't have a nuclear device," Camellion said evenly. "They wouldn't need one to track the satellite.

Keifer said in a businesslike manner, "I'll report our operational plan to the Center as soon as we put one together. I'll double scramble and use the 'squirt box.' We'll have to get approval from Operations."

"Oh no, you won't!" His voice as sharp as the crack of a whip, the Death Merchant turned on a startled Chief of Station whose face mirrored extreme surprise. "We're not reporting any operational plan. We're not going to report a damn thing until the mission is over with." He jabbed a finger in the air at Keifer. "Don't you dare rattle about 'responsibility.' I'm taking full responsibility."

"What about the Navy?" Keifer, quickly recovering his composure, drew back, his mouth tight, eyes hard. "We can't trot over to Admiral Halloran's office and say, 'Hey, we have to borrow some men and ships for a CIA special operation!' "

"Yes, we can," Camellion said. He smiled at a half-angry, perplexed Keifer. "Word was given to Admiral Halloran weeks ago that you and two other men would eventually approach him about a highly secret operation."

Seething because Cosgrove—a damned Contract Agent—was not only in charge but had information that the Center had not trusted to the Honolulu Company Station, Keifer, with amazing self-control, kept his blue-white temper inside the furnace. He glanced furtively at Sims and Gammill. The joke was on them, too. There they sat, stunned looks on their faces. Two agents of the Office of Naval Intelligence, and they didn't know about Halloran either!

"I presume the special messenger also gave Admiral

Halloran the proper lock-ins?"[2] Keifer said crossly to Camellion.

Camellion shrugged. "Ask Gamberkrone."

Still putting his maps and charts into an oversized attache case, Gamberkrone went right on working. "Admiral Halloran has half of a Brazilian ten-cruzeiro bill. I have the other half. The bill has been cut so that the two halves have to dovetail in a certain way. When the two halves fit, Admiral Halloran will know we're the right people." Only then did Gamberkrone turn and look at the Death Merchant. "Mr. Cosgrove, you have the date of the centavos coin?"

"I have to give the year backward," Camellion said. "Right now, we have some hard planning to do."

"It's your show and your responsibility," Keifer said harshly.

It always has been. It always will be. . . .

CHAPTER NINE

Of all the theories regarding time, the only one that has been proven is that time is relative. To a man about to be executed, time passes with the speed of light. To a six-year-old child waiting for Christmas morning, a week stretches out to eternity.

To the Death Merchant, Time was never relative and was always neutral, just as the ocean, pressing in all around him and the three other men, was impersonal, nonpartisan, and indifferent.

The swimmer delivery vehicle was submerged to only a depth of two fathoms (twelve feet), yet visibility in the clear water was zero. In the daytime one would have had a visibility range of over a hundred feet, but now, at 1400 hours, the water was as dark as a closet. With only a sliver

2. Tradecraft term for proper identification between contracts.

of moon in the sky, the surface was also a field of ebony, eycept for a very faint light dappling the shallows close to the numerous islands and coral reefs.

A very private world, a deadly and sinister world. Just the same, Camellion knew that the ocean was also a world of unparalleled beauty. The moods, the splendor, the diversity of the sea were infinite . . . towering mountains and jet-black trenches, delicate plants of ten thousand different colors and fierce predators, microscopic diatoms and gigantic but gentle whales.

The ocean is the cauldron where life originated, Camellion thought, *a cauldron that retains much of its elemental character. Creatures exist whose heritage precedes ours by millions of years, and to whom we are as alien as visitors from space. How ironic! When we enter their world for more than a few seconds, we must backtrack through evolution and sprout steel gills.*

Sitting in the front of the Trojan IV next to Sterling Whitney, the SEAL driver of the vehicle, Camellion did some hard thinking. The success of the operation depended on coordination. The coordination had to rely on numerous factors, emotional as well as mechanical. A twenty-five-cent fuse could blow in a piece of equipment and wreck operation Harelip.

The U.S.S. *Northampton,* a U.S. Navy CLC tactical command ship, waited sixty-four nautical miles due west of Tukoatu. As a crow or dippy-doodle bird might fly in a straight line, warplanes at Hickam Air Force Base, northwest of Honolulu, were only 178 kilometers from Tukoatu—a mere stroll for TF-15 Eagle warplanes, a walk around the block for the much-slower CH-46 Sea Knight helicopters.

But only if Operation Harelip became a reality.

The operation will never begin unless we find clear-cut evidence that the Soviet Union is using the island as a monitoring station. The only way we can get that evidence is—

"Cosgrove!"

Barney Krestell's voice, sounding tinny and unnatural over the AN/PQC-3 UTEL, interrupted the Death Merchant's thoughts.

"I've a question, Cosgrove. Remember ten days ago when we hit Renton's place?"

"I'd have to be an amnesiac if I didn't!"

One of the traits that Camellion liked about The Bomber was that Krestell had a habit of asking odd questions at the most odd times. *This is probably one of those times!*

"Remember the crumb-bum with the .44 mag., the joker in front of the house? You asked him how many guards were around."

"What about him?"

"You asked him the color of the walls inside the house. I was wondering why you wanted to know."

"When you know the color a man prefers, you know a lot about the man.[1] "For instance, a lot of red indicates aggression, but too much red will cause irritation and headaches and bring out the worst in people. Any traffic cop will tell you that he writes more tickets for drivers of red cars than any others."

"What about blue?"

"Blue indicates a peaceful nature, a positive attitude and levelheadedness. But color wasn't all that important back at Renton's. His wife was probably the deciding factor in decorating the house. Women usually have the last word in such matters."

Ralph Muldane cut in, amusement in his voice, "If blue's your favorite color, Barney, something is way off. You're about as 'peaceful' as a cobra roused out of a sound sleep. Hell, you're not even halfway content unless you're blowing up something."

"I heard that when you were born the doctor spanked your mother!" shot back Krestell good-naturedly and adjusted his face mask, although he was positive that the UTEL was carrying his voice satisfactorily.

---

1. *Green*: balance, poise, concentration, good memory, tolerant, relaxing; *yellow*: self control, ingenuity; *orange*: ambitious, open-minded, an original thinker; *indigo*: proud, idealistic, liberal; *violet*: creative, good intuition, analytical; *black*: morbid, pessimistic. But colors are only suggestive. Colors also have a great therapeutic effect on the human body. Since color is composed of energy waves, and because the photoreceptors in the skin pick up the colors we apply to our body, colors can and do alter the functioning of various parts of the body. At Johns Hopkins University Medical Center, patients who need rest are put in blue or turquoise hospital rooms. Patients who need more energy are placed in pink rooms. Yellow rooms minimize pain.

The UTEL is a device designed to permit a scuba man to communicate with another swimmer, a submarine, or a surface vessel. There are four major components to the UTEL—receiver-transmitter, mike (lung or surface), headset, and transducers. The transducer output pattern is in the form of a directional beam approximately 100 degrees in width. To make use of its directional response, the transducer must be pointed like a flashlight, directly at the other station. To be used omnidirectionally the transducer must be pointed at the ocean floor. While using the UTEL submerged, a swimmer can receive voice communications, but if he is to transmit by voice, he must be wearing a full facemask with a lung microphone embedded in it. On the surface, he can transmit by means of a surface mike. Either way, a swimmer could always transmit and receive a homing tone, whether submerged or on the surface. This homing tone could be used either as a vector, to allow a sub or another swimmer to find the user, or as a means of positive communications, if a code has been previously agreed upon. The advanced UTEL, such as Camellion and his three companions were using, had a "talk" line which one diver could plug into another man's suit. In this manner, two or more divers could become a single closed unit and communications could not be picked up by an enemy.

The four men also wore full scuba gear—full-length suits, full face masks and twin air tanks that were a part of the closed-circuit breathing system which lent itself so excellently to SDV sneak attack operations.[2]

Barney Krestell sat behind the Death Merchant. Ralph Muldane, across from The Bomber, was behind Sterling Whitney, and all four were buckled snugly in the Trojan IV, an SDV that operated similarly to the Slim Jim. There were differences, however, between the two swimmer delivery vehicles. The Trojan IV, larger and more sophisticated, could carry eight men in two rows of four seats each. The fiberglass hull of the T-IV could cut the water on the surface at a speed of 5.6 knots, submerged at a speed of 4.1 knots. In addition to diving planes, the T-IV

2. The system is quiet, can be used very effectively on long, shallow swims, is hard to detect, is economical of gas, and is comfortable to wear. One hundred percent of the gas medium—air—can be used and the gas consumption is dependent only on the work rate, not on depth.

had a 4.8-HP electric motor powered by thirteen twelve-cell, twenty-four-volt lead acid batteries, and a submerged endurance range of 104.07 nautical miles.

The last four seats toward the stern had been removed and in their place were spare tanks of air and thick plastic containers crammed with quick-kill equipment—frag and thermite grenades, CN gas tins, heavy auto-pistols in belted holsters, T20 grease guns that fired 560 rounds of 9mm ammo a minute, spare magazines and gas masks.

Silently, except for a very faint purring sound, the Trojan IV bore east toward the rugged west coast of Tukoatu. The water was not totally black, but only because there were two large underwater night-vision devices, with wide-view eyepieces and wide-view lenses, mounted on the top hull in front of Camellion and Whitney, the bottom brackets on a ball swivel for easy maneuverability. The four men also carried hand-held night-viewing instruments; and so, for 45.72 meters (150 feet) ahead, the ocean appeared to be cloaked in twilight, the infrared images appearing spectral and unreal. Slightly off to port, flat, foot-long garibaldis darted out of the way toward safety like orange flames, their rush carrying them through a swarm of silvery glassy sweepers.

"Damn it, the back of my head itches," announced Muldane miserably, slapping the rubberized material fitting over his head as snugly as an old-fashioned helmet of a 1940s aviator. But the face mask was far different from World War II goggles. Protruding, the clear part of the face mask was one wide, scratch-resistant piece of plastic fastened to the helmet, the large coupling of the mouthpiece of the air hose directly below the shatterproof "windshield."

"Tough it out is all you can do," Krestell said, "and thank God you don't have hives."

"We're only three miles from the coast." The voice of Sterling Whitney floated through the headphones of Krestell, Muldane, and Camellion. "I'm going to submerge to thirty feet to get us underneath the surf." His left hand went to the outboard lever and he pushed it forward, opening the trim tank vent valve, thus allowing water to come into the tank and causing the SDV to descend. He and Camellion both glanced down at the voltmeter and the ammeter. The volts and amps for FORWARD I read 48 and 22 respectively; 96 and 15 for FORWARD II; and 48 and

22 for FORWARD III. The electrical system was working perfectly.

A bronze-faced young man in his mid-twenties and a member of a Marine Reconnaissance Company ("Force Recon"), Whitney and the group to which he belonged were administered directly by a Naval Operations Support Group (NOSG) based at Pearl Harbor. Whitney was driving the Trojan IV for one reason. Not only was Whitney UDT,[3] but he was an expert in navigation. As important as Operation Harelip was, the Death Merchant wasn't going to take a chance on his own ability in navigation, which was considerable. He had to have an experienced expert. Sterling Whitney was the man that Lieutenant Commander Harvey, the UDT company commander, had assigned to the task. So far, Whitney had done an excellent job. But the worst, the really dangerous part, was yet to come.

Whitney levelled off at 31.6 feet. The propeller, now churning deeper water, made a new sound, a higher-pitched sound.

"I suppose what will be will be," Krestell commented resignedly. "If we could only be positive that the Russians don't have sonar grids close to the shore. I don't mind telling you, it's that main cave that worries me."

"We went over that ground days ago," Camellion said, irritated. "I said then that the Soviets wouldn't risk such a warning system being found accidentally. Radar by the island's house can keep track of passing ships from all directions. The entire surface of the island is only nine point six square miles."

"Grids or no grids, none of that explains why the Russians committed piracy against the *Pearl of the Pacific*," Muldane voiced his opinion. "None of the people on that ship could be of any use to the Soviets—not in tracking COM-V-CON-2."

"Maybe the people on the *Pearl of the Pacific* discovered something about Tukoatu, something the KGB didn't want revealed," said Krestell. "The only thing wrong with that theory is that the ship was boarded in the middle of

3. *Underwater Demolition Teams.* A UDT unit is composed of 15 officers and 100 men. The unit is further divided into four operating platoons and a headquarters platoon. Operating, as a rule, in teams of four, UDT members are qualified scuba divers and small-boat handlers. They are also qualified parachutists.

113

Kaiwi Channel. Hell, the Ruskies would have grabbed them the instant they knew the *Pearl* had discovered anything."

"Every silver lining must have a dark cloud," the Death Merchant said. "We'll get the answer to that question after we invade the island."

. . . If the KGB doesn't blow the complex sky-high once they know we're onto them. . . .

Whitney expertly guided the Trojan beneath the booming waves lashing and breaking against craggy sea stacks in front of the towering cliff walls of the west coast of Tukoatu, the churning rocking the SDV from port to starboard, from stem to stern. Whitney fought the wheel to keep the double rudder straight and the Trojan on course. All the while he leaned forward to peer through the wide viewplate of the night-vision device. One mistake, like slamming into a pinnacle rising from the depths, and the show would be over even before it had time to get off to a good start.

It took just over a minute for the Trojan to navigate beneath the pounding waves above and to reach the shallows near the northwest coast of the small island.

"Any change in plans or do we explore one cave at a time?" Whitney glanced down at the voltmeter and the ammeter.

"Cave by cave," Camellion said. In his cramped position, he leaned over and studied the Hawaii geological survey map of the island's west coast. The map was fastened to a drop-plate inside the forward hull, and illuminated by a green glow from a light stick only four inches long.[4]

We have our work cut out for us! There were twenty-six openings to caves on a coast that was as jagged and cut up as boulders smashed by the hammer of some giant Thor. In some places the water, before it dissolved into foam and was blown away by the wind, was less than twenty feet deep. In other place there were dropoffs that were hundreds of feet deep.

"You fellows start using the Zons," Whitney said. "Keep me posted on anything you might see that is unfavorable to

4. A chemical flare, a flameless, heatless liquid light that requires no batteries—activated mixed chemicals provide illumination. Commonly used by police.

us. I can detect any rocks that might rise from the depths forward."

Impatience was heavy in Krestell's voice. "Look Cosgrove, why waste time in fooling around with the caves that lead nowhere? The charts show that the entrance large enough for a sub is toward the center of the coast. Why don't we go directly to the big cave?" A man who had the habit of answering his own questions, The Bomber did so now. "Sure, I know why we have to explore those passages. We have to be positive." He adjusted the focusing knob of the Zon-3 hand-held night-vision instrument, and, with Camellion and Muldane, began scanning the water and the seabed on the sides of the vehicle.

The electric motor making a constant low whirring sound, the Trojan passed over a bank of tube sponges clustered on purple coral. To port, a school of grunts darted by, shooting first in one direction and then another. Everywhere was life . . . strange life, with some animals resembling plants and some plants looking like animals. In Mother Ocean[5] color often belied a creature's identity.

Whitney cut speed. The sound of the motor decreased. The Trojan began to crawl along. The vehicle was equipped with a metered depth sounder and the latest-type diaphone, a sound-producing device that was tied into Whitney's headphones. A highly experienced UDT specialist, Whitney could tell by the loudness of the "pings" if the SDV was within ten feet of scraping the sea floor.

The Death Merchant said, "You're headed for the entrance to the first cave northwest?"

Replied Whitney, "Affirmative. We're roughly a mile from the first entrance. We can't rush anything. This coral could rip open the trim tanks."

"I'm not complaining. You know your job."

A loud attention-getting sign came from Barney Krestell. "It will be dawn before we even get around to the

5. There would not be any ocean if it were not for one peculiarity—the fact that water is most dense just before it freezes. Ice therefore floats on the surface instead of sinking to the bottom. If conditions were otherwise, all rivers and lakes and even the sea itself would freeze solid from the *bottom* up. As it is, the ice that floats on the surface insulates the water below, allowing it to stay in liquid form.

beach on the east side," he grumbled. "We should have come up with a better plan than this."

"We can defray the east beach, if time runs out on us." Concern did not evidence itself in Camellion's tone. "There's only two cabin cruisers moored at the pier. If anyone tries to escape in them, how far do you think they'd get?"

"The UDTS in the chopper had better not goof," interjected Muldane, "or we'll be left in the bleachers, with the ball game not even in sight."

"They'll be there," snapped Whitney, his voice indicating that he considered Muldane's remark an insult. "My platoon is not one of the best. It is the best."

"I'll take your word for it," mused Muldane, who, looking through the Zon-3 N-V scope, saw that the Trojan was passing over a jungle of kelp. A well-read man, he knew that the kelp sheltered numerous sea creatures that had to depend on camouflage for survival. Snails and crabs grazed along the swaying blades, and there would be three or four species of sea stars moving among the kelp plants to feed and breed. Further out, Muldane could barely distinguish the sleek body of a white shark cruising slowly along.

"I've spotted a great white," Muldane said. "He's not interested in us, for all the good it would do him." He thought of the telescoping shock rods that he and the others carried. Each rod could deliver 10,000 volts of shock, more than enough to make any shark turn tail and retreat.

"Prepare yourselves," anounced Whitney. "We're almost to the entrance of the first cave."

By 1523 hours the SDV had investigated fifteen of the smaller caves, although twenty minutes of this time had been spent strapping on full tanks of gas.

Some of the caves were short, only a few hundred feet long, with some of their pitch-black interiors above water. Other caves were longer and competely under water. The fifteen caves did have one thing in common: they all came to a dead end, to a wall of solid rock. The caves were empty, devoid of all life. "Surface" fish could not find any food in the caves, and the water was much too shallow for creatures that inhabited the deep waters.

Whitney guided the Trojan directly through the center of the large entrance of the main cave, the entrance that was 86.5632 meters (or 284 feet) wide. Regardless of its width

116

and the depth of the channel—105 fathoms—only 34.4424 meters (113 feet) of the entrance was from two and a half feet to four feet above the waterline, that is, where the waves lapped gently at the bleak, barren rocks. Most of the entrance was free from the pounding surf because of the large granite stacks that, forty-six meters to the west, received the full assault of the angry waves. . . .

"If the Ruskies have a grid laid, they know we're here," Muldane said as Whitney guided the SDV down the center of the channel, the craft submerged only two fathoms.

"The chart shows that this baby is damn near a mile long," Krestell said, all business. "Either we find something worthwhile in this deal or I say we've pulled one big boner."

"We had better come up with Leonid Brezhnev himself!" Muldane said. "Admiral Halloran's aides are already complaining about the cost of the operation."

At a speed of only two knots the SDV made its way, like a giant bug, down the length of the passage, as Whitney checked ahead through the large NV device, occasionally glancing at the volt and amp meters, and listening to the pings of the diaphone, while Camellion watched the special mileage gauge which he had turned back to zero when the Trojan had entered the cave.

The mileage gauge was illuminated by a soft green light, the glow of which did not extend beyond the cockpit of the Trojan. When the needle on the gauge was at 964 feet, Camellion ordered Whitney to surface.

"We still have a long way to go," Whitney said.

"I know we do, but I want to have a look around," Camellion replied.

Whitney opened the air valve, blew water from the trim tanks, and the Trojan rose to the surface.

Total darkness. Through the Zons, Camellion and his three companions saw only water and rock. The uneven ceiling was only five to six feet above their heads.

"I wouldn't even condemn the ivans to a place like this," Krestell said. "This place is as useless as a prick on a paralyzed man."

"We'll stay on the surface," Camellion said, surprising the others. "We'll make better time."

"Don't switch off your gas and breathe the outside air," cut in Whitney anxiously. "Switching from the mixture we're using to stale air could cause severe nausea and vomiting."

At 1,413 feet (on the mileage gauge), the low ceiling came to an abrupt end, and the overhead rock took a sudden rise to forty feet. A long look through the Zons revealed that the ceiling slanted very gradually upward.

"Man, this is eerie," whispered Whitney. "There's not a single stalactite hanging from the ceiling."

"So far we know that a Soviet submarine would have more than enough room in the channel," Muldane said. "A sub couldn't turn around, but it could easily come in forward, then back out."

"I'm only glad we brought along a hundred pounds of RDX." Krestell sounded grimly determined. "Even if you guys did disagree. You never know when big blast stuff like that will come in handy."[6]

Muldane looked pained behind his face mask. "When do you think you'd have time to use the stuff?" he demanded. "Why it would take ten minutes or more to open the container and get the packages out. We're a recon group, not an attack force."

"Negative on the time. I've rigged the drum itself." There was a hint of pride in The Bomber's voice. "All I have to do is pull off the water seal, turn the timer on and set the dial."

The Death Merchant lowered the Zon night-sight device. "We're not going to find anything—or do anything—sitting here. Whitney, start her up. Stay on the surface."

Soon the Trojan was again moving inward through the dark cavern passage, the only sounds the very low humming of the electric motor and the lapping of the water being knifed by the prow.

The green-lighted needle of the milometer was on the 2,151-foot mark when the four men spotted the far-off glow. For a full minute they studied the brightness in the distance.

"It sure as hell isn't sunrise." Krestell lowered the night-vision Zon scope. Like the others, Krestell knew that the brightness did not come from one light but from a whole series of lights, lights that were almost 2,000 feet away.

6. RDX is Cyclonite, the most powerful of all military explosives. It is used primarily as a component of explosive mixtures.

"It's the Soviet base," Muldane said grimly. "What else could it be?" He turned his masked face toward the Death Merchant. "I say it's time to get out of here. We've done our job."

"Whitney, take her down to three fathoms," Camellion ordered, his low voice calm and relaxed. "We're going to see what that light really is. We have to be absolutely certain."

"Suicide! Plain suicide!" Whitney flung out the words. His hand pulled the outboard lever. There was a slight clicking sound. The valves opened and water began flooding the trim tanks.

"He's right, Cosgrove," Muldane said firmly as the Trojan submerged. "There's that light for anyone to see. The Ruskies have to have some kind of warning system. They couldn't risk having anyone coming in and seeing what they have."

Even Krestell agreed with Muldane. "No doubt the Hammer and Sickle boys already know we're here," he warned the Death Merchant. "We're pushing our luck too hard."

Camellion waited until Whitney had leveled off the Trojan, then said, "None of you are using common sense. With all the pleasure ships that pass by, we're not the first outsiders to enter this cave. Use your heads. The Russians aren't going to grab every scuba enthusiast who comes in. If Joe Blow and Sam Smith come swimming in here, they have to swim back to the vessel they came from. Constant disappearances would cause an intensive investigation, and half of the Coast Guard would end up in this area."

"Try telling that to the people who were grabbed from the *Pearl of the Pacific*!" Muldane was openly hostile.

Barney Krestell went right to the heart of the matter. "What's the bottom line, Cosgrove?"

"There is some kind of barrier up ahead," Camellion said. "Hiromori Nagai owns this island. He has every right to have some kind of metal fencing stretched across the channel. The lights are probably on top of the fencing, perhaps illuminating 'Keep Out' signs. Or the lights might be around a natural rock pier. So what could anyone see that could be incriminating, except when the submarine is docked, in which case the pig farmers will no doubt have close-in sonar."

"Uh huh, and Soviet Navy scuba boys to go with it,"

Krestell said doggedly. "The bottom line is, what do we do if a Soviet U-boat is moored up ahead right now?"

The Death Merchant was brutally blunt. "I'm gambling that there isn't one. Stay on those Zon NVs. Whitney and I will keep a close eye forward. Barney, you take the starboard watch. Ralph, handle the port side."

Conversation ceased, the men intent on their work. All that Muldane and Krestell could see to port and starboard was dark water, devoid of even a single fish.

Earlier, while travelling on the surface, they had noticed that the walls of the monstrous cavern were not straight but curved inward and outward on both sides, so that the distance from one wall to the other was never constant. At one point it seemed that the width of the channel was less than 150 feet. Even the rock of the walls was black, revealing that the stone was igneous. On close inspection, one would have noticed the flowing of the wavy surface, like a giant slab of swirl cake cut down the center, as though the rock had once been chocolate and, mixed with other material, had been "frozen." In a sense, the rock had been. The cavern had been formed millions of years ago and was only a long, large bubble in a mass of pyroclastic rock—fire-fragmented rock ejected from a volcano.

The surface of the water began to glow slightly as the Trojan drew closer to the end of the channel. By now, adrenalin was pouring into each man's bloodstream, and they were prepared for anything, even death itself.

"Make sure your shock rods are ready," ordered Camellion, his eyes straining through the $5'' \times 2\frac{1}{2}''$ viewer of the large night-vision scope mounted on the top hull of the SDV. "Whitney, how slow will this buggy go?"

"Half a knot."

"Cut speed then to half a knot."

Whitney cut electric power and the Trojan began to creep along, prompting Muldane to say, "I could move faster on my hands and knees."

"This kind of no-speed reminds me of when my third wife and I were on a vitamin kick," Krestell said. "She was taking vitamin E. I was on iron pills. What happened is that every time she was ready, I was rusty."

"Knock it off, Barney," Camellion said, in spite of his amusement. "We're about to close in. . . ."

A few long minutes ticked into the past. By now the

entire surface of the water over the Trojan reflected light. Close. We're very close.

The Trojan was, in fact, only 209 feet from the steel-mesh fence. The SDV slowly covered 59 feet, and the Death Merchant and Whitney, both men staring intently through the two high-resolution infrared night-sight scopes, caught their first glimpse of the steel barrier.

"You were right, Cosgrove," Whitney said, "There is a barrier. It looks like heavy mesh, so thick that each strand is almost a bar. Full stop or get in closer?"

"Stop twenty-five feet in front of the fence." Camellion glanced at the mileage instrument. The needle was on 1,998 feet.

On hearing Camellion and Whitney, Muldane and Krestell turned their hand-held, smaller night-vision scopes forward. Gradually, as the Trojan narrowed the distance, they too could clearly see the steel-mesh fence stretched across the width of the passage.

Closer and closer drew the Trojan. Then it came to a full stop, its propeller no longer moving. Beyond the barrier was a sight that the Death Merchant and his three companions had not expected to see. Resting in the water and illuminated by halogen lights mounted to the tops of four triangular girder towers was a submarine, a Soviet Z-III cargo-type submarine, its port side presenting itself to the four men in the SDV.

"Cosgrove, you had better never go to Las Vegas," sighed Krestell. "You make a hell of a lousy gambler."

CHAPTER TEN

More bad news! The Soviet submarine was alive with activity. Several officers were standing on the deck of the conning tower, one of them giving orders through a bull-horn to a group of sailors on the forward deck who were using a gin pole rigging to unload cargo from the hold and to swing the cargo to the dock, a pier that was a tremendous shelf of pyroclastic rock. Already on the dock were several large piles of crates, drums, and other containers. In front of the submarine and facing its starboard side, was the entrance to another cave, and, as the Death Merchant and the other men stared at the large nuclear-powered U-boat, they saw a lift truck, its fork piled high with boxes, roll through the entrance and disappear. A few moments later, another lift truck, its fork empty, came through the entrance from the opposite direction.

Unexpectedly, the sailors on the forward deck of the sub stopped work, turned and looked in the direction of the barrier fence, then hurriedly jumped from the deck to the pier. The two officers on the deck of the conning tower— Camellion and company could see only their heads and torsos—turned and stared at the steel-mesh barrier which rose ten feet above the surface.

For a short moment, the Death Merchant studied the two officers and the sub through the night-sight device, the full image appearing slightly wavy because of the thickness of the quiet water.

"They know we're here," he said. "The grid maybe has a motion alert, or else they've transponders laid in a grid. Now is the time to turn around and run like hell on full power."

"If only we could!" barked Krestell savagely. "Take a look."

Just as the Death Merchant finished speaking, a small bright light appeared 175 feet to the right of the Trojan. Then another light, thirty feet to the left and to the rear of the first light.

Wink! Wink! Wink! Three more lights, all moving in a crescent formation to the left of the Trojan. These three were almost 200 feet away. Wink! A third light went on to the right of the SDV.

Russian scuba men! The lights were on their helmets! *Damn!*

"I can't get us out of here in time to outrun them!" Whitney almost shouted from within his helmet. At the same time, his left hand switched on the electric motor.

Unsnapping his seat belt, Camellion's face became inflexible, ruthless. "Whitney, turn around and take her out 200 feet from the fence. Wait and we'll contact you on the UTEL. If the Ruskies smear us, get the hell out. Once you're in the open, radio the *Northampton* and tell them

'The Sheep Have Been Found.' Everyone unplug communications. Ralph, take the left. We'll take the right-side jokers. Turn your shock rods to full power."

"The next time we do this, remind me to be someplace else!" Muldane pushed with his legs and his body shot upward from the seat. At the same time, Camellion and Krestell left the Trojan, Camellion saying, "Are your regular UTELS on?" Muldane grunted. "Screw you," Krestell said.

The battery-powered lights on the helmets of the Soviet divers supplied sufficient illumination for Camellion and his two men to see much of the watery area around them. The three, closing in on the six Russian divers—or vice versa—soon saw that the six Russians were in full scuba gear, including flippers, and carried six-foot-long shark weapons—tubes that fired a charge similar to a 12-gauge shotgun shell. *Which sort of evens the odds! The muzzles of the tubes have to be within a foot of the target's body in order to be effective. But how many shells does each tube hold?*

One of the three divers wriggling toward Muldane detached himself from the other two and headed toward the Trojan. Whitney had turned the SDV around and was taking it at full power—4.1 knots—toward the outside entrance, practically 2,000 feet to the west.

The two other Russian underwater fighters closed in on Muldane—confident of a quick kill.

The three other Soviet scuba men spread out, two jack-knifing through the water like monstrous black fish toward the Death Merchant, the third man toward Krestell, their six-foot-long firing tubes extended.

His eye on the two Russians determined to kill him, the Death Merchant waited until the last possible moment to dodge the muzzles of the silver-gray shark-kill tubes. *Damned pig farmers!* He dove a second before there was a muffled boom above him, but the twenty-seven 0.24-inch (6.1mm) pellets missed. Twisting his body to the left, he rolled over and thrust upward with the shock rod, which he had extended to its full length of six feet.

The beams of their helmet lights knifing the water, Genrikh Altunyun and Petr Fomin couldn't stop their momentum from carrying them over Camellion. They both guessed his intention and tried to roll over and away from the shock rod. Fomin succeeded. Altunyun failed. The flat end of the knob touched him on the side of the left foot and Camellion, feeling the contact, pressed the button in the rubber-covered handle of the rod. *ZZZzzzzzzzzz!* Ten thousand volts of electricity sizzled through Altunyun's body. Shocked into instant unconsciousness, he went limp. The firing tube fell from his hands and started to sink to the dark depths. His body slowly began to rise to the surface.

Petr Fomin completed his roll, jerked his body, moved away from Camellion, kicked powerfully with his legs, jabbed downward through the swirling water with the firing tube and pressed the button twice. He had not even waited to find Camellion and had fired from instinct. Fomin was first surprised, then angry and afraid when his helmet light knifed on Camellion coming in fast from the right. Frantically, Fomin attempted to move the tube toward the black-clad figure, who was still too distant to use the shock rod. The Russian was three-fourths successful. The last one-fourth belonged entirely to the Death Merchant, who reached out with his left hand, grabbed the rounded tube a few inches from the muzzle and shoved the tube away from him as Fomin pressed the firing button. Another muffled BOOM. Again all twenty-seven pellets missed, each BB leaving a long trail of tunnel-bubbles as it went on its individual way.

Very quickly, the Death Merchant pulled vigorously on the Russian's shark-gun tube. In a panic, Fomin let go of the weapon, realizing that Camellion was trying to pull him within range of the shock rod. Fomin's gloved fingers opened, but he had forgotten that each *Sunoinonoi* tube had a heavy strap to insure the user that he could not drop and lose the weapon.

The tightened strap pulled against Fomin's wrist and his body was jerked through the water toward the Death Merchant. The white-yellow beam of the Russian's light raked for one brief moment across Camellion's shock rod and he saw the flat end stabbing up at him. There was only an instant of blinding pain, such intolerable agony that the Russian felt his brain was being pulled apart by red-hot pliers. Next—total darkness. . . .

Emilya Piogorovov, the diver going after Whitney, assumed he had a sitting duck for a target. He knew there wasn't any way that the man—who he presumed to be an

Amerikanski—could fight and drive the SDV at the same time.

Piogorovov was only thirty feet from the Trojan when, without any warning, a cloud of dark dye spurted from the port and starboard sides of the vehicle, a dye of such India-ink blackness that it was only a matter of seconds before Piogorovov found himself in a world of watery tar, an environment of such Stygian gloom that the light on his helmet could penetrate only a few feet. Piogorovov couldn't even see his hands when he stretched his arms! Not realizing that Sterling Whitney had turned the SDV sharply to starboard and had dived the craft two fathoms to a new position, Piogorovov kicked himself around and began swimming toward the barrier, feeling, however, that he wouldn't be needed. Five against three were good odds.

A ruthless realist, Ralph Muldane knew that there were many things he could do a hundred times better than the average. Fighting two expert Russian scuba men wasn't one of them. With Ladislav Gribti coming at him from the left and Osvald Ioffe from the right, Muldane (wishing he was shacked up somewhere in Malta) made his move when the muzzles of the Russians' firing tubes were only six feet from his shoulders. Muldane kicked as hard as he could, arched his back, stroked violently upward, executed a complete rollover and began to swim toward Krestell. Pure joy made his heart pound harder when he saw the surface of the water glowing, the two beams of light from the helmets of dead Russians sending a wavy brightness filtering down through the murky water.

There was a third beam of light, this one darting about like a roadrunner with a bag of Mexican jumping beans jammed up his butt. The frantic movement of the beam was caused by Dmitri Levitin's maneuvering in a frenzy to get into a position that would enable him to blow twenty-seven 6.1mm pellets through Barney Krestell, who was using every stroke he had ever learned in an effort to touch Levitin with his shock rod.

Nonetheless, Muldane remained extra cautious when he detected another dark figure—this one without a light—swimming toward the two other men, both of whom were swimming around one another, keeping out of range of each other's weapons. That third man! It wasn't impossible that one of the commies had turned off his helmet light and was trying a bit of trickery.

"The two of you without a light, ID yourselves," Muldane snapped. "I have two of the enemy right behind me."

"Krestell here. Don't get nervous and muck things up." Krestell was breathing hard. "I do have a momentary problem."

"This is Cosgrove. I'm coming your way, Ralph."

"OK. I'll let The Bomber do his own mucking up!"

In another fifteen seconds, the Death Merchant came slicing through the water like a miniature black submarine. Camellion was twenty feet to the right of Muldane, who did some lightning-fast thinking and ended up with the conviction that if he could electrocute the vodka-and-borsch bastard trying to exterminate Krestell, the odds would then be three to two. It would take only a minute or two. In the meantime, Cosgrove—*that son of a bitch must have been born in the water!*—could duck the two other Russian bedbugs.

Muldane swam straight toward Krestell and Dmitri Levitin. Only fifteen feet behind Muldane, Osvald Ioffe and Ladislav Gribti began to have serious second thoughts when their beams picked up Camellion to their right. They didn't feel any better when they saw him arch his body and dive. Ioffe swam after Muldane. Gribti dove to the right.

Gribti did a fast rollover, kicked with his legs and, when his light caught Camellion, thrust out the tube and pressed the firing button, relishing the sound of the muffled report. But he had misjudged the distance. Some of the 0.24-inch pellets made contact with the top of the Death Merchant's air tanks and the top of his head. Camellion had taken the chance because it had been the lesser of two evils—and he had won. The muzzle of Gribti's tube had been too far away. The water did the rest, slowing the pellets, decreasing their force to the extent that they could not have even penetrated a single sheet of a newspaper.

Bunk and bull! Camellion had no intention of sparring around with Gribti. He swam straight toward the Russian, who was desperately trying to move the long tube through the water and press its muzzle against him. In order to accomplish this, the Russian had to back up—which was exactly what Camellion was counting on, plus the moment it would take to swish the metal tube through the water.

126

Camellion let the shock rod fall from his right hand, reached out and wrapped his gloved hand around the forward end of the Russian's firing tube. With his left hand he pulled a Chris McLoughlin-designed Jakal from its sheath on his weight belt, jerked the Russian toward him and used the double-edged knife to slash the pig farmer across his right wrist. The razor-sharp blade severed the strap of the tube, cut through Gribti's rubberized suit and sliced through flesh to the bone.

Ladislav Gribti yelled within the confines of his scuba suit. His mike was open on the Russian version of a UTEL and the three other Soviet divers heard him, but there was no way that Ioffe, Levitin, and Piogorovov could help him.

The tube slipped from Gribti's fingers. Water began pouring into his cut suit at the same time that blood began gushing out of his severed radial artery. The Ruskie was further demoralized when the water around his wrist changed color, turning a glaring crimson in the glow of his helmet light.

Shock had made Gribti hesitate for only a few seconds; yet in those two ticks in time the Death Merchant had twisted in behind him. Gribti was helpless. Camellion's right arm went around the man's neck, the pressure from his arm squeezing the two air tubes that led from the single tank on the Russian's back to the mouthpiece assembly attached to the face mask. Camellion's legs locked around Gribti's preventing the Russian from kicking them both to the surface. The Russian made a final effort to save himself, his arms going up and trying to reach Camellion's mouthpiece. His hands never got past his own temples. The Death Merchant plunged the Jakal inward, the blade tearing through suit and flesh and opening up Gribti's stomach. Camellion ripped upward, then jerked out the knife, released the limp and dying Russian and watched two streams of bloody air bubbles rise from Gribti's now useless suit, one from the slashed stomach region, the other from the Russian's cut arm. For a very short time, the dead man didn't sink nor rise. He merely hung in the water, his head bent forward; gradually then, as the gas mixture rushed faster through the two rips in the suit, the corpse began to sink into the depths.

The Russians' underwater communication system was turned to a wavelength that could not be picked up by the UTELS worn by the Death Merchant and his men. Camel-

127

lion couldn't hear Dmitri Levitin shout a warning about him to Emilya Piogorovov—"*Polundra* ("watch out below"), Emilya!"

For what seemed to be an hour but which actually had been only three minutes, Levitin had done his best to maneuver Krestell into a favorable position and had failed. Yet he had succeeded in keeping the *Amerikanski* from touching him with the electric shock rod. Levitin's hope for victory had diminished when he saw Muldane swimming toward him and the other *Amerikanski*, then had burned bright once more when he spotted Osvald Ioffe right behind Muldane.

Nothing changed. The battle continued to be a standoff, with the two Russians and Muldane and Krestell churning up a lot of water, swimming in every position possible, but unable to make contact with either the shock rods or the *Sunoinonoi* guns.

Emilya Piogorovov had not actually seen the Death Merchant turn Ladislav Gribti into a corpse. He had been too far away. However, he had swum closer and, within the beam of his helmet light, had seen the black-clad scuba-suited figure swim to the left as the dead Gribti started to sink slowly to the dark depths.

An angry Piogorovov, a tough, ruthless fighter, assumed that the *Amerikanski* would try to come up underneath him. Therefore, the Russian acted accordingly. He dived to the right, his firing tube held out in front of him. Ten seconds later, the Russian leered in triumph when he saw that he had guessed correctly. The beam from the light on his helmet grabbed the Death Merchant, who continued to swim straight toward him. And without a shock rod. There was only a long flashlight with a wide round front in the American's hand. A knife in his other hand!

Piogorovov was too experienced to believe that Camellion was being either foolish or crazy-brave, which is really one and the same. *Nyet!* The American had to have a plan. But what was it?

Camellion thought of what Grojean's note had said about the Intruder Glare-Flare device. *It works better on the surface. Test results under the water are almost as good. Should you have the opportunity, test it for the OST boys.*[1] *Maximum range is thirty-five feet.*

1. The CIA Office of Science & Technology.

"Almost as good!" It had better be very, very good! Ralph and Barney are a hundred feet to my left. The flash won't affect them.

Swimming straight toward Piogorovov, the Death Merchant waited until the muzzle of the puzzled Russian's tube was only ten feet away, then brought up the Intruder Glare-Flare, pointed it at Piogorovov, closed his eyes and pressed the button in the top of the rounded handle.

It was as if the sun had turned nova! There was a brilliant burst of light as the very special bulb produced ten million lumens of light, 85,000 times brighter than a 100-watt lightbulb.

It works, Grojean!

His eyes saturated with light, Piogorovov was instantly blinded by the intense flash. He had no way of knowing that the effect was only temporary and that he would be able to see within the next ten minutes. Terrified, the Russian lost his nerve and perspective. So did Osvald Ioffe who, during the burst, had seen the flash of light. For only a moment he hesitated in disbelief. Taking advantage of the opening, Ralph Muldane thrust in quickly with his shock rod, the tip touching Ioffe on the left arm. Ioffe's body jerked and went limp. The *Sunoinonoi* slipped from his hand. His arms and legs and head hanging downward, Ioffe started to rise to the surface.

Dmitri Levitin died at about the same time that the Death Merchant terminated the blinded Piogorovov. Levitin, knowing he couldn't last long against two of the *Amerikanskis*, tried to make a run for it—in this case, a swim for it, a swim for life—in a direction away from Muldane and Krestell. Dive and cut back toward the barrier. The Russian cockroach had just begun his dive when Krestell's shock rod made contact with his right shoulder. Electrocuted into unconsciousness, Levitin jerked, then relaxed.

Emilya Piogorovov, as blind as a statue, began to jab out in all directions with the *Sunoinonoi*, all the while knowing his efforts were useless, that he was a dead man. Moments later he was. The Death Merchant, swimming in from the rear, grabbed the *Sunoinonoi* and with two quick upward thrusts of the Jakal severed the two air hoses attached to the air tank on the Russian's back. Camellion felt merciful. As the pig farmer began to choke to death from lack of air, the Death Merchant reached around and, with another expert motion, cut Piogorovov's throat. With equal swiftness,

Camellion backed off and called out to Muldane and Krestell over the UTEL. "Ralph, Barney? How's the weather your way?" Camellion watched the beam of Piogorovov's light sink into the depths. The beam became dimmer and dimmer; then it was gone.

"Remind me to ask you what it was that caused the bright flash of light," Muldane finished. "Back in the SDV, I thought it looked like an unusual flashlight."

"Whitney, answer me," Camellion said. That damned Muldane. He knows damned good and well I was testing a device for OST!

"I'll turn on my UTEL's homing tone." Whitney said, his voice crisp and calm, "and you men can follow it home." He paused slightly and added, "I presume you're all alive."

Barney Krestell did not belt himself into the seat in back of the Death Merchant. He did squeeze himself into the rear area of the Trojan where the plastic containers were belted down, holding onto the port top of the SDV as Whitney fed full battery power to the electric motor.

"Settle down back there!" Whitney's voice was sharp. His right hand moved to the starboard vane lever. "You're throwing us out of trim."

Quick thinkers, the Death Merchant and Muldane guessed at once what The Bomber was going to do.

"Barney, I suppose you know that the place to dump the RDX is where the cave is the narrowest?" drawled Camellion. He pulled around the Intruder Glare-Flare on its ring-slide so that the device rested in front of him.

"Don't tell me how to set off firecrackers!" Krestell was genuinely angry. "Where else would I push the container overboard? We can easily spot the place through our Zons. Then Whitney can pull over close to a wall. You got that, Whitney?"

"Affirmative. But let me know several hundred feet in advance. This is not a roller coaster we're on. Cosgrove, you want me to go all the way to the surface?"

"Look, Whitney! These hand-held Zons only have a decent range of a hundred and fifty feet," Krestell said impatiently. "We'll have to make do with a hundred and fifty."

"To the surface," Camellion replied to Whitney. "Then open her up. We can go a knot faster on the surface."

Muldane said heavily, "The ivans could have surprises waiting on the surface, Cosgrove."

"Negative," Camellion disagreed. "We would have run into anything they have when we came in. Those divers were waiting by the fence because the sub was there. If the sub hadn't been inside, we wouldn't have seen anything or anybody. Neither would any vacationing scuba divers from a passing pleasure craft. The fence would have kept them out."

"I don't necessarily mean inside this cave," Muldane remarked, an urgency in his voice. "We still have to go along the south side and be picked up by the chopper when the main force moves in. And if you think we're going across the southside beach to see what's inside the house, you're out of your mind. The Ruskies know we're here. By now, the entire island is on alert."

"He's right, Cosgrove," Krestell's deep voice floated through the headphones clamped to Camellion's ears. "But you're wrong, Muldane. The Russians won't send out a ship to look for us. They realize that Uncle is wise to their setup and that we're only the toenail on the foot of the body of the main assault force. Right now I'll bet they're worried about getting their sub out."

Muldane said vehemently, "KGB security must have some kind of contingency plan worked out. They considered the possibility of discovery before they even set up shop on this hunk of rock. All of you know that."

"The submarine is not really a problem," Camellion said. "If they can't get it out past the legal limit, they'll blow it up. Barney, how much damage will that RDX do?"

"Plenty. It will blow out enough rock to keep a fleet of trucks busy for a week. It all depends how deep the channel is at the point of the explosion."

"I'll take a reading at the spot," Whitney said, sincerely wishing that his commander hadn't chosen him to be the pilot for these crazy spooks. "I guess all of you know it will be daylight by the time we get to the outside."

The Trojan moved through the dark water, Whitney and the Death Merchant peering through the forward high-resolution Zon devices that had a range of slightly over 210 feet. Muldane and Krestell, using the small portable NV devices, watched the port and the starboard sides.

We have the advantage, thought the Death Merchant.

131

*The Soviets don't want a full-scale nuclear war any more
than we do. We can blow hell out of the pig farmers on this
piece of real estate and Moscow can't say a single word,
not that first tiny complaint. The Bear has secretly taken
over a dot of the territory that belongs to the Eagle. On
that basis, not even the Soviet Union's allies in the Third
World can offer excuses in that joke of a windbag society
called the United Nations.*

The Death Merchant felt a deep satisfaction. At least
this operation, unlike the hostage "rescue attempt" in Iran,
would succeed. Then again, the Iranian deal had worked
perfectly for certain political interests in the United States.
The rescue mission was never intended to succeed. The entire purpose of the mission had been political, with the hos-
tages serving as sacrificial goats to high-level Machiavelli-
anism, a conspiracy that had deliberately deceived, and
was still deceiving, the American people.

Sterling Whitney was the first to spot the area where the
channel of the cavern tapered to its most narrow point. "I
think I see the spot," he said. "I can't be sure, not yet."

"And you were the one who jumped down our throats
with your 150 range," Krestell reminded the UDT man.
"So is it or isn't it?"

"I think so," Whitney said.

"It is," confirmed the Death Merchant. He blinked rapidly and moved back from the face plate of the night-sight
device. "Whitney! Get as close to the east wall as possible.
Barney—"

"Yeah, yeah, I know. I should give us enough time to get
out of here," Krestell snapped fretfully. "I'm going to set
the timer for fifteen minutes. By that time we'll be in the
Pacific."

In another five minutes the Trojan glided to a complete
stop, its port side only eight feet from the cavern wall. In
the rear of the SDV, Krestell, using a small light stick for
illumination, pulled the water seal from the plastic drum
and carefully turned the black knob to 15-M. He waited
until the automatic circuit check mechanism turned on the
tiny red light, the signal that the timer/detonator was in
perfect working order. Gloating inwardly, a twisted smile
on his thin lips, he unstrapped the plastic drum, braced
himself with his legs, picked up the drum by the handles
on each end and dropped the hundred pounds of RDX
over the side of the Trojan.

Camellion glanced at the depth sounder meter. "We have about four hundred feet of water under us, Barney," he announced. "I'd say the Soviet sub has a fifty-fifty chance. The sub might be able to slip past the exploded rock, if she has a good skipper."

"We've done all we can in here," The Bomber said. "The drum's over the side. Let's get out of here."

The SDV swayed violently from port to starboard and moved up and down like the board of a teeter-totter, Whitney holding firmly the wheel that controlled the rudder. In the "cargo" compartment, where there weren't any seats or seat belts, a cursing Krestell held himself in place by holding onto the sides of the vehicle, both his legs wedged underneath wide straps holding the firearms and ammo drums.

The turbulence and seesawing subsided and the Trojan, four fathoms below the surface of the Pacific Ocean, resumed its plunge through the dark waters.

The Death Merchant instructed Sterling Whitney, "Go straight west for two miles and I'll pop up and have a look."

Krestell looked at the luminous dial of the diver's watch strapped to his left wrist. "Three minutes to detonation." He spoke so tersely he sounded bitter. To make himself more comfortable, he uncoiled some of his communications cord, one end of which was plugged into Ralph Muldane's helmet. Muldane's wire was plugged into the Death Merchant's, and Camellion's into Whitney's.

The hundred pounds of RDX exploded on schedule, the blast sounding like loud thunder. Grinning from ear to ear, Krestell was as excited as a ghetto child getting off the bus at summer camp. "Hot diddle damn! That should have shaken up the commie trash but good!" His tone changed to one of doubt. "But I don't think the channel will be blocked enough with rock to stop the U-boat."

"Take her up to the surface." Camellion touched Whitney on his right arm. He scooted down and began working on the snap rings of the square watertight container attached to the underside of the forward hull.

"We're not even a mile yet!" protested Whitney.

"Take her up to the surface, and when we get there, none of you unplug your communication lines. We have to get those planes here to seal up that cave entrance."

133

In another minute the Trojan was on the surface, bobbing gently in the waves. Around the Trojan and the four men was that kind of twilight that comes with a brand new day, just before dawn becomes a thin line in the east. Not far behind the SDV the bleak cliffs on the west side of Tukoatu loomed starkly, ugly and threatening in their barrenness, the sound of the waves smashing against the tall stacks like a monotonous dirge.

No vessels were in sight.

"It's peaceful enough. We don't have to guess what the Russians are doing right now," said Muldane, who had halfway expected one or both of the island's cabin cruisers to be in the immediate vicinity.

"It will take them almost an hour to get that sub ready," Krestell said, staring at the cliffs, and another half hour to get past the crushed rock—if they can slide by the mess. RDX is powerful stuff."

The Death Merchant pulled the square case from the underside of the forward hull, placed the case in his lap and unfastened the six clasps that secured the lid. He took off the lid and looked down at the front of a URL-UHF radio. He took the HF loop, attached it to the set and went about getting ready to transmit. He pushed the transmission power switch of the power unit to the "High" position and placed the "Off-Receive—Transmit and Receive" switch to the "Transmit and Receive" position. He threw four other switches and finally was ready to transmit. He picked up the mike and pushed the end of a coiled cord into the female opening of one side of the mike. He used the single-prong plug at the other end of the line to set up communications with the mike of the UTEL.

"The sheep have been found," he said. He repeated the vital message. "The sheep have been found. Proceed with Operation Harelip. Once we are in position for the pickup, we'll radio and the chopper can home in on our signal. Acknowledge."

The URL-UHF had a bursted/digitally compressed group transmission format, and the entire message had gone out over the air in only 100.4 microseconds.

The answer from the *U.S.S. Northampton* was immediate.

"Acknowledged." The single word came through the Death Merchant's headphones and through the headphones of the three other men.

Krestell chuckled. "And now the fun starts, or it soon will start." He watched Camellion unplug both ends of the mike/UTL-UHF communications cord.

The Death Merchant unscrewed the loop antenna. "At this moment the *Northampton* is getting the word to Pearl. The planes will be blasting away at the cliffs within—I should say twenty minutes."

He put the loop antenna into the case, put on the lid and began to secure the clamps.

"It will take longer for the destroyer to get here," Muldane said dully. "By then it won't make any difference. The fly boys will have brought down half the cliff side and sealed the entrances forever. It's those damned cabin cruisers that bug me."

"You're just a worrier," Krestell said. "Three Coast Guard cutters are waiting six miles to the east. The instant those boats move, CG radar will pick them up."

The Death Merchant secured the closed radio case to the clip rings of the underside of the forward hull, saying to Whitney, "Take her down to twenty feet."

"How far out before I turn to the southeast?"

"Five miles, then head straight south."

Krestell frowned behind his full scuba face mask. "Why not remain on the surface?" He sighed loudly. "Damn, I wish I could smoke."

"We're not going to take any unnecessary chances," Camellion said. "There could be pig farmers up in those cliffs with surface-to-surface missiles. Should there be, I don't think they would waste any on us. But you never know. The Russian is a revengeful piece of trash. Lying and deception are second nature to him." He turned around and looked first at Muldane, then at Krestell. "Have you two been checking your regulator and pressure?"

Krestell nodded. "I'm okay."

"No problem," Muldane said. He added, "If the Russians inside the Soviet base can't fight any better than those divers we met, we'll have half a turkey shoot."

There was a click from deep inside the Trojan as Whitney pulled the lever and water began pouring into the trim tanks.

"We might have tangled with the *Mokskaia Pekhota,* or what the Soviets call 'naval infantry,'" Camellion said. He watched the Trojan tilt downward and the water close over his head. "They're the Soviet Marines, even though the term *marine* doesn't exist in the Russian language."

"I've heard of them," Krestell said. "They're elite fighters and called 'Black Berets.'" He laughed lightly. "Can you imagine a Russian pig in a beret? It's as silly as a jackass in a tuxedo! Come to think of it, the Soviet Defense Ministry uses the term *marine* in its English-language translations. I suppose the sons of bitches think it's a more accurate description than the term 'naval infantry.'"

"It would be a dangerous mistake to underestimate the Soviet Black Berets," the Death Merchant warned, watching several lion fish swim by on the port side. Deadly denizens of the sea, the lion fish had spread their featherlike fins—sharp dorsal spines charged with poison. "They're well trained and experts with their weapons, mainly AKM assault rifles. The pig farmers, however, prefer to use the term submachine guns."

His eye on the compass, Sterling Whitney said, "The Russians are weak on communications and too rigid in their chain of command. But they do have good weapons. Some think their 7.62mm (X54R) sniper rifle, with its PSO-1 scope, is the best up to a thousand meters."

"The ivans are also poor on tactics," Muldane said. "They're not a technology-minded people."

The Death Merchant checked his watch—0451 hours. "The profile of an integrated non-high-weapons technology system for a small defense force isn't difficult to erect. A small unit should avoid close-quarter combat, attack from not less than 400 meters and provide quick-retreat rendezvous points. First you destroy enemy helicopter air support, then fixed-wing aircraft, using laser-guided, head-on-mode, ECM-resistant, ground-to-air weapon missile systems. Antiarmor attack range should be 2,000 to 4,000 meters, using latest ATGM anti-tank guided-missile systems. The trouble with the Russians is that they refuse to consider retreat as part of their tactics."

"I suppose that proves that you can lead a horse to water but you can't force a jackass to drink," laughed Muldane.

Barney Krestell snickered. "Or that a man with a pebble in his head is smarter than 240 million dummies with rocks in their heads."

"I suppose it all depends on one's point of view," mused Krestell. "We're not planning any possible retreat today."

"But only because we don't have to," pointed out Krestell. "You can't make a comparison between the Soviet Army and what we're doing here today. Who knows? Some day the Russian high command might wise up in planning tactics. All things change."

"Except death," Camellion said quietly.

The Trojan cut through the water, its electric motor humming with full juice from the batteries. Now that the sun had risen, the water had changed from black to a soft blue. All around the SDV, in the shallow depths, was a world of vivid color—and so was the surface of the water. Shimmering like quicksilver, the surface mirrored the jumbled faces of red and black coral reefs, contorted fingers of red sponges, intense green fronds and filigrees of sargassum weed. At slightly lower depths spidery lobsters scuttled over coral, and crabs climbed along twenty-inch-long tubeworms attached to volcanic rock.

"See what's ahead?" said Whitney. "We'll take a course around them." He turned the wheel sharply to the right to avoid the five Portuguese man-of-wars drifting on the surface with the tide, their poisonous tentacles dangling fifteen feet deep to snare prey. The tentacles couldn't have harmed the men in their full scuba suits, but the possibility of becoming entangled in the thin tentacles and pulling down the drifting creatures was too great.

The Trojan was at 4.6 miles when the four men heard the distinct sounds of approaching aircraft.

"This is far enough, Whitney. Let's go to the surface," ordered Camellion. "We have to change air tanks anyhow. We have only a fifteen-minute supply."

"That will be a lot of work for no good reason at all," protested Krestell. "The helicopter will be here in fifteen minutes, perhaps a little sooner after you radio."

A click, then the hiss of air forcing water from the trim tanks. The Trojan began to rise to the surface.

"We're changing to fresh bottles," Camellion said firmly. "Something could go haywire and we might have to resubmerge. Should that happen, I want us to have a full supply of air. After we surface and change bottles, open your face masks and breathe ordinary air. No use wasting the bottled mix."

The SDV popped to the surface, this time into bright sunshine, the sun a good foot above the horizon.

Krestell began unbuckling the air bottles in the rear of the vehicle, and while he worked the TE-15 Eagles from

137

Hickam Air Force Base began peeling off and screaming in toward the bleak west side cliffs of Tukoatu, the two Pratt & Whitney turbo-fan engines of each warplane shrieking.

The "talons" of each Eagle consisted of a M61A-1 rotary cannon fitted into the right fuselage fairing, a weapon that had 1,000 rounds of 20-millimeter ammunition. Permanent attachment points were located on the outside bottom edge of the fuselage. Four AIM-9L Sidewinder air-to-air missiles could be placed on underwing pylons, and a center pylon was also available. But on this strike, none of the fifteen Eagles carried Sidewinders. Instead, their pylons were loaded with AGM-12C/D air-to-surface "Bullpups."

Muldane took the air bottle that Krestell handed him and looked up at the first approaching Eagle. "I almost feel sorry for the Russians." He chuckled in glee. "It's going to be a turkey shoot."

"Never mind the planes," Camellion said briskly. "Let's get the air tanks changed. I'll then radio the *Northampton*."

Muldane made a face but didn't say anything. He knew a stone killer when he met one, and the man called "Cosgrove" was definitely one of the best in the business. Cosgrove's only trouble was that he had a nasty streak of morality about him. . . .

Right on target, the first Eagle streaked down and, at 4,000 yards, the pilot shot off his four Bullpups. One after another the missiles stabbed toward the cliffs. Powered by a Thiokol LR62 storable liquid-propellant rocket motor, the Bullpup was 13 feet 4.25 inches (4.07 meters) long and contained a 454-kilogram (1,000 pounds) warhead of TNT.

All four Bullpups exploded in a line a hundred feet above the large cavern entrance. There were tremendous *BEROOOOMMMMMSSSSS*, microsecond flashes of flame, and tons of rock flew outward. At the same time long slabs of stone—some fifty feet long—began sliding down the fractured face of the cliff. A few seconds more and they knifed into the water with loud splashes.

The second pilot was slightly off target. Only two of his Bullpups hit the cliff face over the cavern entrance. The remaining thirteen Eagles were one hundred percent accurate. The cliff side shook and shuddered as the Bullpups exploded, each explosion ripping out tons and tons of granite which could only fall to the entrance of the channel. It took the fifteen Eagles only twelve minutes to send their sixty Bullpups at the lower portion of the cliff's face.

The cliff above the wide entrance of the cave had been transformed. For several hundred feet above the entrance there was an enormous indentation—thirty feet deep in some places—as though someone or something had tried to carve out a new cave. Something had—fifteen Eagles and sixty Bullpup missiles.

With their fresh air tanks in place on their back boards and their face masks open, Camellion's men stared at the still-smoking face of the cliff.

"A bedbug in a test tube couldn't get out of that cave," Krestell said happily. "That entrance is sealed forever."

A total pessimist, Ralph Muldane was not so sure. "It's possible that the U-boat got out before the planes got off their missiles. I don't think so, but we can't discount the possibility."

"Yes we can." Whitney sounded positive. "The Soviet sub didn't escape. Such a mass of metal would have made our sonar ping the hit tune of the year."

"You're sure about that?"

Whitney stared hard at Muldane, his eyes mirroring insult. "Do I tell you how to be a 'spook'?—and that's what you are, though I don't expect you to admit it. I'm damned good at my job, mister. I'm telling you the Soviet sub didn't get out. The sonar didn't ping once. I know."

"OK, don't get your balls in an uproar," Muldane said good-naturedly. "So the sub is bottled up."

Camellion had contacted the *U.S.S. Northampton* on the UTL-UHF and had attached the long homing whip antenna to the radio. Now he continued to scan the Western skies through a pair of MK II 8X 50mm wide-angle binoculars. Presently he saw six specks spread out in a row.

"I see the choppers," he said, his voice pleased. He handed the binoculars to Muldane. "Take a look."

Muldane had the binoculars up to his eyes and was adjusting the focus when he and the other men began to hear a faint thump-thump-thump-thump-thump of helicopter rotor blades.

"Praise the Lord!" joked Krestell. "The cavalry has arrived."

"Only now the 'Indians' are Russians," the Death Merchant said.

"So what's the difference?"

"Plenty. The Indians were, and are, a moral people who only wanted what was theirs. . . ."

CHAPTER ELEVEN

Sheer madness! Feeling that they were in a wilderness of lost souls, Colonel Anton Zimovniki, Major Valery Marleoff, and Major Sergei Amosov stared in disbelief at the two officers from the *Stalingrad* and at Captain Anton Tikhvin, the officer in charge of the *Mokskaia Pekhota* unit. The three were talking like stupid *mouzhiks*, like stupid peasants. *Nyet!* They were mouthing the words of idiots, of men who had lost the perspective of reality. Part of their proposal made sense. The *Stalingrad* did have to be destroyed. To have the submarine fall into the hands of the Americans would be as tragic as permitting the Americans to capture Dr. Mkrtchyan and the other scientists and to learn of the existence of the Bio-Memory Scanner. But the second half of their scheme was pure lunacy.

"Comrade Commander Dubokinsko, there is no doubt that the entire entrance is blocked with rock?" Anton Zimovniki tried to keep incredulity from his voice as he addressed the skipper of the *Stalingrad*. "No mistake has been made? The submarine is trapped?"

"There is no more entrance. There is only rock," Josef Dubokinsko said haughtily. "The divers could not even find an opening large enough to admit a single man."

"We doubt if we could even take the vessel through the narrow part of the channel," added Lieutenant-Major Boris Skayiski, Dubokinsko's second-in-command. "That section is also clogged with rock. We must destroy the *Stalingrad*."

While Commander Dubokinsko was a small man with hairy hands, a pot belly, and an enormous nose, Skayiski was tall but not overweight, thin-featured, and with an upper row of gold-capped teeth in his mouth.

"What about radiation?" inquired Major Amosov. He ran the fingers of his right hand through his thick black-gray hair, a nervous habit he resorted to when he felt he was not on safe ground.

"This is a poor time to worry about radiation," sneered Captain Tikhvin, who was a large, tough-looking man with close-cropped hair. He jammed out his cigarette savagely in a massive blue glass ashtray. "The Americans are about to invade this base and you're worried about radiation."

"And you had damn well better concern yourself about it, Comrade Tikhvin!" declared Amosov angrily. "Before this day is over, the Americans will be inside these caves and all of us will be dead."

"We'll take a lot of them with us before they get us!" Tikhvin announced fiercely. "We'll die fighting for the Motherland."

"You're not looking at the implications of what is happening," Colonel Zimovniki said roughly. "We can't stop the Americans, but the world will never know anything about this island and our base. The Americans will not report the incident to the world's press. To do so would make them look like fools."

"And cowards, if they didn't retaliate!" Major Marleoff got in grimly, then lit a cigarette.

"Moscow will also keep silent," Zimovniki went on. "But if radiation from the sub's reactor contaminates the waters around this section of the Hawaiian Islands, there will be no way to keep the secret. The whole world will know what happened and the full blame will fall on the Soviet Union."

"We'll be dead," Boris Skayiski said in a so-what tone.

"But our wives and children and other relatives back home won't be!" Zimovniki said reproachfully. "We all know how the bosses get even with men who fail in highly important missions."

Commander Dubokinsko, pacing back and forth in the meeting room, stopped and looked intensely at Colonel Zimovniki. "Moscow can't blame me and my crew for this monstrous debacle," he protested sourly. "Why, we don't even know the nature of your work in these caves."

"We can destroy the *Stalingrad* with individually placed charges," Boris Skayiski said, "in such a way that the nuclear reactor will remain intact. It's the detection gear the Americans will want to study. We can destroy our sonar and other detection systems completely."

"The fault lies with Moscow." Colonel Zimovniki's bluntness surprised the other Soviet officers. Instinctively they knew the reason for his frankness. He was doomed and within hours would be a corpse. They were all walking dead men. Surrender was out of the question. "The Center outsmarted itself. Not only should this base never have been established on American territory, but . . ." He paused as Amosov and Marleoff looked worriedly at him, silently saying, *Why tell them secrets they have no business knowing*? Zimovniki continued anyway. The time for extreme caution had passed. The Americans knew the base existed, and there wasn't anything Moscow could do about it. "But we should never have been made a part of Tavern Melancholy. There should have been no connection between us and the others."

"Tavern Melancholy?" repeated Anton Tikhvin, his brow furrowing into a big V of puzzlement.

Dubokinsko and Skayiski locked eyes, then looked suspiciously at Colonel Zimovniki.

"An intelligence-gathering network throughout the north and the south Pacific," explained Zimovniki bitterly. "We had no contact with the *Apparat* in the Islands and vice versa. I think that somehow the people in the Honolulu *Apparat* made mistakes that led American intelligence to this base." He turned his head slightly and glanced at Major Marleoff, who was sitting across the table. Thinking of the missing crewman of the *Pearl of the Pacific,* the seaman who could not be accounted for, Marleoff looked away.

Captain Anton Tikhvin, who was also pacing up and down like a caged animal, turned on Zimovniki challengingly. "What's the difference how the Americans found out? They know and will soon be attacking."

"*Da,* they know and will soon attack," responded Zimovniki, dismissing Tikhvin's manner, "and you would take your thirty Naval Infantry and my security people and fight the Americans on the surface!"

"Exactly!" Tikhvin's dark eyes blazed with determination. "We will do the unexpected. We will meet them where they least expect us, on the beach when they come ashore. We can gun down half of the stupid Americans before they have a chance to regroup and start searching for any entrances to the complex."

"You simple-minded idiot!" spit out Colonel Zimovniki. He pushed back his chair and got to his feet. "The Americans aren't stupid; you are. The only thing you would accomplish with such ridiculous tactics would be to make it easy for the Capitalist swine. They're not going to land on any beach! *Chort vozmi!*[1] This is not World War II!"

Captain Anton Tikhvin was so enraged, he turned purple and sounded as if he might be choking. Surprised at Zimovniki's brutal insulting of Tikhvin, Commander Josef Dubokinski and Lieutenant-Major Boris Skayiski stared at the KGB officer.

Zimovniki said in a cold, ruthless voice, "The Americans won't attack any beach! They'll blow that house to pieces from the air. They're not going to take the time to climb mountains and search for entrances. By some method of technology they've found out where we are, and they probably know about the satellite-tracking device. The Americans will land on Mount Haleatimu." He glared at the somewhat mollified Anton Tikhvin, who was nervously lighting another cigarette. "If you and your men are caught out in the open, you won't live five minutes."

Tikhvin, taking off his gray utility cap and sitting down, didn't say anything.

"We'll make our stand inside the base," Major Amosov declared, wiping sweat off his forehead. "We're 350 meters below the summit of this mountain. In that respect we're in luck. There are only three entrances from the top. One is a shaft we drilled with a laser. It contains an elevator and leads to the reflector. The other two are slightly below the top on the north side. They are natural caves that slant down to this base. We can easily defend those natural passageways, and they won't dare try to use the elevator."

Commander Dubokinsko sat down heavily, all the while staring at Zimovniki. "My God, Colonel! Do you mean this place has been tracking American satellites with a parabolic reflector microphone?" His voice cracked from astonishment as he asked the question.

1. "Devil take it." The approximate Russian equivalent of "damn."

"You heard Major Amosov," Zimovniki said mildly. "Technicians raise and lower the dish each morning." Reaching for his own cigarettes in his shirt pocket, he added drily, "This morning was the exception."

"It's crazy," Dubokinsko said dully. "A tracking station on American soil! What could Moscow have been thinking?"

"There is also a very special laboratory on the bottom level." Zimovniki gave a tight-lipped smile and assessed the sub captain who would soon be without a vessel. Zimovniki wasn't fooled. In spite of his tough exterior, Commander Dubokinsko was terrified. So was Boris Skayiski, who had the same helpless look about him.

In contrast, Anton Tikhvin was intensely interested.

"Experiments? What kind of experiments?"

Zimovniki finished lighting his cigarette, exhaled, and tossed the paper match to the floor. "We can't allow the scientists and any information about their work to fall into the hands of the Americans. I have already given orders that Executive Action be taken against the scientists."

Commander Dubokinsko was not certain what "Executive Action" meant, but he suspected it meant liquidation— a bullet in the head. He remained silent, the helplessness of his position numbing his mind.

But Anton Tikhvin, who was also a secret officer in the KGB's *Napravleniye*, the Political Security Service, knew exactly what Executive Action was. He too remained silent, secretly thinking it was a government of swine that would terminate its own people needlessly. Naturally such action was necessary since the scientists were on the island. But they shouldn't have been sent there in the first place.

Tikhvin turned with the other men toward the door as it opened and Captain Vadim Arkadevich hurried into the room. Of medium height, Arkadevich was in charge of all internal security within the Soviet base in Mount Haleatimu. He was thickset, had a small mustache, very large ears, and small eyes set too closely together.

Arkadevich was so agitated that, when he walked up to Colonel Zimovniki, he didn't bother to salute.

"Comrade Colonel," he said breathlessly, "the door to the laboratory is locked and Doctor Mkrtchyan refuses to open it."

Major Valery Marleoff got to his feet, alarm all over his face.

"The son of a bitch knows!"

Colonel Zimovniki inhaled sharply, frustration twisting his features. The unexpected had become reality.

The door to the laboratory was four inches thick. . . .

CHAPTER TWELVE

The noise from the rotor blades of the six Boeing-Vertol CH-46 Sea Knights was tremendous, especially the roaring from the CH-46 SK hovering only twenty-five feet above and slightly to port of the bobbing Trojan.

An assault transport, the Sea Knight could carry up to twenty-five fully equipped troops, could cruise at 130 mph, and was powered by two 1,870 h.p. General Electric T58 Gnome turboshafts. The diameter of each three-blade main rotor was fifty feet. All six helicopters carried two Hughes electric chain guns mounted toward the rear of the fuselage, in pods on the port and the starboard sides. Each multi-barrelled electric cannon could throw out hundreds of 20-mm shells per minute.

The drums of arms, ammo, and grenades were hoisted on a winch line into the chopper, after which a chainmesh ladder with steel bar rungs was dropped through the doorway to the SDV. Carefully the four men left the Trojan—it would be picked up later—and started to climb the ladder, the Death Merchant going up last. Once the four were safety aboard and the door secured, the pilot revved up the engines and lifted the big bird at a slant to the south, preparatory to rejoining the five other choppers hanging at 2,000 feet, only four kilometers southwest of Tukoatu.

There were nine UDT men and nine United States Marines aboard the chopper. Olin Gammill, the ONI spook, and Simon Kirkland, the Company man, were also on board, sitting on one of the forward benches on the starboard side, both looking uncomfortable and out of place in their helmets, tiger-stripes, combat boots, and battle gear.

Three Marines and two UDTs began opening the large

canisters; other men began helping Camellion and his three companions out of their gear.

Supported by a Marine who was hanging onto a handhold on the rounded ceiling, the Death Merchant was stepping out of his black suit when a tall, muscular black man in his early thirties made his way from the forward section and looked over the new arrivals. His skin was the color of coffee and he was sucking on a lollypop, the stick protruding from the left side of his mouth.

"Who's Cosgrove?" His voice was a deep bass.

"Yo," Camellion said, accepting a gun belt and holsters filled with two Backpacker Auto Mags.

The black man shifted the sucker to the right side of his mouth.

"I'm Captain Robert Webb, the Marine officer in charge of this force." He eyed the Death Merchant up and down. "You must be something special out of a box of Crackerjacks. My orders are to follow your orders. How do you want to do it? Your way or the tactical way?"

A tough dude who resents a civilian taking over—and he's honest about it. Good. We'll get along. Camellion finished buckling on the gun belt with its pocket full of spare clips and accepted a canvas shoulder bag of grenades and a bag crammed with eleven spare magazines for a T20 submachine gun.

"We'll first blow apart the house on the east beach," Camellion said pleasantly, glancing at Webb. "One chopper will then land in the area west of the house and secure that section of the island. Our bird and four more will rake the summit of Mount Haleatimu, then land on the mountain top. That's my way. It's also the tactical way. And if you say it isn't, I'll tell you that you should resign your commission and go into another line of work."

Webb grinned from ear to ear, then shifted the sucker to the other side of his mouth. "Affirmative. Landing on the damned mountain is the only way to do the job, But how do we get inside—and are you sure there's a Soviet base inside? It's so damned incredible!"

"The base is there and so is a Russian sub," Camellion said between clenched teeth. "But it's not going anywhere; neither are the Russians inside the mountain." He and the three men who had been with him in the Trojan had worn extra-large scuba suits over their tiger-stripe fatigues. Camellion now reached into his top right breast pocket, pulled

146

out an oilcloth map and, rocking back and forth as the helicopter veered to starboard, handed it to Webb. "There are two entrances, natural caves. Each entrance is on the north side, about fifty feet from the top. The terrain is on a wide slant. We shouldn't have any trouble climbing down."

Webb gave Camellion a piercing stare. "Do the caves lead to the Soviet base? We have plenty of special light sticks, but there's no sense in wasting time in stumbling around the wrong caves. What's your evidence?"

"Only theory," Camellion told Webb the truth. "The Ruskies had to make use of natural openings. Blasting with explosives would have been heard by passing ships and would have attracted attention."

Webb, his body swaying as he hung onto a handhold, was skeptical.

"Suppose those caves come to a dead end? Then what?"

"In that case we'll have to do it the hard way. We'll have to blast an entrance in the blocked-up channel—if it is blocked—and go in with SDVs. Anymore questions?"

"How come you haven't asked me why I have a sucker in my mouth?"

Smiling, the Death Merchant buckled the chest crosstrap of the two snap-spring shoulder holsters, each of which contained a 9mm Beretta auto-pistol.

"Maybe you like suckers," said Camellion. "Personally, I don't care if you have wheels for feet, as long as you know your business."

Webb swung in closer to Camellion. "I'm going up to the cockpit and radio orders to the other birds. You didn't say, but I don't think the chopper that will secure the beach area should land without cover."

"We think alike, Webb," the Death Merchant said. "You know your people. Choose the craft you want to smear the house and the rest of us will act as air cover."

Webb grinned again. "Good enough. I'll contact the other birds on the radio and we'll go in. Any evidence that the commies have rockets or anything else that might bring us down?"

"It's as long as it's wide." Camellion shrugged. "But I doubt if they have any high-powered stuff. The base was built for secret activities, not for defense."

"I hope you're right, Cosgrove!" Webb gave Camellion a long look. He turned and, via the handholds on the ceiling, moved toward the cockpit.

* * *

The six Sea Knights swung toward the east end of Tu-koatu at a height of 2,500 feet, gradually losing altitude. Three stopped over Hiromori Nagai's house at an altitude of 1,000 feet. Spread out in a line, they hovered. Two more descended to 500 feet. The sixth chopper, the copilot and gunner raising and lowering the electric cannons and moving them horizontally on their ball mountings as the chopper dropped lower and lower, stopped 150 feet over the house and the gunner opened fire with the two Hughes chain guns. It took only ten seconds for the flood of 20-millimeter shell heads to dissolve the red tile roof. Slowly the pilot began to move the helicopter in a large circle. All the while, the two electric cannons continued to fire, the roaring one continuous *bruuuuuurrrupppppppppppp*, the two streams of fire one continuous line of 20-millimeter shell heads that began ripping apart the house. The big shell heads broke two by fours, smashed larger beams into kindling and turned plaster walls into chunks of rubble. And as the house was sawed apart by the unbelievable tornado of steel, furniture and valuable objects of art were also destroyed.

Total destruction time was only 4.6 minutes. Where the house had stood was complete wreckage . . . broken boards, shattered tile and debris that had been furniture. Over the entire mess rose a cloud of gray dust that drifted slowly toward the beach.

In the wreckage were also three corpses, so torn apart by shell heads that they were no longer recognizable as human beings—three Hawaiians, all underworld characters from Honolulu, two men and one woman, all three of whom had been hired—at the insistence of the KGB—by Hiromori Nagai to replace his honest servants.

Colonel Zimovniki had not seen any need to warn any of the Hawaiians, including the hoods who had helped Major Marleoff, Nikolai Aninin, and Pyotr Stashynsky kidnap the people from the *Pearl of the Pacific*. Seven of the trash were sleeping in the *Golden Swan*, a sleek Viking double-cabin cruiser with an open bridge deck—the same vessel that had been used to pirate the *Pearl of the Pacific*. Three other of God's rejects were in dreamland in the *Mermaid*, a smaller Kipper 44-foot Pacifica cruiser. The loud sound of the rotor blades of the six choppers had awakened the men bunked down in the *Golden Swan*, but the three in the

Mermaid were in a drunken stupor and kept right on sawing logs while the one Sea Knight demolished the house. Four of the Hawaiian triggermen had managed to jump from the *Golden Swan* onto the wooden pier by the time the Sea Knight zoomed over the two cabin cruisers. Three men were on the stern deck of the *Golden Swan*, falling all over the place trying to get to the pier as the two chain guns began firing. The three men in the *Mermaid* were still sound asleep.

Brrruuuuuuuuuurrrrrrrrrrppppppppppppppppp. A monsoon of 20-millimeter shell heads rained down and exploded, turning the four men on the pier and the three goons on the *Golden Swan* into one big bloody mess of severed body parts. Bathed in blood and gore, a man's head exploded. Another man's arm and one leg, cut from the body by shell heads, shot from the deck and dropped into the water. A third man dropped in three different parts, blood gushing as if from a fire hose. Hearts, lungs, and livers were torn from bodies, bones broken and shattered into flying chips. Within ten seconds the hundreds of shell heads had turned the *Golden Swan* into useless scrap metal. Several seconds more and a dozen shell heads found the engine and fuel tank.

BERRRROOOOMMMMMM! A large ball of red-orange fire, ringed with black smoke, shot up and the *Golden Swan* exploded, hot, jagged pieces of metal flying upward and outward in all directions.

Brrruuuuuuuuurrrrrrrrrrrppppppppppppppppp. Shell heads ripped into the *Mermaid* and she too disappeared in a rolling ball of fire and smoke, parts and pieces of the demolished cabin cruiser falling over a hundred-foot radius.

Watching through a pair of binoculars, a thousand feet up and to the right of the carnage below, the Death Merchant compared the chain guns to sandblasters. The two did achieve the same results. The only difference was that the chain guns, instead of using grains of sand, used 20-millimeter shells.

"That seems to be that!" said Olin Gammill, who was watching the destruction below with the Death Merchant. "Now for the big one."

The five choppers hovered and waited. The Sea Knight that had done the attacking swung 700 feet to the west and began to descend to an area covered with short *tekki* grass. No sooner had the tricycle landing gear touched ground

149

than UDTs and Marines in full battle gear began pouring out of both doors, each man carrying a Colt CAR-15 heavy assault rifle.

Camellion, Gammill, and the other men in the helicopter braced themselves as the pilot swung upward and to the northwest, gravity tugging at their bodies and intensifying when the pilot banked, turned the big bird and pointed its nose toward Mount Haleatimu. Looking out of the windows, the men saw a green canopy far below, a field of uneven forest cut with gorges and large and small valleys. Some small mountains were almost devoid of vegetation; others were thick with trees and ferns and bushes. If the attack force had gone in by ground, it would have taken them a week to reach the summit of "The House of the Moon."

There was more expert maneuvering as the pilots of the five Sea Knights arranged themselves in two lines that stretched from east to west, two helicopters in the first line, three in the second, the chopper in which Camellion rode being number three on the east end of the second line.

The first two Sea Knights made the run, their electric cannons beginning the vicious firing at a distance of 500 feet (150 meters), when the choppers were only several hundred feet above the terrain. Hundreds of 20-millimeter shell heads chopped into koa trees, shredded guavas, pandanus and wild orchids. Small rocks, exploded when struck by the rocketlike shell heads, giant chips zinging from larger boulders.

The two helicopters rose, headed west and waited, hovering several miles to the northeast. The last three big whirlybirds moved in over the mountain top, their six electric cannons roaring, six lines of steel projectiles raking the summit. Nothing could stay alive in such a downpour of steel death. The top of the mountain, shaped in the form of a lopsided triangle, was half the size of a city block, and not a single yard escaped the impact of 20-millimeter shell heads.

The five choppers came down, two landing 30.5 meters (100 feet) from the north rim, three, 68 meters (225 feet) from the east rim. In a large semicircle, the attack force moved inward, toward the center. First they had to find the large cover over the shaft. They soon did. They discovered that the covering was composed of large logs fastened to a framework of steel girders. Large rocks—chunks of granite—were fixed to the logs by means of thick steel strips, the strips bolted solidly to the logs, the rocks fastened to the rocks with mollybolts.

Hugh Hale Gamberkrone had been only half right. The shaft was not round. Quick measurement revealed that the opening was fifty-four feet long and forty-eight feet wide.

"Gamberkrone was right about the dead wood and the rocks," the Death Merchant commented. "The blue lines he mentioned were the metal strips holding the rocks to the logs. . . ."

"The Ruskies really goofed," Simon Kirkland said. He shook his head wonderingly. "Evidently they forgot that the metal strips would give off emanations. I suppose one of those pointy-headed liberal morons in D.C. would say it only proves that honesty is the best policy."

"Maybe, but insanity is still the best defense." Barney Krestell turned to the Death Merchant, who was down on one knee with Captain Webb, studying a Hawaiian geological survey map of Mount Haleatimu. "Look, Cosgrove. Is this a cliché festival or are we going to get on with it?"

Camellion and Webb glanced to the left toward Lieutenant Vernon Flint and six other Marines, all of whom were coming toward them in an easy run. Camellion and Webb stood up.

Lieutenant Flint— he was an athletic man with a firm jaw and steely eyes—stopped before Captain Webb. "We found the other entrance, sir." His manner relaxed, he didn't salute (proving to Camellion that Webb was a good officer). He turned and pointed to the west across the shaft covering to a large pile of rocks, the tallest of which was thirty feet high and deeply pitted from the impact of scores of 20-millimeter shell heads.

"Double doors, sir, over by the tall rock, like elevator doors," Flint said. "The Ruskies must have drilled a shaft right up through solid rock." He spit on the ground. "Painted gray and solid steel."

"Thank you, Lieutenant." Webb pulled the stick out of his mouth and tossed it to the ground; the lollypop that had been on the end of the stick had dissolved. He turned to Camellion. "We'll set contact charges in front of the doors as well as around the shaft. We've got to be certain that our rear is protected." He waited for the Death Merchant's confirmation. He got it promptly.

"An excellent precautionary measure," Camellion answered, "although I have a gut feeling that none of this is necessary. The Ruskies aren't going to come out to us. We're going to have to go in and get the scum."

He turned and looked at the UDT men placing five-pound blocks of Composition C-4 around the edge of the shaft, a block every thirty feet at a point where the ends of the logs fitted snugly into the top of the steel-sheet sides of the shaft. A trip wire would be run from the electric blasting cap inside each block and the battery-powered detonator pronged in on the outside of each block. Should the Russians attempt to open the cover, which was in two sections—BOOOOOMMMMM. No more lid! No more Russians! The detonators, however, would not be activated until that last man was ready to enter the two entrances on the north slope of "The House of the Moon." The same trip-wire arrangement would suffice in front of the elevator doors.

A final conference was held. Camellion, Olin Gammill, Lieutenant Fling and six Marines would go down on the north side and search for one entrance. Ralph Muldane, Simon Kirkland—who was photographing everything in sight with a small motion-picture camera—Sergeant William "Wild Bill" Hurt and four UDTs would search for the second cavern entrance.

The Death Merchant also decided that, after the men were ready to go into the two entrances, the five helicopters would leave the mountain top and fly back to the beach area.

"What about the three shields?" inquired Webb, putting another lollypop into his mouth. "Do we unload them now or wait until we find the two entrances?"

"We'll be able to lower the shields to precise positions after we locate the openings," the Death Merchant said. "And the sooner we begin the better."

"You mean the quicker we'll get our butts shot off," Muldane said dourly. "I never did like caves."

On both knees, Barney Krestell continued to study the geological survey map. "Unless this map is wrong, we have to go downward—inward—on a slant for sixteen hundred feet. That's a long way to go. The Russians—what do you call them, Cosgrove? 'Pig farmers?' The pig farmers could have explosive charges set and all kinds of barriers set up." He got up and started to fold the map.

"We'll have to chance it," Camellion said lazily, a slight

152

twisted smile on his lean face. "The other way, through the channel, would be even more dangerous.

Sergeant Wild Bill Hurt spoke up. "What about air? So each man has a small bottle of oxygen and a gas mask. Neither one is very good for very long if there's no air."

"Engineers tell us that caves act as natural flues," Camellion said. "There should be plenty of air."

"There should even be a slight draft," Olin Gammill said.

The Death Merchant made an impatient gesture with his left hand.

"Let's go find the entrances."

The climb down the north slope was not difficult. The rocks were solid, the slope was not steep, and there were ample hand and foot holds. But since the possibility existed that the Russians could be waiting below to fire on them, there was still a very real and very deadly danger involved. To offset this danger, three men went ahead, taking the "downward" point as it were. Not a shot was fired. There was only a slight breeze and breathtaking beauty. To the north a miniature grand canyon sliced through lava slopes. Below, ridges rose, embracing small jungle valleys. Wild ginger, bright red anthuriums and 'ohi'a mingled with ferns, vines, and other growths on the mountain slope.

Camellion and his group began searching through thick foliage on the fifty-foot level, where a long ledge poked out from the slope. Without any difficulty, they found the cavern opening. It would have been impossible to miss it. They estimated the mouth of the cave to be forty feet wide and thirty feet high. The sides and top of the entrance were jagged with black volcanic rock overgrown by un'illa vines, thick with big yellow and white flowers dangling down from the top of the opening. Inside . . . blackness. Three Marines posted themselves on each side of the entrance, Colt CAR submachine guns ready.

The Death Merchant pulled a Tadiran PRC-601 from the case on his belt and switched on the six-channel receiver. "Captain Webb. Camellion here."

"You've found the cave? Over."

"Affirmative. I'll stand on the ledge and you can use me as a marker for your position when you let down the two shields."

Ralph Muldane's voice broke in. "We found ours, too.

It's a big son of a bitch. Osgood, is that ledge the one above all the *iliau* trees? Over."

"You got it."

"In that case the caves are about two hundred feet apart. There's nothing to stand out on here. I'll climb back up and drag a line as a marker. Out."

"Good, let's get on with it—out," Camellion said. He switched off the transceiver and shoved it back into its case.

Let's walk into the mouth of hell. . . .

The question was suddenly there in his mind: *What could be so earth-shaking that Grojean himself is coming to Hawaii to brief me?*

CHAPTER THIRTEEN

One of the prime functions of a leader is to keep the flames of hope burning brightly. Under prevailing conditions in the cavern-tunnels, the Death Merchant and Captain Webb found sprinkling encouragement an almost impossible task. Not even Camellion wanted to die, although, unlike the other men, he wasn't concerned about being dead.

There was more than ample room in both caverns, the width and the height of the tunnels such that the men could have turned handsprings under different conditions. Nor was it the semidarkness that ate at the confidence of the force. Each man had a light stick tucked into his belt—burning time, two hours and twenty minutes. In addition, each man carried a battery-powered light that could be attached—in an emergency—to his ballistic helmet.

The Death Merchant and Captain Webb each wore a sophisticated night-vision goggle. Known as a Holographic One-Tube Goggle, the device employed thin-film diffraction optics and advanced electronics, both of which worked together to amplify dim visual light and near-infrared radiation, superimposing the image over the view of the wearer. The image intensifier tube, extending above the bridge of the nose, did not block any portion of the wearer's visual field.

Olin Gammill and Sergeant Hurt also wore the Special goggle.

Sixty-three men, including Camellion, were in the Death Merchant's force. Gammill and Hurt, in the second cave, led sixty men.

In spite of the largeness of the two caves, the men had to stay close together and move forward in a hunched-over position. At no time could any portion of their bodies extend beyond the top and side edges of the two shields at the head of each column. Designed by Camellion in Banana Bread Box 1, each shield, weighing 310 pounds (140.616 kilograms), was six feet (1.8 meters) high and seven feet (2.1 meters) wide, and was fastened to a square horizontal aluminum frame with a rubber-tired wheel at each corner. A hand lever at the bottom center of the rear girder could brake all four wheels.

Each shield was composed of sheets of "Armadillo" laminate, each sheet one inch (2.54 centimeters) thick. From the front side, there were first three sheets of bullet-resistant laminate, then a one-inch-thick sheet of solid steel (85 percent of the weight), followed by two inches (5.08 centimeters) of Kevlar and Ballistic Nylon and three more sheets of one-inch A-laminate—nine inches that, all bolted together, could stop any kind of small arms fire and even (possibly) heavy caliber machine gun projectiles, but not under sustained firing.

The difficulty was that the weight of each shield, coupled with the fact that each shield was resting on a slightly downward incline, tended to pull it forward under its own momentum. To compensate for this tendency, an eyebolt was bolted through the center of each shield and one end of a hundred-foot (30.5 meters) "Army green line" attached to the eyebolt. Each line was held by a dozen men. In this manner each shield was prevented from rolling forward and downward under its own momentum.

The greatest danger was that the leaders of each column had to look around the edges of the shields to see what lay ahead, to see where they were going, and at times they had to leave the protection of the shields to remove small rocks too large for the wheels to roll over.

A further complication was that communication between

the two columns was difficult. The Tadiran transceiver was one of the best in the world; however, the device had not been designed to operate clearly through hundreds of feet of rock. The result was that conversation between the two columns was garbled and unclear.

Without interference from the Russians, the two columns proceeded slowly into the guts of the mountain.

The Death Merchant was to the left side of the shield. Behind him were two Marines—Corporal Paul Gibbreth, who carried the latest kind of flame thrower, and Private First Class Carey Thrug, to whose Colt CAR-15 was attached a CGL-4 40-millimeter grenade launcher.

Barney Krestell and Captain Webb were first behind the right-side shield. The first two men behind them also carried a flame thrower and a grenade launcher.

Camellion checked his pedometer and found that they had reached the 741-foot mark of the cave that, according to the survey map, was 1,600 feet long.

"We've come two hundred and twenty-five meters," he called out. "Two hundred and sixty-one meters (859 feet) to go."

"I don't like this quietness," Krestell growled. "The ivans are slime-balls dipped in shit, but they're not cowards."

"They're not foolhardy either," Camellion retorted. "They're not going to make any stupid charges and let us burn them down. Their Achilles heel is that they don't have any heavy stuff. As I said earlier, this base was never intended to be defended."

"If you ask me—and you're not—we're going to have to have Ph.D.s in weak heels to secure this base. It's the weapons that they might have on the sub that worry me."

The Death Merchant, who knew that The Bomber's pessimistic talk was all cackle but no eggs, all an act, looked around the thick edge of the shield, blinked and saw what he knew he had to see sooner or later. One hundred and fifty feet ahead (45 meters) was a metal barrier of some kind. Staring through the HOT goggle, Camellion got the impression that the barrier, stretched across the sixty-foot width of the cave, was made of sheet steel braced with wooden crates. Toward the center of the makeshift wall several men were hunched over a light machine gun. Two other Soviet slime-balls were staring through night-sight devices in the direction of the approaching column.

156

Either they saw me or they didn't! If we can get closer, we can cremate them with the flame throwers!

The four Soviet *Morskaia Pekhota* had not spotted the Death Merchant. They had, however, seen Captain Webb peering around the right edge of the right side shield. Realizing that the *Amerikanski* could not see in the dark, the Soviet Marines guessed he was wearing some kind of night-sight device and had seen them, which Webb had. At once the Russians opened fire, the snarling of the LMG breaking the uncanny silence.

Zing! Zing! Zing! Zing! Zing! And ripping and tearing sounds, muffled ricocheting whangs, as 7.62mm projectiles tore through the laminated sheets and were stopped by the steel in the center of the shields.

"Lob several grenades over the top of the shields," Camellion yelled at the Marines. "Make damn sure you don't hit the ceiling near us."

Private Thrug and Prive Lawrence Minton, the second Marine with a grenade launcher, were cool, well trained, and very fast. With precise movements, they first tossed up small light sticks to get the height of the ceiling, then cut loose with the two CGL-4 grenade launchers. Two 40mm grenades whooshed from the launchers, shot at an angle toward the jagged ceiling and exploded with loud, eardrum-stinging roars a hundred feet ahead.

The light machine gun stopped firing. The Death Merchant knew why: due to the nature of those silly creatures called human beings, the explosion of the grenades had forced the machine gunners into automatic reflex lag time.

"Now," snapped the Death Merchant. "Two grenades each around the side, four feet from the ground, straight in."

Thrug and Minton responded like well-oiled robots.

Two more slight whooshes and two more grenades were on their way, on a straight course toward the barrier harboring the Soviet Marines. Instant flashes of fire and the grenades roared off by the time that Minton and Thrug were dropping two more grenades into their launchers.

The previous two grenades had exploded on target slightly to the left and right of the machine gunners, the detonations sending sheets of steel upward and sideways and showering the Russians with shrapnel. The man feeding the belt into the machine gun let out a high-pitched scream as chunks of shrapnel stabbed into his left side. The

157

machine gunner yelped and fell backward when part of a ripped sheet of steel smashed him flat in the face and broke his nose and shattered his teeth. Oddly enough, Gleb Passeyro, one of the men with a night-vision instrument, was struck by only one chunk of metal, a piece of shrapnel that lodged in his thick black beret, barely stinging his skull. The other Soviet marine with a night-sight device was stabbed in the right side, right shoulder, and right cheek and temple. Howling in pain, he dropped the N-S device, fell to his knees and, muttering curses, clawed at himself.

He didn't mumble for long. The next two 40mm grenades exploded closer toward the center of the barrier. One explosion tore mutter-mouth's head from his shoulders and sent it rolling west like a bloody bowling ball. Shrapnel erased the wide face of Gleb Passeyro and changed it in a blink of an eye into shreds of bloody meat hanging over the front of a skull that had been fractured in three different places.

The Slav who had been feeding the machine gun lost the left side of his head from shrapnel. The left side of his neck, torn open, gushed blood, great spurts of red that ran down his front and back and sprayed out over the shattered wreckage of the barrier.

Only the Soviet slob who had triggered the Kalashnikov (RPK) light machine gun escaped shrapnel, which *pinged*! *pinged*! *pinged*! against the metal sheet on top of him. A different fate was in store for the pig farmer from Mother Russia. A large piece of metal torn from one of the sheets came down edgeways on his left leg, slicing downward like a warped blade of a guillotine. The sharp edge slicked through black uniform cloth, cut through flesh and neatly severed the femoral artery, the "blade" stopping only when it struck the long femur bone in the upper leg. *OHhhhhhhhhhh!* Letting out a cry, he fell back and started to bleed to death.

With the smell of burnt TNT in their nostrils—a pleasurable odor to the Death Merchant—Camellion and Webb looked around the edges of the shield. For all practical purposes the barrier was gone. Only one pig farmer was moving, the joker trying to crawl out from under a piece of sheet metal.

"Dosvidanya, trash. You won't be remembered in the cemetery of nameless men!" Camellion said and drew the

right Backpacker Auto Mag from its specially designed holster, switched off the safety, raised the stainless steel weapon and snapped off a round. The big flatnosed .44 Magnum projectile shot through the Mag-Na-Ported barrel, zipped through the thin sheet of steel and blew a hole in the Russian the size of a half-dollar. The pig farmer jerked once, kicked twice, then lay still.

"This is one fine crock!" complained Ralph Muldane, who was standing next to Barney Krestell. "It will take us an hour to clear a space for the shields."

"A minor inconvenience," said Webb. "The loss of those men won't boost the morale of the enemy either."

Camellion, reholstering his AMP, remarked, "Cheer up, Ralph, me boy! It's like my pappy used to say, 'Son, you gotta chop the cotton before you go to town.' We'll get to the end of the tunnel and find the Ruskies because we have to."

The Bomber gave a mirthless chuckle. "Hell yes we will. We're miracles of creation, we are! Hell, we're fighting for God and Country. Ask any stinking Congressman."

"Why ask windbags anything?" Camellion said. "Let's ask Gammill how he and his group are doing." He pulled the Tadiran PRC-601 from its case, switched it on, pressed the TALK button, and held the device close to his mouth.

"Olin, come in. Come in, Olin. Over."

The Death Merchant did not make contact until the sixth attempt.

"Gammill here—over."

"They were waiting for us. A barrier. Four of the trash with an RPK light. They lost. Give me a report of your condition."

"I can't hear you. Plea—" Gammill's voice, coming in very weak, faded out entirely.

Due to the interference of the rock between the two caverns, it took Camellion twelve minutes to tell Gammill what had happened, that it would "take every bit of an hour for us to clear the rubble," and to learn that Gammill's group had not encountered any difficulty. Furthermore, the ONI officer and his group had made better time than Camellion and his party. Gammill's force had covered 293 meters or 964 feet, and had only 636 more feet (193 meters) to go.

"We can even see dim light ahead," Gammill reported. "Stay where you are and give us time to catch up.

We'll—" The Death Merchant's voice was cut off by pure static—*I might as well be under a bridge with a 1955 car radio!*

"The Soviets in the base are jamming us," he said sorely, a vindictive flame flaring in his cobalt blue eyes.

Ralph Muldane lit a cigarette, then sighed. "The trouble with what we are doing is similar to an alcoholic's having to stay sober—he's aware of every moment and always knows how he really feels. It's the same with us."

Captain Webb turned to Camellion, his black face shining eerily in the glow of the light stick dangling from his belt. "How good a man is Gammill?"

"Exactly what is he?" asked Lieutenant Flint, speaking without thinking. "I mean, what organization does he belong to?"

"He's an agent in the nefarious Society of Necrology," Camellion replied with pseudoseriousness.

No one smiled but Barney Krestell, who reminded himself to look up the word in the dictionary, provided he lived to get to a dictionary.

Lieutenant Flint felt embarrassed but managed to maintain a sober expression.

"Lieutenant, he's telling you to mind your own business," Webb said in a monotonous tone, all the while looking at the Death Merchant and waiting for his answer.

"Gammill's a pro in his field," Camellion said. "He knows we're being jammed in communications. He'll wait an hour for us to remove the rubble and another twenty to thirty minutes for us to catch up, to make up the hundred-and-five-foot difference."

"Olin's the cautious type," Barney Krestell said. "He'll wait anyhow an hour and a half."

"Let's move," said the Death Merchant.

Like a lighted snake with a stiff spine, the column moved ahead, in a short time coming to the grenade-demolished barrier and the dead Soviet marines. With Camellion and Webb acting as lookouts, which meant looking down the length of the tunnel through the HOT goggles, seven of the men began clearing a path through the rubble, one of them almost vomiting as he kicked the Soviet marine's head to one side. It was the eyes that startled the UDT man. The head had been lying in a pool of blood, resting on its back, and both eyes had been wide open.

160

Clearing the path took only thirty-six minutes.

"We should stay here and wait," Captain Webb suggested, "or—unless we've guessed incorrectly about Gammill—we'll be out in front of him."

Camellion smiled. "My way or a tactical way, right?"

"You're the one who said it."

"We'll wait fifty-four minutes, then make the final stretch," said Camellion.

Private Gibbreth was the first to hear the very faint thuggg-thuggg-thuggg that was interwoven with a louder but smoother and faster sound. The sounds were familiar to the Death Merchant—air compressors and an electric generator. A further indication that the force of sixty was getting close to the Soviet base was the greenish-tinged glow the force spotted when it was at the 985-foot (300 meters) mark.

Camellion and his men pushed ahead as fast as was possible under the conditions that prevailed; yet they didn't relax their vigilance. To the contrary, every man became more alert, more aware, the tension increasing. At the edge of each man's mind was the same unanswered question, the same ice pick chopping worry—had the Russians mined any part of the 615 feet (187 meters)?

At 300 feet from the greenish sheen was pure light, the kind of radiance that pours out from batteries of sodium vapor lights.

At 240 feet the force heard a series of half a dozen muffled explosions, far ahead to the west. Camellion's column halted.

"Whatever it was, it wasn't directed at us," Ralph Muldane said and lit a *Vantage* cigarette.

"It was the Soviet submarine," Camellion said, noticing that Barney Krestell was pulling what resembled a larger portable radio from a shoulder bag.

"A nuclear sub means radiation," Webb said, his voice as miserable as his expression. He pulled the lollipop from his mouth and tossed it to the ground. "The hell with this torture." He looked from face to face, at the men in his vicinity. "Any of you have a spare pack of ciagarettes?"

As Sterling Whitney handed Webb a pack of *Kent III 100s*, the Death Merchant and the other men watched The Bomber put the explosives detector into operation. A Leigh Marsland Model S201, the device was designed to sense vapors from a broad range of civil and military-manufactured explosives. The L.M. M-S201 was powered by rechargeable nickel-cadmium batteries and the ten-kilogram main unit could easily be carried by hand or on a backpack.

The light ahead provided a mild twilight, and Krestell didn't need a night-sight goggle to see ahead. Standing by the side of one shield, he moved the foot-long probe up and down, then from side to side. Camellion watched the needle on the large dial. The needle did not move.

Home! The Death Merchant and his force covered the remainder of the distance, and when the shields came to a halt, they were forty feet from the end of the cavern-tunnel. To have moved closer would have enabled the Russians in the base to fire down on the force. Except for Richard Camellion—*this cave is small compared to the one in Asia*[1]—the other men at the head of the column were awed by the size of the area beyond the forty-foot mark, although they could see only a portion of it. If the cavern-tunnel was huge, the "hollow" that held the Soviet base was gigantic. Just beyond the forty-foot mark, the cavern-tunnel extrance merged with the opening of the hollow. Beyond was a 100-foot (30.5 meters) gradual decline. At the end of the slope was the south side of the four-story complex, a huge chunk of prefabricated building a hundred feet long and seventy-five feet wide. It reminded some of the men of a giant brown candy bar without the wrapping. The rock ceiling was sixty feet above the flat-roofed building complex.

The strange silence was unnerving. There was only the thuggg-thuggg-thuggg of the three air compressors and the whirrrring of the two electric generators.

Lieutenant Flint's square jaw quivered slightly from tension.

"This is too fucking easy," he commented nervously, pushing back his helmet. "Only that one light machine gun and no explosives. It doesn't make sense."

"Lieutenant, stop that dirty language," Webb said irritably. "It isn't necessary." Although he didn't say so, Captain Webb agreed with Flint. To the Death Merchant, Webb wore an expression like a man who is sick on his day off.

1. See Death Merchant #30, *The Shambhala Strike.*

"Oh, but it does add up," remarked Camellion. "Winning half of any battle with the Russians is being able to predict what they'll do next. This cave wasn't mined because the pig farmers didn't have the explosives. And if they have anymore RPKs, you can bet your last cigarette they're pointed at the end of this tunnel."

Sweat dripping from his face, Muldane reached for a handkerchief.

"They didn't seem to lack explosives when they blew up the sub," he said. "But I suppose all Soviet subs carry charges?"

Captain Webb took the cigarette out of his mouth and looked calmly at the Death Merchant. "Cosgrove, we're about to stick our head into the lion's mouth. There's—"

"Into the mouth of the Bear," Camellion said, pushing out his lips.

"There's only one way to get across that area without all of us getting cut down. We lob forty millimeter stuff, CN, smoke, and make a straight-in charge."

"You'll not get an argument from me," Camellion said jovially, thinking that even with smoke cover many men would have to die. They'd still be lucky. Some men die only once. Others have to die over and over to pay for past mistakes. . . .

"What about Gammill and his group?" Krestell asked, tightening the Firemaster ammo carrier harnessed over his chest and shoulders. "We should at least try to make contact with him."

"I did try, about five minutes ago," Camellion said. "We're still being jammed. We must assume—"

BLAAAMMMMMMMMM - BLAAAMMMMMMMM - BLAAAMMMMMMMM - BLAAMMMMMMMM - BLAAA- MMMMMM!

A satisfied smile skidded across Camellion's mouth. "The pig farmers aren't throwing those grenades at themselves. It would seem that Olin's already attacking."

"We're next in line," Krestell said, his eyes hard. "That's a cheerful thought, isn't it? We'd better get our asses in gear."

"Webb, pass the word down the line and we'll do it," Camellion said. *And find out whom the Cosmic Lord of Death chooses. . . .*

Privates Carey Thrug and Lawrence Minton first lobbed ten 40mm grenades through the entrance, a few of which fell short of the south side of the building only a mere 42 meters (140 feet) away. The other eight grenades slammed into the south side of the first story, exploded with a crashing sound and demolished large sections of the triple walls made of wood and aluminum paneling.

Following the barrage of grenades, Minton and Thrug used tear gas grenades that could be shot from a CGL-4 grenade launcher—twenty of them, scattering them out. Yet the Russians didn't fire a shot. Even an idiot would have known why. There were two cavern openings. Gammill and his men had already lobbed 40mm grenades, gas and smoke through the opening of the cave they were in. The Russians withheld their fire because they assumed that the attack would be coordinated as closely as possible and would come after Camellion and his people had tossed in their last smoke grenade.

The Russians opened fire with an RPK light machine gun and AKM assault rifles as the last Alsatex smoke grenade hit the wall of the second floor, bounced off, hit the ground and began hissing thick red smoke that, bathed in the greenish tint of the vapor lights and combined with the almost invisible lachrymatory cloud of CN gas, took on a terrifying life all its own.

The Death Merchant and his group charged forward, each man wearing a K. Matter GmbH gas mask (an amplifier was in every mask, to permit the wearer to communicate without loss of speech volume or distortion). With Camellion out in front, the group raced through the opening and began zigzagging down the slope, 7.62mm slugs cutting the air all around them.

Olin Gammill and his men charged through the mouth of the other cavern entrance.

The Day of Judgment had arrived for the Soviets on Tukoatu. . . .

CHAPTER FOURTEEN

Colonel Anton Zimovniki and the rest of the Russians found themselves in the position of men too poor to paint, yet too proud to whitewash. All they and the KGB Sluzhba guards could do was fight and die. All the KGB guards were armed with automatic rifles and sidearms; they were well trained and would give a good account of themselves. "Household" help and the scientists and technicians who had tracked the American satellite were all armed and, with the Sluzhba guards were placed strategically on all four levels. One group was the exception: Dr. Yuri Mkrtchyan, Doctor Anatoly Gavvda and the scientists and technicians working in the Bio-Memory Scanner laboratory on the bottom level, or the first story.

Zimovniki and his people had not had the time to cut through the thick steel lab door with an electric cutting torch. Explosives were not feasible. The blast would have blown up a quarter of the complex even if they had had explosives and they didn't. The charges aboard the *Stalingrad* were already in place.

Standing by a window on the south side of the third level, Zimovniki spoke extra loud so that he could be heard through his gas mask. "The Americans will have to enter from the lower level, and we know they have forty-millimeter grenades they can throw from launchers."

Major Amosov, a PPS submachine gun in his hands, was way ahead of his superior. "The safest position for us is in the northwest corner of the fourth floor." His voice, too, was muffled through the gas mask he wore. But the masks were absolutely necessary. Already the air was thick with smoke and tear gas.

Commander Josef Dubokinsko swallowed, his prominent Adam's apple bobbing up and down. "Comrade Colonel, there must be some solution to our predicament? We can't just stand here and do nothing!"

165

"I'm not your 'comrade,' you idiot." In spite of the insult, Zimovniki spoke resignedly. "The only thing we can do is die like men and take as many of the Americans with us as possible."

"Twenty of my Naval Infantry and I will go with you," Anton Tikhvin said harshly. The entire facepiece of the Russian gas mask was a single lens, and the other men could see that Tikhvin's features, molded by revenge, were frozen in determination. The commander of the *Morskaia Pekhota* unit was thinking of the four men he had lost in the cavern.

The sound of an RPK and AKM assault rifles exploded in the air.

The *Amerikanskis* were attacking.

"Let's get to the fourth level," Major Valery said urgently.

During the charge that would last only a few minutes, there could be no guarantees as to who would live and who would die. Whether a man was struck by a bullet and wounded and would survive, or was hit by a slug and killed on the spot, would be decided by the Cosmic Lord of Death.

With red smoke (tinged green in places) rolling around them, the Death Merchant and his force of 124 raced for the south side of the complex building. Keeping as low a profile as possible, they ducked and dodged and weaved, all the time knowing that their divergent motions would not save them from a projectile. The Russians were firing indiscriminately into the boiling smoke, raking the area from side to side with streams of fire. Psychologically, however, racing in at a crooked angle gave the Americans confidence, making them feel they could duck a slug.

At one time or another, almost every man felt a Russian-manufactured bullet graze his fatigues or clip a piece of equipment. A spitzer-shaped projectile cut through Captain Webb's right hip holster and clanged loudly against the top part of the slide of his nine-millimeter Browning autopistol. Two more projectiles tugged at his left sleeve.

Other U.S. Marines and U.S. Navy UDT men weren't so fortunate. They caught slugs in vital parts of the body and some were killed instantly; others, falling into unconsciousness, would take longer to die. The unluckiest of all were

166

those few men who were hit, fell, and remained conscious while they died.

Lieutenant Vernon Flint was one of the men whose time had come. A bullet caught him in the right shoulder and knocked him round so that, for only a shave of a second, he was turned toward the east instead of facing the south. During that microsecond another high velocity AKM projectile bored through his left side just below the ribs, the projectile tearing through his pancreas, ripping through a part of his liver and going out his right side. His mouth pulled tight in an obstinate grimace, Flint began to feel detached from his own body. *Ridiculous!* he thought. And he didn't feel any pain, only an intense throbbing from the waist down—and where were his legs? He knew that the body *he* inhabited was falling, but found it difficult to accept that he was witnessing his own demise. A roaring filled his ears. The cries and the chattering of weapons began to fade and a wall of total blackness began rushing toward him. His last thought was of necrology and he wondered what it was. . . .

Slam! The bullet struck the front of Ralph Muldane's ballistic helmet so suddenly that his first awareness of it was that he was falling backward from the impact. Yet he was still alive! It was then that he remembered that the ballistic helmet was made to withstand the grand slam of a .357 mag slug fired from a range of three meters (ten feet).

The helmet saved my life! Thank you, God! Muldane scrambled to his feet and raced on, anxious to meet the enemy, anxious to kill the Soviet sonuvabitches face to face.

At the same time that the Death Merchant saw that his force and Olin Gammill's had merged, he felt a sharp burning sting on his left side, along the rib cage, and knew that a bullet had cut through his fatigues and had barely opened the skin for a length of several inches.

CLANNNGGGGGGggg! Another projectile struck the tip of the inside end of the curved shoulder piece of the single-frame stock of the T20 submachine gun and jerked his arm outward. But he did not drop the weapon. Nor did he hate the Russians ahead, any more than an exterminator "hates" the cockroaches he exterminates.

Abruptly the run was over, and the Death Merchant, Krestell, Muldane, Gammill, Kirkland, and the rest of the men found that they were through the thickest part of the smoke and CN gas and only ten feet from the south side of the complex building. There was an instant of seeing hate-filled but frightened faces at windows and at doors, of glimpsing men—and women too—pointing hand guns or AKMs.

Another blink of a moment and scores of Colt CAR-15 submachine guns were roaring and raking open windows and doorways with hundreds of 5.56mm projectiles. Forty-six citizens of the Soviet Union were snuffed in a fifth of a minute. Other pig farmers lost their nerve and won the rubber-backbone award for cowardice. Then again, one could not blame the men and women who were base maintenance people or technicians. They were not supposed to be soldiers. The Soviet "marines" had retreated for tactical reasons, because the Colt CAR-15 machine gun fire had been too intense. They would live to kill more Americans on the upper floors.

It was an irony of Fate that while the steel door of the laboratory had prevented Colonel Zimovniki and his KGB agents from reaching Dr. Mkrtchyan and the other Bio-Memory Scanner scientists, it had not stopped four 40mm grenades from ripping large holes in the south side wall of the lab. Mistrusting the KGB, Dr. Mkrtchyan had brought arms with him from the Soviet Union, and now he and his people in the lab used them in an attempt to repel the American invaders. Two U.S. Marines stormed through one of the holes and were promptly cut to pieces with 7.62mm PPS machine gun slugs.

Other Marines tossed in fragmentation grenades that exploded, wrecked a lot of equipment and killed Doctor Ludvik Svoboda, the Czech cytologist. Then Corporal Paul Gibbreth stuck the nozzle of his flame thrower around one edge of a hole in the wall and pulled the trigger—WWWHHHHOOOOSSSSSSSHHHHHHHHHHHH. A tongue of red-orange fire, bordered in rolling hoops of black, jumped from the nozzle and engulfed Doctor Todor Zhikov, the Bulgarian geneticist, Doctor Paul Janos Ceausescu, the Romanian genetic engineer, and six laboratory helpers. All eight uttered short high-pitched screams before the inhaled fire ate out their lungs. Clothes and hair ignited instantly. Flesh turned red, then brown, then black, then shriveled under the intense fire.

Gibbreth swung the nozzle back and forth. Another WHHHHHOOSSSHHHHH and the river of red fire ran across the room, baked Doctor Sonya Zupik, the Soviet electro-biologist, to a crisp, ignited four women lab technicians and flowed over part of the Bio-Memory Scanner machine, a large contraption that resembled something from a Grade B science-fiction movie. Parts of it resembled Van de Graaff generators. There were enormous coils and circuit breakers, and a long control panel filled with dials, knobs, switches, and rows of multicolored lights. On a platform was a large metal chair that—complete with rounded headpiece but minus the ankle electrodes—looked like an American electric chair. This was the chair in which the test subjects were strapped, the chair in which hundreds of victims had been driven mad.

The thought of surrender never crossed Doctor Mkrtchyan's mind. *Nyet!* Better to be dead than a prisoner of the Americans! He shouted through his gas mask for the rest of the people in the lab to get behind the Bio-Memory Scanner machine, finishing with screaming, *"Davai bistre! Davai bistre!"* ("hurry up, hurry up").

Doctor Anatoly Gavvda, the Soviet psychiatrist, had a backbone made of half-frozen jello. He and the nine lab technicians left alive would have surrendered to Satan himself in order to live . . . if Dr. Mkrtchyan had not been present and if they had had the opportunity. But American-made 5.56mm projectiles were flying too fast. There were a hundred loud Zinnnnngggsssss and the Bio-Memory Scanner machine was filled with holes and turned to junk, broken circuits and slug-sliced cables arcing blue electricity.

U.S. Marines tore around both ends of the long, wrecked machine, their Colt CARS roaring, the volume of the firing tremendous. Doctor Zimovniki's body dissolved into a shower of torn smock particles, flesh, chips of bone and a wide spray of blood—torn apart by a cloud of CAR projectiles. Dr. Gavvda died the same way—blown apart by full-metal-jacketed 5.56mm projectiles.

Irena Posnoganavitch, her face black with smoke, tears flowing down her face from CN gas, for she did not have a gas mask, tried to throw up her arms and scream "SURRENDER" in English. A bullet zipped through her mouth and blew out the back of her head before she could even begin to form the word. The other eight technicians died as quickly. Riddled they fell. Bloody they died.

Sergeant Wild Bill Hurt, a tough-faced career man, who

weighed 231 pounds and not a gram of it fat, looked down for a moment at the bloody bodies. Near the shot-shattered head of Dr. Gavvda, Wild Bill saw the convoluted windings of part of the scientist's brain. Morbidly fascinated, he stared at the various folds, some pink, others grayish-blue. The hell with it.

"Let's go, men," Wild Bill shouted. "Gibbreth, get that flamer ready."

The muzzle of the Death Merchant's T20 grease gun flashed spurts of fire, the weapon roaring, the stream of 185-grain, Jacketed Hollow Point .45 slugs stabbing all over the four Russians in black berets leaning out from the sides of the doorway. The four *Morskaia Pekhota* fell all over the place in their hurry to hit the ground—not that it made any difference to them. They were already dead.

The Death Merchant smiled—*they remind me of contortionists dying in their own arms!*

Coming in to the left of Camellion, his legs pumping like runaway pistons, Barney Krestell triggered off a long burst of .45s at the windows of the first floor. To the left of The Bomber, Simon Kirkland, Ralph Muldane, ten Marines, and four UDT men raked the windows of the second, third, and fourth levels with streams of high-velocity swaged slugs, their efforts rewarded with cries and screams and the smashing of furniture.

Fifty feet to the right of the Death Merchant, Olin Gammill and more U.S. Marines and UDT fighters were systematically demolishing the other south side front of the building. While most of the men sprayed the windows and several doors with machine gun bullets, Jerry Asperch and Sonny Lapata, the two men who had used CGL-4 grenade launchers with Gammill's group in the cavern-tunnel, began zooming 40mm grenades through the windows of the second, third, and fourth levels, the violent explosions ripping apart portions of the mess hall, storage rooms, sick bay, and the relaxation area on the south and southeast. Twenty Russians were burned within a few minutes. Whole sections of the body-and-debris-littered floors began to groan and sag as TNT explosions turned braces and small metal beams into splinters and twisted, useless metal.

There were more grenade explosions and the blurrrr-blurrrrr-blurrr-blurrrrrr of Colt CARS from the far east and the northeast corner of the quivering, smoking building. Captain Webb, twenty-three U.S. Marines and ten

UDTs were hosing down the windows with streams of sub-machine gun slugs and Carey Thrug and Lawrence "Nickie" Minton were lobbing in 40mm grenades. Half of the officers' quarters was blown into bits of metal, wood, and ripped bedding. The kitchen was changed into hot twisted metal. Propane gas tanks exploded and killed five Russian women and three Russian men, two of the bodies and a cloud of metal flying outward, one piece with such momentum that it impaled a Marine in his chest. He fell to his back with part of what had been a table leg protruding from his torso.

Captain Webb and his group began to close in, their attack coordinated with the attacks of Olin Gammill and the UDTs and Marines with him. Toward the southwest, the Death Merchant, Krestell, and the others charged through two doors and a nine-foot hole created by two 40mm grenades.

With Kirkland and Krestell, Camellion ducked down behind several low steel locking cabinet tables and three overturned heavy-duty lateral file cases. The Death Merchant had already used three magazines of .45 cartridges in the T20 sub-gun, and he had no intention of reloading the fourth time. Not only was the weapon not cost-effective, but it was downright unhandy in close-in combat. What was really needed inside the building was automatic shotguns. But no! None were available in Honolulu. Washington was on another "let's-all-save-money" binge as the dear, dumb liberals (who would soon be dear, dumb, and dead liberals) pretended that a world of mega-death didn't exist.

Camellion strapped the T20 over his back, pulled the two Backpacker Auto Mags from their special holsters and glanced at the horse-faced Krestell, then at Kirkland, who looked as if he had black ammo pouches under his eyes. Both men reloaded their T20s, but used the straps to sling the machine guns crossways over their backs. Their common sense surprised the Death Merchant, who liked both men in spite of their being career "Government Employees," as they called themselves. For professional Company Case Officers, the two exhibited excellent know-how in kill-and-survive tactics. Barney Krestell's hands dipped to his belt holsters and he pulled two Smith & Wesson nine-millimeter M-59 auto-pistols from the oiled leather. Simon Kirkland filled his hands with two nine-millimeter Hi-Power Browning auto-loaders.

171

Ralph Muldane and several Marines furnished cover fire, and Camellion, Krestell, and Kirkland leaped up and, jumping over litter and debris, darted and dodged their way toward a door on the north side of the room. Simultaneously, several Marines tossed frag grenades through a doorway in the east wall and Muldane and other fighters stitched the ceiling with slugs. The projectiles cut right through the aluminum and plywood ceiling, but all the lead was wasted. The bullets hit only dead bodies. The ivans who had been there alive had fled to the third and fourth levels.

Crouched against the wall to the left of the north side door, the Death Merchant suspected that Russians were concealed and waiting in the room beyond. Camellion signaled Krestell, who was on the opposite side of the doorway, and Barney pulled the pin from a fragmentation grenade and flipped the grenade around the edge of the doorway, tossing the small bomb into the next room. In five seconds the 56.7 grams (two ounces) of TNT exploded, the shrapnel pinging all over the room. The smoke was still so thick it could be cut with an ax when Camellion charged low into the room, threw himself to the left and, seeing forms rearing up from overturned desks to his right, began firing. As Krestell tore into the smoky room—Kirkland right behind him—Camellion's first .44 Magnum slug struck Serge Mulkelsky in the tip of his nose and performed the worst plastic surgery in history. The big flatnosed projectile erased Mulkelsky's face and exploded his skull and brain, part of the red, sticky mess—bits of flesh, blown-apart gray matter, and bloody bone fragments—splattering over Mikhail Agayanta and Robert Bannikov, the two *Morskaia Pekhota* closest to the decapitated Mulkelsky. With three other *Mokskaia Pekhota*, Agayanta and Bannikov were trying to get into action with stubby-barrelled Koski-PPdP submachine guns. Agayanta and Bannikov didn't have any more luck than Mulkelsky. Camellion, Krestell, and Kirkland saw the five Russian marines swing up the muzzles of their Koski-PPdPs and threw themselves downward, firing as they dropped to the floor. The Death Merchant's twin AMPs roared and the big .44 Magnum projectiles bored into Bannikov and Agayanta just as the former pulled the trigger of the Koski and Vladimir Groik and Oleg Tremmel swung their submachine guns toward Krestell and Kirkland. Georgi Stoubui, the fifth Russian marine, at-

172

tempted to line up the Death Merchant with an APS Stechkin machine pistol, to the lower butt of which was attached a wooden shoulder stock.

Bannikov's stream of 9mm semi-spitzer shaped slugs passed thirty-eight millimeters over Camellion's right shoulder. The sixteenth bullet tugged at the collar of his fatigues but kept going on its way. The seventeenth slug cut halfway through the leather strap over his right shoulder, the sling holding the T20 across his back.

Stobui triggered off a short burst of 9mm projectiles with his Stechkin M.P., but he had fired too quickly and his instincts were off. The copper-sheathed slugs burned smoky air over the Death Merchant's head and narrowly missed the left shoulder of Krestell who, with Kirkland, fired at the same time that Camellion's Auto Mags roared again, the two .44 Magnum projectiles smashing into Mikhail Agayanta and Robert Bannikov and lifting them off their feet.

Kirkland's two Hi-Power Brownings roared in unison with Barney Krestell's two Smith & Wesson auto-loaders. Georgi Stobui cried out when a 9mm Browning bullet poked him in the chest and another stabbed him in the middle of the stomach. Two of Krestell's S&W 9mm bullets caught Oleg Tremmel in the chest, dead center in the sternum, killing him instantly by turning his heart to bloody mush. A third S&W 9mm ripped into Vladimir Groik's throat while a 9mm from one of Kirkland's Brownings tore into Groik's upper chest—both slugs killing him twice over.

The Death Merchant and Krestell and Kirkland were getting up off the floor when Ralph Muldane, followed by U.S. Marines, rushed into the room, Muldane's Indianlike face bathed in sweat behind the full face lens of his gas mask.

"Listen, I just made radio contact with Webb and Gammill," he said happily to the Death Merchant and the two "government employees." "They've shot the bejesus out of the east end and a lot of the building on the north side, up toward the east."

"What are the positions of Webb and Gammill now?" Camellion shoved a full magazine into one of the Auto Mags.

"They've linked up with Sergeant Hurt and are waiting at about the center of the third floor. Webb said there aren't any ivans in sight. He said that as best as he can figure out, the Russians still alive must be holed up toward the west end of the fourth floor."

The Death Merchant's eyes narrowed. All sound of firing had stopped.

"They could be on the roof," Kirkland offered.

"Why the west end?" asked Krestell.

Muldane laughed and glanced upward. "Are you kidding? Why, you can't tiptoe on the thin floors above without the people below hearing you."

"We'll go to the second floor," Camellion said. "We'll head east then go up to the third floor." He pulled the Tadiran PRC-601 from the case on his belt. "I'll call Webb. We're lucky that one of the grenades blew hell out of the jamming equipment. . . ."

Only the sounds of the air compressors and the generators filtered in through the broken windows on the fourth level. With the Death Merchant were nineteen men. Twenty-seven Marines and four UDT men had been killed. Seventy-four of the force were spread out on the first, second, and third levels—spread out, watching the outside through windows, waiting. . . .

Camellion's reasons for advancing on the fourth floor with only nineteen men were purely tactical. To have the entire force on one level was not practical. Bunched up, the men would be easy targets. And would the floor of the fourth level support the weight of ninety-four men? The building, as large as it was, had not been built to withstand the bombardment of 40mm grenades. The east wall had been eighty-five percent demolished by explosions. A portion of the north wall, toward the east, had been blown into kindling and twisted aluminum. Inside the building, floors and walls tilted, doorframes hung off center.

The Death Merchant looked cautiously toward the west, staring down the corridor, his thoughts revolving around what Sergeant Hurt and his men had found. *A cell full of people!* Hurt had said. *There must be sixty or seventy men and women, all as naked as jaybirds. But their minds are gone. They didn't even know we were there!*

The corridor was empty. At the end of the corridor was a wide doorway, the double doors closed. *And no doubt locked.* Camellion pulled back from the edge of the doorway.

"Well?" demanded Captain Webb. Behind him was Olin

Gammill and the other members of the small group, some of them watching the doors and windows of the sleep room they occupied.

"Twenty-two meters to the west is a double door," Camellion said. "Unless all the pig farmers are dead, they must be in that room behind the double doors. It wouldn't make sense for them to be scattered out in the smaller rooms on either side of the hallway. We could pop them off too easily."

"Hold on! How do we know they're not on the roof?" asked Olin Gammill, wiping sweat from his face with a Marine issue handkerchief. By now, almost eighty minutes after the first shot had been fired, the smoke and the CN gas had drifted up toward the rock ceiling of the giant cavern and Camellion and the men had removed their gas masks for the sake of convenience and comfort.

Captain Webb clicked his tongue impatiently. "Negative! The ivans wouldn't be stupid enough to be on the roof," he said to Gammill. "If they stood up, our boys could smoke them. The Russians have no way of knowing if we have men spread out far enough from the building to see what's on the roof." Webb's eyes jumped to Camellion. "What's your opinion, Cosgrove?"

"It makes sense," Camellion agreed. "The KGB is never downright stupid, and they would have to have a bad case of the galloping sillies to be on the roof."

Webb finished lighting a *Kent III*. "OK. We'll blow the doors with forty-millimeter stuff, slam in four or five more grenades, then go in. Unless you have a better plan, Cosgrove?"

"Well, the infantry always follows the infantry," Camellion said. "Get one—no! Get two of the launchers up here."

The Death Merchant was not immune to mistakes and he had made one now by underestimating the determination of Colonel Anton Zimovniki. The KGB security expert, deducing that the Americans would use grenades, had no intention of letting the enemy slaughter him and the thirty men with him. He would die and his men would die—but not without a fight! And certainly not without Americans dying.

Zimovniki and his men had removed several panels from the ceiling of the Officers' Briefing Room at the end of the hall, and had begun climbing onto the flat roof as the

Death Merchant and his men approached the west end, Zimovniki and his gunmen barely slithering along on their bellies, inch by inch. Zimovniki's intention was to reach the east end of the building where the roof was partially destroyed. Here, he and his KGB men would be able to leap down to the fourth-level floor and come in behind the Americans. It was risky and there was only a slim chance that the plan would succeed. But if they remained in the briefing room, they wouldn't have any chance at all.

"They have not used a single grenade against the west side," Zimovniki had told his men. "On that basis, it's reasonable to suppose they assume we are at this end of the building."

But because Zimovniki and his men had to crawl very, very slowly in order to avoid making the least sound, they were only sixty feet (18.3 meters) east of the double doors of the Officers' Briefing Room when Lawrence Minton and Sonny Lapata began loading the CGL-4 grenade launchers and Camellion and the rest of the men were running forward to position themselves in rooms closer to the double doors.

The first two grenades blew the doors and their frame into a million splinters and blew a six-foot-wide hole in the wall to the left of where the doors had been. The wider the entrance, the faster the Death Merchant and his men could charge in.

The next two grenades exploded with tremendous bangs and further widened the rent in the wall—and further weakened the ceiling, which in this case was the roof. The roof started to bulge downward along the section where the double doors had been as Minton and Lapata fired off two more 40mm grenades, both of which shot through the smoking, jagged hole. As Fate would have it, one grenade struck one of the main supporting I-beams in the center of the large briefing room, the explosion tearing the top section of the I-beam from the ceiling, which had been none too solid to begin with. Now that it was further weakened and had to support the weight of thirty-one men, the ceiling-roof could not withstand the strain. Bolts began bending. Braces and supports began cracking. With a loud series of snappings, crackles, and pops, an 80×40-foot section of the roof fell inward.

The Death Merchant and his men were no less surprised than Colonel Anton Zimovniki and his people. Camellion and company could not prevent the ceiling from falling in. Zimovniki and his KGB agents could not prevent the roof on which they lay from crashing downward.

Amid the tearing of aluminum sheeting, the snapping of beams, and the cracking of plywood paneling, Colonel Zimovniki and his men collided vertically with Richard Camellion and his group.

Pandemonium became King of the Mountain. Struck by pieces of the roof and falling KGB men, some of Camellion's men had fractured or broken bones, with some of Zimovniki's agents sustaining similar injuries.

In the long hallway and in four of the rooms, dazed, cursing men—both Russians and Americans, only now realizing what had happened—struggled to their feet and reached for weapons, any kind of weapon.

A born survivor, the Death Merchant managed to pull both Auto Mag pistols from their holsters as he struggled to his feet and, with his shoulder and upper back, pushed from his body a dazed KGB agent lying on a sheet of twisted aluminum. The Russian went down in a pile of arms and legs and stopped trying to get up after Camellion turned and blew open his chest with a .44 Magnum bullet. At such close range the projectile blew a hole the size of a football in the KGB man's chest and caused bits of clothing and pieces of flesh, slivers of bone and a large splat of blood to go skyrocketing in every direction.

It was now every man for himself—*at least until the boys downstairs get here. Damn! This is worse than cigarettes, whiskey, and wild women!*

In a death-dealing crouch, Camellion began triggering the stainless steel Auto Mags. *A pig farmer shoot*! Snap aim at KGB men crawling out from under the caved-in ceiling. *Fire and watch the trash die.*

A .44 projectile popped Viktor Grott in the vicinity of the navel and kicked him back against John Uritsky, who had suffered a broken left wrist in the fall. Camellion exploded Uritsky's skull with a .44 AMP bullet and with the other Auto Mag slammed a dynamite projectile into the groin of another KGB goon getting to his feet. At the same time he noticed that, in front of him and to his right, Barney Krestell and Captain Webb had gotten to their feet, Webb's black face dripping blood from a long gash on his left cheek. Yet Webb was more than able to cave in the face of a Russian by stamping on the man with his right foot; and he had managed to hold onto his Colt CAR submachine gun. Barney, however, had only one of his S&W auto-loaders in his hand.

Hearing the high-pitched snarling of a Koski-PPdP in the vicinity of a doorway behind him and to his left, Camellion spun and saw that the Russian submachine gun was in the hands of Ralph Muldane, who was spraying four KGB men attempting to crawl from the wreckage of the roof. Twenty 9mm slugs jumped from the muzzle of the weapon. Two Russians cried out in agony. All four fell back and lay still in death, blood oozing from their freshly butchered bodies.

Sterling Whitney, Simon Kirkland, Olin Gammill, and the other Americans were somehow able to stand up. They weren't any faster than Colonel Zimovniki and his men, most of whom had crashed down in the hallway in front of the Death Merchant and the other Americans. Neither force had time to regroup and retreat. The prize now was survival. It was kill or be killed.

A lightning-fast thinker, Colonel Zimovniki had fallen thirty feet in front of the Death Merchant and, even while in the air, between roof and floor, had been able to retain his hold on the Koski-PPdP. He fell with a sheet of aluminum under him and crashed down onto a Marine, the Marine losing consciousness when his head struck the floor. Zimovniki had not been foolish enough to jump up and start firing. While Camellion and his AMP had killed Grott and Uritsky, Zimovniki had lain quietly, pretending to be dead. After other Russians and the Americans were on their feet and struggling with each other, only then did Colonel Zimovniki push himself up and open fire. His first burst caught Ralph Muldane, three 9mm slugs hitting him in the right-side rib cage. Dead and not even knowing it, Muldane was knocked against a sagging doorframe, his right side dripping blood. The corpse fell forward, face down.

The Death Merchant and Colonel Zimovniki spotted each other, but before Camellion could fire at the square-faced Russian with the short black hair, or Zimovniki tattoo him with slugs, a half-dozen struggling men locked in combat got between the leaders of the two groups. A combat-wise man, Zimovniki recognized an expert when he saw one. He could tell by body posture, by the way an opponent held a weapon as though it were an extension of his own body. *Nyet*. Zimovniki was not going to chance it. He jumped across a cracked panel of plywood, ducked through the doorway of a ceilingless room, looked around and was instantly grateful for the manner in which the officers' quarters had been designed. To save paneling in the walls and to cut down on weight in shipping the materials in a sub, each room had only a thick curtain in the hall doorway. Further weight had been saved by giving each room a doorway in the side walls, these too filled with thick, dark curtains.

Zimovniki realized that while he could move east through the curtained doorways, Americans could use the same doorways to move west!

Filled with more hatred than fear, Zimovniki waited. . . .

The Death Merchant, also a genius at judging another human being, had used the same tactic as Zimovniki. He too had ducked into a doorway, one four feet ahead and on the same side as the room into which Zimovniki had retreated. Camellion's reason, however, was different from Zimovniki's. Camellion had retreated because he had seen two other Russians—behind and to the left of the big Russian—trying to aim down on him with deadly little Koski-PPdPs. One man was a little joker with a pot gut, a bald head, and the longest nose that Camellion had ever seen on any man, anywhere. The second man was tall, with narrow, sharp features.

Once he was safe in the room, Camellion very quickly shoved fresh magazines into the AMPs, all the while eyeing the dark blue curtain hanging crookedly on the doorway facing the west. There were only three small bedrooms between him and Colonel Zimovniki. Camellion recalled how the Russian had chopped Muldane—*I have a score to settle with that son of a bitch.* . . .

Sterling Whitney was lucky one moment and unlucky the next. At a distance of six feet and using a S&W Bodyguard revolver, he pumped three .38 slugs into the left side of a tall, thin-faced Russian with a large mane of black-gray hair. Major Sergei Amosov, who had just killed Marine Private Barry Melody with a Stechkin M.P., let out a long, painful sigh, half-turned and had only one thought: he never thought he would die on a Thursday. . . .

Whitney was next to die. A few moments before Simon Kirkland could reach out for the KGB Captain, Nikolai Aninin slammed the side of an AKM assault rifle against the back of Whitney's head, crushing his skull as though it were wax. Aninin's feeling of victory dissolved into naked terror when he felt an arm slip across his throat, tighten, and a knee press into the small of his back. He felt his body being bent, his head pulled backward, the knee in his back forcing out his stomach—and heard his own scream as Kirkland's Marine knife ripped into his stomach and cut upward toward the sternum. Aninin's world became pure pain. He had the feeling that he didn't exist, that he no longer had a body, that if he let go of the thin fragment of consciousness, the real him would disappear. The real him did! Aninin became a corpse. The corpse slumped. And so did Simon Kirkland—before he could rear up as he was pulling out the knife. The last four 9mm projectiles from Anton Tikhvin's K-PPdP stitched him up his right side and slammed him unconscious and dying toward the dirty floor. Tikhvin threw away the empty machine gun and, seeing a fierce-eyed Barney Krestell coming at him, tried to pull a holstered 9mm Makarov PM pistol. The Russian *Mokskaia Pekhota* leader's hand was wrapped around the butt of the pistol, the Makarov still in its holster, when Krestell slammed him in the groin with a right-legged spin kick, the exploding agony paralyzing every nerve in the Russian's body, the pain freezing the scream in the long hollow of his throat. Reflex forced Tikhvin to double over, and his face met Krestell's knee in a terrible uplift that broke his nose and smashed his front teeth. In a flash, The Bomber was behind the helpless KGB officer, his arms darting out in a Commando neck-breaker hold.

Krestell was snapping Tikhvin's spine as Lawrence Minton went down, his body almost dissolving under the impact of three lines of fire, one coming from a Colt CAR-15 that had been picked up by Vadim Arkadevich, the other two streams of projectiles from the Koski-PPdPs fired by Commander Josef Dubokinsko and Lieutenant Major Boris Skayiski. In turn, Captain Webb and Sergeant Wild Bill Hurt raked all three Russians with long bursts of CAR-15 5.56 projectiles, Wild Bill thinking that one ivan had such a long nose that his mother must have been an anteater!

* * *

The Death Merchant crept forward, using a simple but effective teachnique. While standing to one side of a doorway, he would poke at the curtain with a long piece of wood—a large splinter from a broken beam. When the curtain wasn't riddled, he would go in quickly. He paused and listened by the west door in the second room east of the room harboring Anton Zimovniki. Camellion did not know that Major Valery Marleoff and Pyotr Stashynsky had crashed in from the roof into the room just ahead of him and were keeping very still, playing a waiting game. By like token, neither was Colonel Zimovniki aware that Stashynsky and Marleoff were in the northeast corner of the next room to the east, anymore than the two KGB officers suspected the existence of Zimovniki and the Death Merchant in adjoining rooms.

Camellion poked at the curtain with the long piece of wood, and Major Marleoff, watching the east doorway, fired five rounds with a Stechkin M.P. The five slugs made the curtain jump and passed in front of Camellion who, in the next room, was against the wall to the right of the doorway. Pyotr Stashynsky, standing next to Marleoff and keeping an eye on the hall doorway, spun around, a Makarov PM in his right hand.

An odd, bright glow flamed in Camellion's eyes. A trace of a smile appeared on his lips—*I have stared into the face of Death. I have looked into the mouth of Hell. I have smelled that bitter breath. I have glimpsed where Demons dwell. One more time!*

He carefully placed the piece of wood on the floor, stepped sideways, fired four AMP projectiles through the curtain, then dived in, fast and low. And almost collided with Marleoff and Stashynsky, both of whom had decided to get what they considered the edge. They had crept closer to the door.

In the next room to the west, Colonel Zimovniki had been pleasantly surprised to hear a Stechkin machine pistol firing in the very next room. With his back to the east wall, he had begun creeping toward the doorway, all the while watching the hall doorway and the doorway to the east. Then had come the loud explosions of the AMP, the four .44 Mag slugs also striking the curtain of the doorway to the left of Zimovniki. A look of alarm on his face, Zimovniki pulled up short.

181

Camellion's fast reflexes saved his life. At point-blank range, he pulled the trigger of the AMP and shot Valery Marleoff in the lower chest. All in the same motion, his left hand shot out, closed around Pyotr Stashynsky's right wrist, shoved the wrist and pistol away from him, and twisted.

The explosion of the Auto Mag ringing in his ears and with Marleoff's blood splattered all over him, Stashynsky attempted a simultaneous left-handed knife-edge strike to Camellion's face and a right knee lift to the groin. But in spite of his fear, which gave the Russian extra strength and crazy-brave courage, he was no match for the Death Merchant. Camellion easily blocked the knife-hand with his right forearm and the knee lift with his left leg. He twisted Stashynsky's wrist. The Makarov PM slipped from the Russian's tortured fingers.

Chain-lightning fast, Camellion released the Russian's wrist and delivered a left *Goju-Ryu Tettsui* fish hammer to the bridge of the KGB officer's nose. To prevent Stashynsky from staggering back, Camellion grabbed him by his shirt front and slammed the barrel of the Backpacker AMP across his left temple—at the same time, from the corner of his eye, seeing Colonel Zimovniki coming in through the doorway to the west. *And he has a damned Koski!*

Before Zimovniki could raise the machine gun, Camellion jerked the sagging Stashynsky around and pushed him with all his might at the startled Russian colonel, who could not dodge in time. The unconscious Stashynsky slammed into Zimovniki and both men went down, Zimovniki falling to his back. His finger tightened on the trigger and the machine gun vomited out a blast of slugs that shot upward through the roofless room.

Camellion could have killed Zimovniki on the spot. A .44 Jurras mag projectile would have gone all the way through Stashynsky and Zimovniki. But the Death Merchant didn't fire.

I want this pig farmer alive!

A right-footed kick broke Zimovniki's wrist and sent the machine gun clattering across the room.

"Sookyn syn, Amerikanski!" Zimovniki screamed, his rage greater than his fear of dying ("American son of a bitch!").

"Idyi v Zho-poo!" snarled Camellion ("Go to hell!").

He stamped on Zimovniki's face with his right heel. Zimovniki quit trying to shove the unconscious Stashynsky from him and tried not to choke on his own blood and broken teeth.

Camellion kicked Zimovniki in the side of the head, just hard enough to send him into dreamland, and the KGB colonel lay still.

Camellion paused and listened. The firing and the sounds of men locked in a death struggle had stopped.

"STOI! IDI SUDA!"

"RUXI VERX! RUXI VERX!"

The "Come here" and the "Hands up" were shouted in Russian, but the voices belonged to Barney Krestell and Captain Webb. . . .

EPILOGUE

Banana Bread Box 1.
Two days after the battle of Tukoatu.
1400 hours.

The Death Merchant rocked slowly back and forth in the swivel chair, studying the 8 X 10 photograph that Courtland Grojean had handed him. He had never met the man, but the high cheek bones, the hawknose, the black eyes and black hair were familiar.

With a half-smile, he handed the photograph back to Grojean, who carefully inserted it into a blue folder.

"Do you know him?" Leaning to one side, Grojean returned the folder to his attaché case.

"Sure, he's that ding-a-ling the press calls *The Penetrator*." Camellion said. "I hear he's very intelligent and has a lot of savvy. But remember, I choose the people with whom I work. If *The Penetrator* is going with us on this next mission . . . ?"

"He isn't." Grojean leaned back in the chair, carefully pulled up his trousers and crossed his legs. As usual, the

Chief of the CIA's clandestine division was immaculately dressed, this time in a pearl pinstripe suit—white shirt, wine four-in-hand tie, and matching handkerchief.

"I would ask you his name, but of course you wouldn't tell me!"

Grojean's smile was equally as cynical. "I'll tell you instead about what we found on Tukoatu. It's fantastic!"

Speaking rapidly and in a low tone, Grojean explained that the secret Russian base had served a dual purpose—as a tracking station and as a laboratory in which monstrous experiments had been conducted. CIA experts had found a safe hidden in the laboratory, the safe crammed with meticulously kept records of the experiments that had involved "racial recall."

The concept was not new to the Death Merchant. According to some theoreticians, the activity of thought extended beyond the physical body and partook of a "field of mind" surrounding the planet and extending into space for . . . how far? This mind field was composed of the collective experience of the human race: our thoughts, our feelings, our actions.

"All these trillions of thoughts exist in one vast thought field," Camellion said, "the equivalent to what Carl Jung called an archetype experience. The totality of this thought field, or archetype, constitutes an 'atmosphere' of thought energy coextensive with the earth's physical atmosphere and beyond."

"Ah yes, what Jung called the collective unconscious," Grojean said. "There is no valid evidence for such a field and most psychiatrists consider it nonsense."

"The Soviet scientists didn't," Camellion said coldly, "and from what you've told me, Doctor Mkrtchyan and his people proved the validity of the theory. They almost succeeded."

Grojean seemed uncomfortable. "We're not sure that we'll be able to reassemble the Bio-Memory Scanner. It might take years."

"And the mindless subjects in the laboratory?"

Grojean shifted in the easy chair and carefully inspected the fingernails on his right hand. "I admit that Soviet Psychotronic Weapons are a definite threat to our security, and," his eyes became cold, his tone granite, "what they intend to do in the Pacific Ocean is even more dangerous and is an immediate threat." He made a waving motion with his left hand. "I suppose though you're still convinced that full-scale nuclear war is inevitable?"

Camellion stopped moving back and forth in the swivel chair, his gaze boring into Grojean. *Okay! So he doesn't want to tell me what they've done with the zombies in the lab. As if I didn't know.* "With all the new theories involving 'cost effectiveness'—how cheaply we can kill millions in one stroke—and of 'counterforce' and 'countervalue,' the scenario has already been opened. Civilization, such as we know it, is in its very last years."

For a long time Grojean didn't speak. He only looked at the Death Merchant. At length he said, "You might be right, Camellion. In the meanwhile, we have to do all we can to make sure your prediction doesn't come true—if you don't mind!"

"I don't!"

"You know the setup. You leave tomorrow for Los Angeles. And like I said, be damned careful. I'm almost positive there's a mole in the Deputy Director's Office."

"Speaking of moles and doubles, what about that *hapa haole*, Eddie Ogden, the yoyo at the Tattoo Palace on Kapiolani Boulevard? If he set me up, I'm going to hammer out his eyes with a railroad spike."

"He didn't," Grojean said. "The KGB had mikes planted all over the place in the Tattoo Palace. More evidence of a mole—but that's in my department. Don't push it. You just worry about L.A. Like I said: *watch yourself.*"

The Death Merchant nodded.

The *Rim of Fire* mission was about to begin. . . .